Clean Slate

ALYSSA LASTELLA

Starlight Publishing LLC

Starlight Publishing LLC

www.AlyssaLaStella.com

Cover art by LA Cover Designs

Printed in the United States of America

ISBN:

Ebook: 978-1-7356366-0-3

Paperback: 978-1-7356366-4-1

To everyone that has supported me throughout the start of my journey, I could never thank you enough.

To the dreamers who are just starting their journey, you're capable of more than you know or believe.

CHAPTER ONE

DYLAN

I heard the slightest knock on my bedroom door, not long after the muffled sounds of yet another screaming match had started under my feet. I turned to look towards the door and saw my little sister Natalie's tall, rather slender frame leaning against the molding, jingling my car keys.

"Let's get out of here, I'm sick of hearing the same argument every week." She nodded, gesturing down the stairs.

"I'm in. Where do you wanna go this time?" I asked, shoving my feet into my sneakers, and grabbing my jacket from the computer chair as I made my way out of the room.

I jogged down the stairs behind her while she divvied out my options, "We can go to the diner or the park, and since you're my favorite brother, I'll let you pick which one."

"First of all, I'm your only brother. Second, we'll grab milkshakes to go and then head to the park?" I raised my left eyebrow as I waited for her response.

"I like the way you think. Dibs on the music choices!" With that, she took off running towards the car so her phone's Bluetooth would connect before mine got the chance to. I rolled my eyes and shook my head while I unlocked the car and watched her scramble in and immediately start fumbling with the radio.

I slid into the car and hummed along to the songs she played while she was full-on belting them out.

We pulled up to the diner and were greeted with the same tacky, turquoise accents of the building that brought a greater sense of home to me than my legal place of residence.

When Nat swung the door to the diner open, I caught it and barely made it through the second set of doors before Martha greeted us with the same warmth that she always did.

After our father died, Delgado Diner quickly became the place we would go to hide out for hours on end and as soon as Martha noticed, she took on the role as our caretaker while our mother was mentally elsewhere.

"Hiya, Darlings! The usual?" She asked, despite already starting to make our milkshakes.

"Please." I nodded.

Natalie excused herself to the bathroom while I waited for the milkshakes at the front counter. Once she was out of earshot, Martha asked, "Your mom fighting with her boyfriend again?" The sympathy and slight disapproval in her voice were both unmistakable.

"Yeah, I just want to try to keep Natalie as far away from any toxicity as possible, it's not good for her. I can tell it bothers her, but she would never admit it, so I try to let her come to me." I leaned my elbows on the counter with my arms crossed.

"I'm sorry, hon. You two are planning on getting out of there soon, right?" Usually, she would've apologized for having her back to me, but today she just listened while I talked.

"Yes, I'm just waiting for her to graduate so nothing holds

her in one town. I know I'll watch over her better than our mother would. She doesn't even see how incredible Natalie is, it's making Nat small. She doesn't think her own mother cares." I shook my head.

I grabbed my wallet from my pocket and slid a ten-dollar bill across the counter.

She turned back towards me and slid two vanilla milkshakes with extra whipped cream towards me. "If it's any consolation, I think you're doing the right thing by Natalie. Just do me a favor and make sure you're also doing right by yourself." She offered a small smile as she handed me my change.

"Making sure Natalie's happy, and flourishing is the right thing by me," I tell Martha, taking pride in the magnitude of truth in the sentiment.

Martha cleared her throat when she noticed Natalie was coming back and finished popping the lids on with a smile.

"Here ya go, hon. Where are you two off to today?"

I shot her an appreciative smile and let Natalie answer. "We're heading to the park," she held her hand up to hide her mouth from me but loudly whispered, "we have to talk about prom stuff!" She and Martha snickered at my expense and I threw my head back and groaned, earning a punch and a cocky smile from Natalie.

We grabbed our milkshakes before thanking Martha, hugged her goodbye, and headed out the door to the park.

Spotting our favorite two swings all by themselves, we headed towards them and took our designated seats.

Gently rocking while we sipped, we found ourselves bouncing between talking about school, work, and the latest shows that we'd been binging separately while we pondered which one we should tackle together next. Much to my surprise and desire, prom was barely touched on. "I don't know about you, but I really hope that this argument doesn't get in the way of the little getaway that they're about to go on." Natalie let out an amused snort.

"Oh, no, that would be tragic. How long are they going away again?"

"A week. I think they're leaving around noon tomorrow after Mom's shift."

"Impeccable timing as always." I cracked my knuckles, hoping the tension that I felt would be released.

Natalie shrugged and I internally fought to leave well enough alone and not twist the knife.

"Do you ever get scared that your life isn't going exactly the way you planned?" Natalie's seriousness was abrupt and unexpected. She was looking down at her feet, digging the toe of her sneaker into the mulch beneath the swing set.

"What do you mean?" I stopped moving and gave her my full attention.

"I don't know what I want, I just know what I don't want. I have to commit to a college in a week and I don't know which major I want to pursue. If I'm gonna be fooling around with liberal arts, then I don't think I should go away. We can't really afford it anyway." She shrugged apathetically but the crinkle in her brow gave her away like it always has.

"I thought you were thinking about being an English major. You love words, hell, your first word was 'book'! And I don't want you worrying about what we can and cannot afford, we'll figure it out, we always do. You just go and chase whatever it is that you dream about, okay?" I looked at her, waiting for a response.

She nodded, shyly. "I want to get published. I have most of my material ready, I just need to find someone who's interested in me and my work."

"Do you have it all laid out like you'd want the book to be?"

"Yes, I'm actually waiting to get my proof of the book in

the mail. That way, even if I can't get published, at least I'll have a copy on my bookshelf. It should be here in a few days." She smiled at the idea of it.

"Well, when it gets here, I hope you'll show it to me, I'd love to see it." I gently and playfully bumped into her to try to lighten the mood.

She looked away, off into the distance and I watched her face twitch as she changed the subject. "Do you think mom and number four are done screaming yet?" She attempted a laugh, but it came out flat and dry.

"Maybe. I don't think Chris has the stubborn patience for fighting that Rick had."

"No, no, that wasn't Rick, Rick was number two, he wore all the sweater vests. Dante was number three. He was the one who loved dragging fights out, he had a lot of fedoras." She chuckled, "You can't make this stuff up."

"Nobody was or ever will be as bad as that abusive asshole, Jack." I shook my head. "I can't believe that they've all had some kind of tragic flaw."

"I can't believe that Chris still lives with his mother at 49 years old. Or how *disgustingly* unlucky he is when it comes to all the scratch-off tickets he buys. I don't think he's ever won more than a dollar and he just won't quit!" She looked up at the sky as she leaned back in her swing.

"Well, when you're always wasted, it's kinda hard to be a winner." I sighed. "Mom really didn't have high standards when she got back into dating after dad died."

"I know, it's like she got it so right the first time and still lost the love of her life, that she's scared to find someone who's actually good. I loved her and dad's love story. I miss him a lot. Maybe things wouldn't be such a mess if he were still alive... Mom would still be her normal self and we wouldn't have to deal with all the drama she brings home." Her voice was drenched with disappointment and the familiar sadness graced her features again.

"Nat, I hope you know Dad would've been so proud of you for who you are and your writing and everything in between. I hope you know that he *is* proud of you and that he's with you every day." I grabbed her hand and held her wrist up in front of her. "Remember what he said when he gave you this bracelet and reminded you about every time he would get you a new charm?"

She nodded and her nose crinkled as she battled her emotions. "He said, 'Nat, when you find your dream, you have to be persistent and chase after it because if you don't, then who will?'" She smiled through watery eyes and continued "And then he said, 'You have to be like a gnat, Nat.' and laughed for like twenty minutes. He really was his own biggest fan." She closed her eyes, forcing them to overflow as she pulled her bracelet close to her heart.

I got off of my swing and turned to stand in front of her, pulled her to her feet, and hugged her tight. "I know, Nat, I miss him, too." I felt her weep softly into my shoulder. I shushed her and rubbed her back until she calmed down and pulled away to wipe her eyes.

"It feels so stupid to be this emotional about it after six years, but he always treated me like his little princess." She went quiet for a minute and then spoke so softly I could barely hear her. "Thank you, Dyl. I know you've been doing everything you can to protect me since Dad died. He'd be proud of you, too."

"None of that, Natalie, I mean it. You are my baby sister, it's my job to take care of you." I rubbed the top of her head quickly, messing up her hair. It earned me a shove, but it was completely worth it. "I've got a confession of my own actually."

"Spill!"

"I think I want to go back to school. I'm not really sure what I'm gonna go for, but I want to make something of myself eventually. I don't want to work these dead-end jobs for the rest of my life because I'm not educated for anything more."

"Dyl, I think that's an amazing idea! Hm... what could you do for a living? You could... be a cop like Dad! Now that I think about it, I'm not sure you need to go to school for that. You can do something investigative! Crime scene investigation maybe? I think you'd be really good at that; think about all the lives you'd change!"

"That actually has crossed my mind once or twice, I'm just worried that I'm not smart enough for that. School has never really been my strong suit, you know that."

"Personally, I think that's just because you didn't give a rat's ass about what you were being forced to learn. You have a selective memory type of thing going on, but I know that if you applied yourself to something that really motivates you and keeps you inspired, you'd make amazing things happen."

"Alright, come on, let's start heading home before this gets too mushy. I'll even let you drive." I took the car keys out of my pocket and handed them over to Nat.

She let out a screech and took off for my car for the second time today. This time, I raced her for the Bluetooth and if you asked her, she'd deny it, but I won.

When we pulled into the driveway, Chris's car was gone and so was Mom's. Looking at the time, I figured she had to go to work since she usually worked afternoon and night shifts.

Natalie and I went our separate ways when we got inside. She said she had some more obsessing to do over her writing and a few new ideas that she wanted to get down before she forgot them while I went into my room to watch a movie or two.

I got about halfway through the first movie I wanted to watch before I decided I couldn't sit still anymore and went to bother Natalie.

I knocked on her bedroom door and when she gave me permission to come in, I just barely caught a glimpse of her closing her laptop and her notebook. She was always so private when it came to her writing; nobody was ever allowed to read it except for our dad.

"Bored already?" She asked cockily. Besides writing, her favorite thing to do was to comment on how I get bored before I finish doing anything.

I ignored her question and the smirk that I heard in her voice. "Are you ready for tomorrow night? Prom's a big deal and I've barely heard you talk about it."

"Yeah, I guess so. It's just so fussed over, but I know I'll be fussing over it, too, once I start doing my hair and makeup." She walked over to her dress hanging on the back of her door and lifted the dry-cleaning bag over it. "I did get the perfect dress after all, even though it weighs more than I do."

Her dress was a beautiful full-length black dress with gold beading running vertically equidistant, but I've carried it and I don't think any dress should ever be that heavy, beading or no beading.

"You're gonna look amazing and you're gonna have a great time. It seems lame, but when you get there, I promise it's not all that bad. If I made it through the whole night, you will, too." I knew high school wasn't her favorite but of all my high school sufferings, prom was a lot of fun and I'd go again if I could.

"Alright, now get out. I'm gonna get ready to go shower and get in bed." She obviously didn't want to talk about prom anymore.

"Aye, aye, captain!" I saluted her before going back to my room to do something that I should've done a while ago.

I pulled out my laptop and looked up the best hairdressers and makeup artists in the area and searched until I found someone who does both with availability for tomorrow around 3:00 p.m. and booked her immediately through her website. I also found a nail salon that I would take her to in the morning.

I want her prom to be perfect no matter what the cost.

She's always so worried about being a burden financially and emotionally when she couldn't be further from it. I know that all of her friends are getting treated like royalty tomorrow to get ready and she feels like she's missing out because, between my mother's minimum wage job and her unpredictable dead-end boyfriends, we're struggling. Even with my job, we don't have much more than what we need to pay the bills.

Fortunately, I've been putting a little bit of money aside every week since I graduated high school a few years ago and now I have more than enough to do this for my sister.

After I made sure that everything was set up and ready for tomorrow, I got into bed and fell asleep almost immediately which I was thankful for. I couldn't wait to see the look on Nat's face tomorrow.

CHAPTER TWO

DYLAN

W hen I woke up, the house was quiet and the sun was just peeking through one of the slats of my blinds, giving the room an orangey glow.

I went for a quick run as the sun finished coming up and showered when I got home. By the time I was done, Natalie was awake, and I heard music playing in her room from the hallway.

I knocked on her door and said "Nat, get dressed, we're going out." just loud enough for her to hear me over the music, but not loud enough to wake up our mother who was sleeping soundly on the recliner in the living room downstairs.

Her door swung open and she popped out of her room to ask where we were going. I already had my back to her as I headed to my room and waved her questions away dismissively. Thankfully, she didn't put up a fight like she usually would and just got ready.

A few minutes later, her long brown hair was thrown into a braid, she had on leggings and a sweatshirt which was perfect for this surprisingly cold June morning and she had thrown on a pair of flip flops. She leaned against the doorway with her arms crossed.

"I'm ready. Wherever we're going, I need to be back by 3:00 to start my hair and makeup." She reminded me.

"Yeah, yeah, we'll see. Come on, let's go! Oh, and any protests will get you nowhere because I'm not giving you an option." I tried to stay one step ahead of her.

I heard her grumble behind me, but she followed nonetheless, knowing better than to bicker.

When we pulled into the parking lot of the strip mall with the nail salon in it, she paid no mind to where we were because our favorite store was in the same shopping center. When I walked straight rather than towards said store and held the door to the nail salon open for her, she stopped dead in her tracks.

"What are we doing here? Are you finally doing something about those disgusting man feet and getting a pedicure? It's okay, I'll show you the ropes *and* I'll even help you pick a color that'll be sure to snag all the ladies' attention!" She teased.

I let her keep going all she wanted because what she didn't know was that I called this morning and all I needed to do was say her name when we walked in. She was immediately taken to a pedicure chair, and I followed behind.

"Dylan Alexander, if you're doing what I think you're doing, please stop," she lowered her voice drastically, "we can't afford this."

I got closer to her ear so that she was the only one that would be able to hear me. "Listen to me, stop worrying about what we can and cannot afford and just sit and talk to me about something else or I won't stay over here with you." I backed up and stood up straight. "Just relax and enjoy this."

I took a second to look around at the people who

populated the salon, the majority being teenage girls buzzing with excitement.

After she was seated in the last open seat, Natalie turned to me while she waited for the nail technician to come back to her station. "Is getting a matching French manicure and pedicure tacky? I'm really not looking to blend in with every other girl there tonight."

Before I got the chance to open my mouth, the nail tech came back. "Would you like French for prom?"

Natalie's polite smile dropped as she turned to me. "Solid it is."

Not worrying about her noticing while she was deep in conversation with the nail tech about which color would complement her dress best and how her night was planned, I slipped away from where she was seated and paid up front.

Natalie glared at me in disbelief after she was informed that the bill was already paid.

"Dylan, what did I tell you about spending ridiculous, unnecessary amounts of money on me? Thank you, but you really didn't have to do that." Natalie caught herself in the middle of her reprimanding me and changed her tune as I shoved my hands in my pockets and continued walking to the car.

After all, she didn't know that we were on our way to get her hair and makeup done.

When we arrived at the hair salon, I stayed up front but while they walked towards the back, I heard the hairdresser start talking to Nat in between snaps of her gum. "Alright, doll, we're going to get you all washed up and then you have the option to cut and then style or just style, we have time for both. So, you tell me, do you want to cut it at all beforehand?"

I watched intently as Natalie grabbed a handful of her

hair and brought the ends up in front of her eyes, examining the ends, contemplating.

I stood up and jogged towards the back where she was now seated in front of a sink with a towel around her shoulders. "Yes, please cut it a little bit." I couldn't bear to keep watching her contemplate every little thing just to say no in the end because of financial issues that she shouldn't be concerning herself with.

Nat shot me an accusing look and when I cocked an eyebrow and looked at her with a 'you're-not-winning-today' look, she huffed at me and said "Just enough to get rid of the dead ends, please. I love the length."

The hairdresser smiled and nodded, "You got it, doll." She turned her attention to me and directed my gaze towards the sink next to Nat with a jut of her chin. "You can sit there if you'd like."

"Thank you." I nodded and took my seat.

The salon was surprisingly empty compared to the nail salon, so I sat with her and filled the time with mindless chatter. As time passed, she seemed to glow more and more as she continued to get more excited about tonight's festivities.

I watched as her makeup was done and absorbed the similarities between the two of us while her features were delicately traced with varying brushes.

Despite Natalie having more of our father's Italian features, hints of the Spanish in her from our mother's side were definitely there. I, on the other hand, took after our mother more so than our father.

Natalie's hazel eyes were beautifully enunciated, whereas mine were undoubtedly brown, not a hint of another color present. Our noses were almost identical, having a similar bump in the middle from our profiles. Our hair was the same deep brown color which was from our mother. We both had full lips and tanned skin. I always tanned easier than Natalie, but she'd always remind you that in the winter, she's naturally a smidge darker than I am.

Her hair was loosely curled and topped off with an intricately braided headband while her makeup was light and natural-looking.

"Are you happy with how it came out?" I smiled at her as she walked over and twirled to show off her hair.

"Yes! How does it look?" She batted her eyelashes.

"Just like the picture you showed the hairdresser which is a relief! Remember when I took Emily to prom and her hair came out nothing like the picture she showed? She was miserable about it the whole night!"

"I know, that's probably the last time Noah goes anywhere with you and a date."

"Was she really that bad?"

"From what I saw when you guys took pictures and from what Kathryn told me based on what Noah told her, she sounded like a nightmare!"

I laughed and followed her up to the front counter where she would attempt to pay for everything that she had gotten done. That was, until her attention was pulled away towards bracelets for sale and her face lit up. "Martha would *love* this!" She picked one up and looked at it adoringly. I suggested that she should put the bracelet on the counter so I could include it while I was paying, and she vehemently refused.

"I want this to be from me. Seriously, thank you, but you've done more than enough. I'm getting paid either tomorrow or early next week and I will give you some of the money back. If you wanna thank Martha for everything, you'll just have to get her your own gift!" She stuck her tongue out at me.

She pulled out the money for the bracelet and paid for it. "We have to stop at the diner before we go home so I can give this to her.

"That's fine, luckily, we still have time before you need to finish getting ready."

CHAPTER THREE

DYLAN

W hen we got to the diner and Martha was given her gift, it brought tears to her eyes and she brought Natalie into a warm embrace. "Thank you so much, Natalie. I love you two so very much. Thank you for being the closest thing to children that I have." I noticed a sadness streak behind her eyes when she spoke, but it left almost immediately.

I knew that she wanted children more than anything else. Unfortunately, having biological children was not an option for her.

She told us the story years ago; she was diagnosed with cancer in her early twenties. Thankfully, she caught it early enough that a hysterectomy and some chemo were able to eliminate the risk. I was beyond honored that she considered me one of her own and I know Natalie feels the same way.

Martha fussed over how beautiful Natalie looked for a while before we eventually excused ourselves so that she could have enough time to get dressed.

"Thank you both for stopping by before you leave for prom, I couldn't imagine missing this! Natalie, thank you for the bracelet. You look beyond beautiful, have the best time tonight and please be safe."

"I will, I promise. We both know Dylan will be lecturing me about safety later, so don't worry." She said excitedly, despite her sarcastic eye-roll.

I nodded. "You bet your ass I'm going to lecture you, it's my job."

Martha swatted at me for my language. Being the semi-religious Latina woman that she is, she always hated even the smallest and least harmful of curse words. "I'm sorry, Martha, allow me to rephrase." I turned my attention back towards Natalie. "You bet your *bottom* I'm going to lecture you, it's my job. Better?" I looked at Martha for approval after wagging my finger at Natalie.

She smiled and nodded. "Much better, thank you." She hugged Natalie again and when she pulled away, she reached into the pocket of her apron and kept her hand wrapped around whatever it was that she took out. She placed it in Natalie's hands and cupped them firmly. "We'll be with you all night long and you know you can call either of us at any hour and we'll be there." She nodded in my direction.

"Thank you, I love you!" My sister beamed just before we turned to leave and headed towards our house. When we got there, Natalie bounded up the stairs to her room.

"If you need help, just call down and I'll come up. Mom's not here." I called up the stairs after her.

I heard her yell "okay" from her room and assumed that her door was already shut since she sounded like she was miles away.

Only a few minutes had gotten the chance to pass by while I sat on the couch, on standby when I heard her bedroom door open and her heels clicking on the hardwood floors upstairs.

She came down the rickety spiral staircase in her new

heels so slowly and so cautiously, it reminded me of the time when I caught her trying to sneak out in the middle of the night to go meet Kathryn at a party.

I reached my hand upward towards her, offering my help and stability which she gratefully took once she was able to reach me.

"You look beautiful, Nat." I twirled her gently before her second foot hit the floor.

"I try." She shrugged and I elbowed her arm delicately, giving her a look of disbelief. She broke character and laughed. "No, but seriously, thank you." She smiled as she grabbed a handful of the beaded fabric and curtsied jokingly.

She's always been good at wearing the smile that showed everyone that she really was as pure and golden as she seems.

"Can you put this on for me? I don't want to chip my manicure trying to do the clasp." She opened her hand and revealed Martha's infamous cross in her palm.

"Sure, turn around." I opened the clasp as I waited for her to turn around and lift her hair out of the way. "Is this what she gave you earlier?"

"Yeah, I'm feeling kinda anxious about having the responsibility of wearing it, I don't want to break it or lose it."

"Assuming you're not planning on being a complete lunatic tonight, I'm sure it'll be fine. This clasp is a pain in the ass to open as it is, I doubt it'll just undo itself." I fumbled with it for a moment. "Well, actually, it looks like it likes to get stuck in the open position. I'm sure it'll be fine, don't stress yourself out too much. Okay, you're good, you can drop your hair again."

"Thanks, Dyl. Now that the pleasantries are over, when are you going to start lecturing me?" She quirked an eyebrow at me.

"Listen, since I can't come with you without mortifying

you, not that I'd even want to go to your grade's prom, it's literally my job to do this, but I know you're not stupid, so I'll make it quick. No booze, no drugs, and no boys." I stood with my arms crossed defiantly.

Natalie stomped her foot in protest and let out a whine as she let her shoulders droop forward to really accentuate her pouting, really portraying the childish image that she was going for. "No boys? You're no fun."

"Fine. One boy. It has to be a good one though, nobody with a vape. I know Mom and Chris left this afternoon, but if you wanna be around a vape god, Chris is always just a phone call away!" I mocked as my poker face faltered. "Come on, it's time to go. I'm gonna run and grab my car keys." I placed my hand on her head, careful not to mess up the hair which she managed to keep meticulous, and twisted her head until she eventually allowed her body to follow as she turned towards the front door.

"Can you grab my clutch off the counter? I'm gonna go wait in the car." She was already halfway out the door now that she was able to walk around like she's been walking in heels that high for her whole life. Stairs have been her biggest obstacle ever since she tripped going up the stairs onto the stage that she walked across for her stepping up ceremony before high school.

I shrugged into my jacket, grabbed her clutch off the kitchen counter, and lifted my keys off of the hook that they were on.

Just before I closed the door behind me, I pushed it open again and ran up to Nat's room to grab her sweater that I knew she probably laid out for tonight but had forgotten. I threw it over my arm and turned the key in the front door, pausing to jiggle the knob to make sure it was locked.

I walked over to my car, holding her sweater up for her to

see. "You forgot something," I said as I walked over to the passenger side where she had rolled down the window.

"Thank you, you know I'm all out of sorts tonight, prom is a *big* deal!" She went to shove a finger into my chest to get her point across before she stopped herself. "Oh my god, I love your clutch! It really pulls your whole outfit together!"

I looked down and realized I was wearing the crossbody chain of her clutch and rolled my eyes. I walked around the car and slid into the driver's seat. By the time I got situated, buckled, and put the car in reverse, she was still laughing, cackling actually, at her own joke.

"Oh, stop it, you're just like Dad." I mocked her cackle, but louder and more obnoxious than she could ever manage.

She whipped her head in my direction to glare at me.

"You're just mad because I wear it better." I flicked my invisible long locks like I'd seen her do countless times before.

"Yeah, okay. You're pretty, but you're not *that* pretty, try again." She shot back. "Okay, sh, I love this song." She nodded at me and spun the dial so my car was basically screaming the playlist she's been perfecting for tonight.

———

TWINKLING, classic white lights came into view as I pulled up to the venue.

Natalie let out an excited screech and tapped the window with her nail as soon as she saw the entrance's elegance. An arch wrapped in the lights that she's always loved, and delicate foliage graced the path.

My amazement from looking at the venue was ruined for me when it hit me just how pissed I was that our mother wasn't here.

I didn't mention it and neither did Natalie. It was finally

her prom night which she has been waiting for forever and in her eyes, she was going to have a good time whether she liked it or not.

After I put the car in park, I jumped out of the driver's seat and jogged around the front of the car to open the passenger door and help Natalie out. She placed her hand in mine to stabilize herself for the second time tonight as she climbed out of my car.

"Dyl, don't forget that I'm going back to Kathryn's tonight, so you won't have to worry about picking us up later."

"Do you have everything you need for the night?"

"Yeah, I think she has more of my clothes than I do at this point."

"Alright, well, if you need anything, call me and I'll bring it to you. And you better text me when you're leaving and when you get to Kathryn's. Remember what I said. Have fun and be extra careful. Boys get stupid when girls look this beautiful. God forbid, if you need to defend yourself, don't forget the self-defense training we went through."

"Okay, okay, I'll be safe, I promise. No booze, no drugs, no vape gods, only good boys, remember the self-defense, I got it. I love you, thank you for being so protective, but you are blocking traffic and everyone's gonna get pissed. Go home, I'll call you if I need a ride!"

I started walking backward as I delivered my last words of wisdom before heading home. "Okay, that's all I ask. I love you, too. Remember, if you need me for *any* reason, I will be here in te-"

"Ten minutes flat, I know. Now go!" Natalie shooed me towards my car before she turned and ran off to meet Kathryn by the door who waved at me from a distance.

I waved back as I closed her door and then ran over to the other side to get in and pull away.

CHAPTER FOUR

ELLIE

The door is only a few feet away, the end is so close, but still just out of reach.

Just as my fingers curled around the doorknob, the creaking floorboards alerted me just in time to drop my bag behind the couch, out of sight from the hallway where he was coming from.

"Where do you think you're going?"

I swallowed the lump in my throat as goosebumps scattered across my body. "Nowhere, I was just going to sit on the porch to get some air."

"Do you know what time it is?"

I nodded and wrapped my arms around my torso.

"You know you're not allowed to leave the house past 9:00 p.m."

"I know, I'm sorry." I left the comfort of my spot by the door and sought the frigidity of the couch.

Please don't be too mad, I didn't leave.

"You're 'sorry'? That's not gonna cut it. You did something you weren't supposed to. You know the rules." He paced around the room with his arms crossed, circling me like his prey and every hair on my body stood as he made his way towards the back of the couch.

I closed my eyes and held my breath, preparing for the inevitable as I heard his foot hit the duffel bag.

"What do we have here?" He picked the bag up and dropped it on the couch next to me, making me jump.

I envisioned myself dissolving and becoming nonexistent and I tried to count my breaths to distract myself.

"Answer me when I ask you a question!" His voice boomed abruptly, forcing me to jump again.

"I was going to go to my mom's. She wanted to have a girls' weekend." I fought to keep my voice steady, squeezing my hands in my lap.

"When have I ever let you go out over night? You never even asked me. If this little alleged girls' weekend theory is true, then why haven't I heard anything about it before right now?" I tried to keep my shiver to a minimum while he picked a piece of my hair to twirl around his finger from behind the couch.

"I was going to come back in and tell you where I was going after I put my bag in my car."

I winced as he grabbed more of my hair and yanked me back by it. "That's not how this works, you don't 'tell' me anything. Not only are you to ask me for permission before you do anything, but you are to ask me several days in advance, not when your keys are already in the ignition." He kept my hair clenched in his fist.

My eyes watered despite my trying to keep them dry. "Please let go of me." My voice wavered from its usual sturdiness.

"I don't think I'll be doing that. The 'please' was cute though."

I tried to look up to his face, but I was only met with the clenching of his jaw from underneath.

"Please, JJ. It hurts." I sobbed, my hands trying to pry my hair from his grip. His fingers being intertwined in my hair complicated the process and his grip only tightened.

"I'll let go when you stop lying to me." He said through clenched teeth.

"I'm not lying!"

"Oh-ho-ho. Look who's being brave!" He thrusted my head forward and released my hair.

My hands flew to the spot of my scalp that was being pulled on as I cried.

"Get up." When I adjusted my glance to in front of me, he stood there, not willing to wait for me to oblige before he grabbed my upper arm and yanked me to stand up.

"Jared, *please!* I told you, I'm sorry! I messed up, I'll never do it again!" I screamed through my sobs, desperate to be heard. *"You're hurting me!"*

He pulled his arm back and sent his fist straight for my stomach, causing me to double over, my arm still in the grasp of his other hand. A few seconds passed by, solely of me gasping for the wind that he knocked out of me, before he dropped my arm and I let it hit the ground next to me as I fell to my knees.

He crouched down next to me. "I'm sorry, babe. You know I hate doing that, but you need to be kept in line. Clearly you forget the rules if I don't enforce them."

He's starting to feel guilty.

I ignored him and saw my window for opportunity start to open slowly. "Can you please get me an icepack from the freezer?" I made sure to keep my gasps noticeable, despite being able to catch my breath again.

"Yes." He turned towards the kitchen before he stopped in his tracks and turned back towards me. "This better not be some sort of trick. Promise me it's not."

I forced a cough and gasped again. "JJ, I can barely breathe right now."

"Promise?" His voice got increasingly sterner.

"Yes." I coughed.

The second he turned the corner into the kitchen, I worked my way upright.

This is probably the last chance I'll have. If he catches me trying to leave a second time, he'll never leave me alone again.

"I'm not seeing it, where is it?" He called from the kitchen.

I strained my voice while I grabbed my bag, wincing as my stomach muscles moved. "It should be on the bottom shelf, maybe in the back behind the frozen dinners."

I pulled the door open as quietly as possible before sprinting through it. Pushing through the pain of today's beating while at a full sprint was one of the most physically challenging things I'd ever had to do.

Jared came into view in the front door just as I closed the driver's door.

I expected him to make his way to the car at lightening speed, but what scared me even more was that he just stood there, hands in his pocket, watching me. His expression was unreadable, something I'd never seen before.

Why is he just standing there? Why isn't he chasing me? He always chases me.

I forced myself to tear my eyes away and turned the key in the ignition before driving to my parents' house, lost in a cloud of confusion, pain and fear.

Maybe calling my mom will distract me a little bit.

It was already late by the time I had arrived, but thankfully, my mom stayed up as she waited for me, worry evident in her own voice. My hands shook as I made my way to the front porch, my head on a constant swivel, expecting Jared to come lunging out of the darkness.

I knocked twice, not willing to let my guard down while I dig in my bag for my keys. I kept my back towards the door as I waited for her to open it.

When I heard the lock flick open, relief flooded my body and I felt the tension dissolve from my shoulders.

"Ellie? What's going on? You're worrying me."

I gently pushed her into the house and stepped in myself before closing and locking the door behind me.

I dropped my bag next to the front door and hugged her. "I haven't been completely honest with you lately and I'm so sorry, but I need you now."

"Okay, come sit. I made some coffee; I figured it would be a long night."

I peeked through the gap between the curtains covering the front window to see if Jared's car would magically show up. But it never did.

I sat on the couch across from her and pulled my legs up next to me. "You remember how I told you that I couldn't come back for your 25th wedding anniversary?"

"Because you were stuck at home studying, yes. I knew that was a lie the second you said it, where were you?" She held her coffee cup in both hands while she leaned forward towards me, waiting for me to continue.

"Okay, well I was home, but I wasn't studying. That was the first time that..." A sudden lump made its way into my throat, stopping my confession altogether.

One of my favorite things about my mother was that she didn't push when she knew something was bothering me. She just sat and let me take the time I needed before I could continue.

I took a deep breath to gather myself, "... that Jared hit me." I kept myself from meeting my mother's eyes, fearful of the judgment they'd hold, but eventually, too much time had passed that was filled with nothing but silence. I allowed my eyes to meet hers and my heart broke instantly.

Her eyes were filled with a sadness that I've never seen directed at me from her. "It happened again tonight, didn't it?"

"It's happened multiple times, but tonight it happened because he caught me trying to leave. I know we've talked about it before and you've always warned me about boys like him, but I didn't know this side of him until it was too late. I'm so sorry. Oh, my god. Dad. I don't want him to know, Mom, please don't tell him." I sobbed.

She came to sit next to me, and she pulled me to lean on her while I had my face buried in my hands. "Ellie, honey, breathe. It's okay, there's no need to apologize. I'm sorry this happened to you, I never would've expected it from him from the stories you've told us. The fact that we've never officially met him in the few years that you've been dating was always a little bit of a red flag, but I didn't think it was this serious. I love you, and I will do everything I possibly can to protect you, and I need you to understand that that means telling your father. He only wants what's best for you, he won't be mad at you, you know that, right?"

"I don't know what to do. I was too scared to leave, and now that I finally did, I'm terrified that he's going to be around every corner or just show up unannounced. What do I do?"

She stayed quiet for a minute while she thought about any of my potential options. "I think the only thing that we can do is make some significant changes. Did you take everything you had at his apartment? Is that what that bag is full of?"

I nodded.

"Okay, good, that's a great start. You've essentially

removed yourself from the situation. What do you say we take a few days away from here? We'll go on a little getaway and see what we can think of, but I don't think you're going to feel safe here over the next few days. I'll tell your Dad what's going on so he knows to look out for any Jared sightings and we'll leave tomorrow afternoon. Sound good?"

"Yeah, I think getting out of here for a little while will do some good."

"I agree. Do you want to invite Allison to come with us?" She stroked my hair as I rested my head on her shoulder.

"I don't think so, I don't want to just interrupt her life like that, she just got a new job. Plus, I think it'll be nice, just the two of us."

"I love that idea."

"I will text her though just to clue her in on what's going on a little bit. I don't want her to think I just abandoned her or fell off the face of the earth."

"Okay, are you okay to go take a shower while I make your bed? The sheets haven't been changed in a while."

"Yeah, I think so. I'm not sure I'll get much sleep tonight though."

"If you need me, you know where I am." She kissed my head before getting up. She gathered the cups and brought them into the kitchen before heading upstairs.

I pulled my phone out to text Allison before I went up to take a shower.

Ellie: Hey, I just wanted to let you know that I'm going to be leaving the state with my mom for a few days. Jared and I are over, and I need to get some space and clear my head.

I didn't get an answer immediately like I usually would from Allison, so I headed upstairs to shower and crawled into bed when I was done. I played a video on my phone to keep me distracted and fell asleep before I got halfway through.

CHAPTER FIVE

DYLAN

I glanced at the time when my phone buzzed.

12:47 p.m.

That was the time that I got the worst call of my life.

My heart was pounding in my ears and my heels were pounding against the floor in the house.

Then the ground outside.

Then the floor in the hospital.

I heard a voice, too, at one point. It sounded frantic and I couldn't recognize it, but it was irritating me.

"Sir? Excuse me, sir?" I hear another voice, a woman's.

I tried to respond to it, but the only thing I heard was the voice of whoever was speaking so frantically before.

"Sir, she's in surgery, please have a seat in the waiting room. When I have an update, I will come and find you."

What was she saying? I didn't answer her, nothing she was saying made any sense.

It wasn't until I felt someone grab my arm that I realized that I *did* know whose frantic voice that was.

It was *mine*.

I turned to look at whoever grabbed my arm, but I could barely make out their gender through my blurred eyes.

I blinked hard enough that my eyes cleared, and I took in my surroundings. I was in the hospital.

I don't remember driving or how I even got here, but I knew one thing for sure: my baby sister was in an accident, and it's not good.

I got a call from a paramedic. He called her first emergency contact. My attention flashed to the memory of when she got her first phone and we set each other as our emergency contacts immediately. We were in the emergency room by the time the nurse finally got me to sit down.

A paramedic came up to me in the waiting room. "Dylan?"

I stood, "Yes, were you the one who called me from the ambulance?"

"Yes, your sister is a real fighter. She should've been dead on impact. Knowing that... I need you to understand and take time to really consider how bad her injuries will be. I know this is awful to think about and more difficult than anything ever should be, but you may want to prepare yourself for the worst-case scenario. If you have any questions, I'll be around." He offered a sympathetic smile which only made me feel worse.

Great, he pities me.

He was walking away when I called out. "I do, actually... have a question, I mean."

The paramedic turned towards me and waited for me to ask. I noticed that his name tag read "Jake".

"What happened to her?" My voice cracked.

"She was driving her friend's car when the vehicle was struck on the driver's side in the middle of the Pleasant Street and West Street intersection. It appears that her head hit the window when they were struck. The driver of the other vehicle, Jared Jenkins, was also injured, though his injuries aren't as bad. He had a blood alcohol concentration of .127 and traces of LSD in his system. As far as I know, the cops are keeping an eye on him while he gets checked out, but there's not much they can do right now except wait for him to sober up." He told me all this as if he had no emotions, completely void of any sincere reaction.

"If you find out anything else, please find me."

Jake nodded at me before walking away. After he left, I felt my body carry me into the bathroom and I heard the door lock behind me

I splashed my face with cold water in a desperate attempt to wake myself up from this nightmare, from this world where someone really suggested that I might have to live without Natalie.

I braced myself using the sides of the sink and stared at my reflection in the mirror. Water trickled from my jaw, down my neck, wetting the collar of shirt. Despite the water's frigid temperatures that sent chills coursing throughout my body, I couldn't wake up.

It wasn't a dream; I couldn't escape it.

I held back the urge to scream and break things and find someone to blame but the only person that might even be somewhat to blame was staring back at me.

I shouldn't have let her go. I knew all about what prom was like. I knew everyone drank and was stupid enough to get behind the wheel afterward, not thinking about the potential consequences.

No, that's crazy. Maybe I should've just taken away her option to drive home with Kathryn. If I drove them to Kathryn's afterward, this could've been prevented.

I took the next fifteen minutes to gather myself to the

best of my ability, unlocked the door, and walked out of the bathroom to find Jake leaning against the wall across the hall.

He stood straighter when he saw me and took a step towards me. "I found this near a bag with her ID in it at the scene of the accident, does it mean anything to you?" He held up a gold chain with a cross at the bottom and I'm not sure if my heart jumped up into my throat or fell into my stomach, but I knew that I felt sick.

"Yes, can I hold onto it?" Part of me feared the possibility of him saying no.

Maybe God will hear my prayers louder and help my sister if her own flesh and blood was holding the cross.

"Yes, of course. Again, I'm praying that she pulls through." He nodded kindly before walking away.

I checked the time.

It had only been a little over an hour, but it was almost two in the morning at this point. I couldn't bring myself to call Martha, so I prayed a little bit for both of us.

We both needed her to wake up and be fine. It felt as if the world would collapse if she didn't.

I'll call Martha when I know more. When I find out that everything's fine and that Natalie's out of the woods.

Our mother was on her little getaway with Chris and wouldn't be able to get a flight back home for a few days. I wasn't worried about her showing up anyway. I didn't want to hear her shrill voice speaking all of my worst fears into reality and acting as if her world will end if Natalie doesn't make it.

Regardless of the reactions that I dreaded, I pulled out my phone to text her and let her know what was happening, Natalie's lecturing echoing in my head.

Dylan: Natalie was in an accident, it's bad. How soon can you get home?

Nobody in this world is closer to Natalie than I am, and if I can keep it together, so can everyone else.

It felt like an eternity until someone came out to speak to me again. I kept my eye on the surgical board, but the only information that was available for her was something I already knew: she was in surgery.

CHAPTER SIX

DYLAN

As time continued to pass, it started to feel like that board was taunting me, and my stomach twisted each time I looked at it and saw no change.

Why don't they have more updates? Are there complications? Should it be taking this long?

When Nat's surgeon came out, her expression lacked the enthusiastic emotion that I was desperate to see. "Dylan? Dylan Fields?" I stood and nodded when I heard my name and walked over to her. "Hi, Dylan. I'm Dr. Jocelyn Marsh, your sister's surgeon. It's a pleasure to meet you."

I shook the hand that she had extended towards me, unable to form any words except for, "Is she okay?"

"She's stable for now. I need you to understand that her injuries were incredibly severe, and the next few hours are crucial. If and when she wakes up, she's going to be in a lot of pain. Her femur has been badly bruised, but luckily, it's not broken. She was asking for you a lot before surgery, you may go sit in her room and wait for her to wake up. I can take you there if you'd like." She offered a crooked smile that didn't hold much promise.

"Yes, please, I need to see her."

The doctor led me down one hallway after another until I felt like we had gone in a complete circle, and everything looked the same except for the all-too-similar sporadic art on the walls. When she stopped walking, she put her hand on the handle that would lead to my sister after what felt like days of separation. She looked at me sympathetically and warned me again, "It looks bad, but remember, she's stable as of right now. It's also imperative that you remember that she has injuries that you can't see as well. If and when she wakes up, if I'm not here to remind you, please remember that you have to be extremely gentle and careful with her. Don't let her push herself too far, too fast."

I nodded and all but ignored the surgeon as I walked into Natalie's room.

No amount of warning could've prepared me for what I actually saw. The beautiful and glowing sister that I dropped off at prom a few hours ago was now weak and hurt beyond belief.

She had tubes circling around her, weaving in and out of her body and her face was littered with cuts, scratches, and bruises while her head was wrapped with gauze.

I swallowed the lump in my throat as I took in the sight before me. I couldn't believe the damage that a mere few seconds had caused. Although looking at her like this pained me, I knew she was alive, and for that, I was thankful.

"I'll give you some time to sit with her. I'll be back to check on her in an hour or so. If you need anything, you can hit that button and a nurse will come in. If you need me specifically, have a nurse page me." She expressed before exiting the room.

"Thank you," I called right before the door shut behind her.

I grabbed Natalie's hand and held it tight. "Natalie, I'm so glad you're okay, and I'm so proud of you for making it through surgery, but now I need to ask you for a favor. Open your eyes. Please, I need you to stay with me and these next few hours are super important according to your surgeon, so I want to keep you awake and talking. Please, wake up." I rested my forehead on our joint hands.

I was just about to ask her to open her eyes again when the door opened to reveal Kathryn.

Kathryn and Natalie have been friends forever which brought Kathryn's brother, Noah, into my life. The four of us are all very close and spend most of our time together.

When I made eye contact with her, I noticed how red her eyes were and that they looked incredibly glassy. Her hair was a mess and she had a cut on her forehead and an IV running into her hand. She came into the room wearing her hospital gown and socks, her IV on a pole next to her. She turned to shut the door behind her and proceeded to completely unravel right before me.

I couldn't make out what she was saying through her sobs, so I hugged her and calmed her down before asking her to repeat herself.

"Dylan, I am so sorry. I should've been the one driving, she doesn't deserve this, it's all my fault and now she might die, and I don't know what I'm going to do with myself if that happens." She was hyperventilating.

"Kathryn, please stop blaming yourself. The paramedic that I spoke to told me that the driver that hit you was under the influence. This is in no way your fault, okay? I need you to stop blaming yourself and try your best to pull it together because if she's gonna make it through this, she needs both of us to be strong. Come sit down and try to relax." I guided her towards the two chairs that sat next to the hospital bed.

I pulled them closer to the hospital bed so we could hold Natalie's hand at any given moment. Kathryn placed a cold hand on Natalie's forearm, while I went right back to holding Natalie's hand.

We're here, Nat.

We stayed like that for hours. My left hand never let go of Natalie's hand and my right hand held onto Kathryn's.

The only thing that I could think in one of the most difficult situations of my life, was: *This is it; this is family.*

"I FIGURED when I didn't see you in your room, you'd be here," Noah said to Kathryn as he came into the doorway. He made his way over to me, clapping a hand on my shoulder and giving it a squeeze. "How is she?" Noah tried to act tougher than he was, but his voice was shaking just enough to notice, and when I looked up at him, his eyes darted around the room, looking anywhere but at Natalie.

"The same. Thanks for coming. How was work?" I asked, grasping at shallow conversation to distract me.

Noah has been going away to school for a few years now and has always been a hard worker, so even when he *is* home, we don't get to see much of him. I try to take advantage of whenever he's around.

I was staring at Natalie, deep in thought and after a long period of silence, Kathryn snapped me out of my thoughts when she whispered, "It just... it happened so fast. I barely even saw it coming and then we were getting hit. I can still hear the whole thing. Her screams were the worst of it. They died down and when I looked over at her, she just seemed so... lifeless."

I lost my ability to form any words. I didn't know how to react to something like this.

The thought of losing my sister was too overwhelming for me to process and after what Kathryn just said, I can't help but imagine exactly what I assume happened in slow motion. I ran a hand over Natalie's hair, her curls limp and lacking the volume they had hours ago.

"I want to try to get her cleaned up tomorrow if she's awake." I tried to take my mind off of the fact that I didn't know if she *would* wake up. I shuddered as the thought crept into my mind. I shook my head to rid myself of the morbid thoughts and, while it seemed to work for the most part, I knew that this was only the beginning. I knew that someone would eventually remind me of the situation at hand and I would be back at square one.

All I had to do to be reminded was open my eyes and look at either her or Kathryn and I felt a fire burning within me.

This shouldn't have happened, not to them.

After Noah left to go back to work, Kathryn and I passed the time by talking about things that didn't matter like the songs that played and who wore what and brought who as their date. Anything to take our focus away from reality.

A while later, Natalie's surgeon came in, as promised, and ran more basic tests to make sure that things were going well. When she was gearing up to leave the room, she had a satisfied look on her face, lifting a weight off of both of our shoulders.

I pulled my phone out again.

Dylan: Mom, the surgeon just came in and she looked optimistic.

The day after prom, Kathryn had to get checked one last time before she was discharged. Once she was cleared with some bumps, bruises, and a minor concussion, I was comfortable stepping into the hallway once Kathryn took my place. I pulled my phone out of my pocket and fiddled with it momentarily before clicking Martha's contact and listening to it ring.

She answered on the second ring. "Hi, hon, what's up? How was Natalie's night?"

"Can you step away for a second?" I fought against my voice's desire to crack.

"Of course, is everything okay?"

"I don't really know how to tell you this, but…" I resented my voice for betraying me. "Natalie was in an accident last night. She's in a coma right now, I'm not really sure what's gonna happen. I guess all we can do is wait."

"Oh, my God. Okay, I'm coming. I'll get Bethany to cover for me, I'm on my way now. I'll see you in twenty minutes." Her voice was thick with emotion, but I found a certain comfort in her coming.

My gut reaction was accurate as Martha calmed both Kathryn and me down and took care of us in the motherly way that she always did. When I caught her up on everything, I apologized for not calling sooner. Thankfully, she understood why I waited so long.

As expected, Martha proved, yet again, to be the comfort that I sought in countless crises.

A few days later, things continued in a pattern. Nat stayed in her coma, Kathryn and I made sure that we wouldn't both be gone at the same time so if she *did* wake up, at least one of us would be there.

My mother, on the other hand, hadn't responded to the texts I sent her.

Dylan: Did you get my texts? I haven't heard from you.

It was easier to remain hopeful when I wasn't alone with her comatose body. Kathryn helped me push through a lot and I wasn't as scared, probably because I convinced myself that if I showed that I was scared, she would freak out again.

Everything will be fine. She'll wake up any day now, everything will go back to normal, and we can all bury this in the past.

CHAPTER SEVEN

DYLAN

On the fifth day of her coma and the Thursday after prom, I was sitting next to her bed, holding her hand when I heard the slightest of grunts.

It was so sudden and such a pleasant surprise that my entire body felt like it was in overdrive as I frantically searched for the button to call the nurse. My hands were shaking, and I couldn't seem to get them under control enough to make myself useful until I gave my hand a violent shake to get rid of the nerves.

After finally successfully hitting the button, I returned my focus back to Natalie whose hand was moving ever so slightly. I grabbed her hand as gently as I could and brushed her hair out of her face with my other hand. "Nat? Nat, I'm here. Can you hear me?"

I didn't have time to say much else to her before the nurse came in.

"She made a noise and then she was moving her hands, I think she's waking up," I explained faster than I had planned to.

"Dylan, right? I'm going to run a few tests to see if she's

made any progress and track any potential changes. Have a seat." She smiled and gestured for me to let go of my sister's hand, possibly out of fear that I would squeeze it until it popped.

Since Kathryn has been released, she's been able to go home for at least an hour or two a day to shower, take a nap and eat something significant, but I couldn't believe she was missing this! I resisted the urge to call her, figuring it's better to hold off until I have something more concrete to tell her.

I sat and watched intently as the nurse ran the tests. I didn't even know this many tests existed.

Can she feel pain?

I had so much time to sit and read different debates that I couldn't separate the truth from the myths at this point.

Almost as if she'd heard my thoughts, Natalie's eyes shot open. The nurse must've seen my excitement because she looked at me sadly, "No, I'm sorry, she's not awake. She's still in her coma. Some people open their eyes in response to pain. Remind me to give you one of the Glasgow Coma Scale sheets so that you can look it over." She offered an apologetic smile that, truthfully, didn't help in the slightest.

I nodded and rolled my lip between my teeth as I continued to wait. "What's your name?" I asked quietly, trying to distract myself. "I'm sorry, it just helps me feel less alone. You're always in here, looking after my sister and I don't even know your name, I'm so sorry." I looked at the back of her head while she worked.

She nodded and I saw an understanding glimmer in her dark brown eyes when she turned to face me. "Denise."

I nodded and let the conversation fall flat.

Denise turned to me after what felt like forever. "Well, I have some good news and some not-so-good news. The good news? There are differences in her test results that suggest that she *might* be waking up, but not-so-good news, we can't be sure if she really is going to wake up. Even if we could be sure, we don't have a known timeframe. She could wake up the second I walk out of this room or she could wake up very slowly and in pieces, which would take much longer. Now, this part is very important: Please, try to be careful with her and let her relax as much as possible. Don't try to speed up the process or force her to wake up, her body needs to take its own desired amount of time to do this." She gave me a stern, very mother-like look that warned me that there will be consequences if she catches wind that I didn't listen. Despite Denise's deeper skin tone, part of me felt like I was staring back at Martha.

"Understood, thank you." I offered a sheepish smile, feeling very much like a child after that little speech.

"You're welcome, hon. You let me know if anything changes. I'll be around." She nodded at me and handed me a sheet that talked about the Glasgow Coma Scale before leaving the room.

As soon as Denise closed the door behind her, I carefully combed through the information on the sheet to see where Natalie fell on the scale. I wasn't sure what to make of the information.

Is this good news?

I stood and made my way closer to the door where I pulled out my phone and called Kathryn immediately. She didn't pick up, so I left a message. "Hey Kat, it's me. I just wanted to let you know that I called the nurse in before and she ran some more tests and said she can't be sure or make any promises, but she thinks Nat could be showing signs of waking up soon. We're supposed to let her rest. I'm trying not to wake her, but I've been staring at her hard enough to wake anybody. Anyway, I don't want you to miss it if she wakes up, hurry back! Call me when you get this, I'll talk to you soon."

I was trying not to get my hopes up, but it felt impossible.

A few hours and a couple of more of Natalie's movements later, I got a call back from Kathryn.

"Please tell me I didn't miss anything! I'm so sorry, I'm on my way now, I just fell asleep when I got home, but I'm up, showered and on my way back. Have there been any changes?" She was talking so fast that she was practically panting afterward, and I could've sworn that I heard her running.

Finally getting the chance to talk when she was done, I told her that there were no major changes and told her to text me when she got to the hospital.

"Drive safe, I'll see you soon."

"I'll be there in ten minutes."

While I waited for Kathryn to arrive, I got a phone call from a number I didn't recognize.

"Hello?"

"Hi, is this Dylan Fields?" I didn't recognize the voice on the other line either.

"Yes, who is this?"

"Hi, Dylan, this is Detective Willis from the Boston Police Department, how is your sister doing?"

"She's still in a coma, but things might be looking up."

"I'm glad to hear it." I expected him to continue, but he didn't and silence came from both sides of the call.

"I'm sorry, what is this about?" I was growing impatient with the small talk. I could miss my sister waking up because of this nonsense.

"I'm calling to regretfully inform you that Jared Jenkins is no longer in our custody. He discharged himself from the hospital against medical advice. We are working to track him down and we will keep you updated. If you have any questions or anything, give us a call and ask for Detective Willis, I'll be the one handling your case."

I exhaled slowly, trying to remind myself that this is not the police department's fault. "Find him. I want him to pay for what he did, that's your job."

Don't make it be mine.

"We are doing everything we can at the moment, and we are carefully monitoring all security cameras and traffic lights to see if we can find him." He explained with a slight edge in his voice.

"Great. Is that all?" I tried to get off the phone for the second time.

"Yes, that's all. I wish your sister a speedy recovery."

"Thanks, bye." I ended the call and resisted the urge to throw my phone at the wall.

If he was being monitored and watched by a cop in his room at all times, how could he have just slipped out?

Focus on the good things. Natalie could be waking up. In either situation, all you can do right now is wait.

CHAPTER EIGHT

ELLIE

A s my mother and I boarded the plane, my heart was conflicted. There was a certain calm in getting away from the city that I knew Jared would be able to find me in, but also an anxiety that I've always found in flying.

When we took our seats, I wiped my sweaty palms on my jeans and reached for my mother's hand.

"Are you gonna be okay?" She looked at me and gave my hand a comforting squeeze.

"Yeah, I think so. Once we're in the air, it'll be easier for me. That's how it always goes. In the meantime, distract me. What's the plan when we get to Boston? And why are we going to Boston of all places?"

"You know I used to live in Boston once upon a time. I haven't been back in years and I think you'll love it there like I did."

"If you loved it there so much, why'd you leave?"

"Sometimes you can't do the growing that you need to do if you never leave home. You have to step out of your comfort zone sometimes. You know, all that nonsense that everyone always preaches about. I hate to say it, but I agree." She brushed off the cliché that was coming out of her mouth.

I sighed, "I think living a life without Jared will be a difficult transition from the life that I used to live and the life I want to live. I just always assumed I'd be in that situation. Now I'm out, but I feel like I have to have eyes in the back of my head and it's almost hard for me to be able to tell which is worse."

"The situation you're finally escaping is definitely worse. If you have to 'escape' it, it's not okay. The fear will fade when he finally gets what's coming to him. On the path that he's on now, there's no way that he'll keep slipping out of sentencing." My mother's sadness had faded into something closer to anger, but it was clear that she was trying to contain the true height of her emotions.

"You're probably right. Anyway, Dad was gone before I woke up this morning, how did he react when you told him everything?"

"Obviously, he wasn't thrilled over the situation, I mean, who would be? He's proud of you for knowing you deserve better, though."

"I just wish it didn't take me so long to figure it out."

"Ellie, when you love someone the way that you loved Jared, it's hard to imagine that those people can have such major flaws. Being a little sloppy or slightly ill-mannered, that's one thing and those are average quirks that can make a relationship a little more difficult, but…" She lowered her voice so that only I could hear it. "physical abuse is not something that can just be overlooked. It can come out of nowhere and that's why it's hard for people to get out of situations like that sometimes. You think this person is fantastic and the love of your life until they show you this side of them that you didn't even know existed. It's a shock to the system."

"I'm just over him having any control over my life. I tried to cover up my leaving by telling him I was coming to your house for a girls' weekend and even that he had an issue with. I had to ask him to see my mother. It's just so infuriating to think about now that I have a minute to breathe and look at it all from a distance." I ran my free hand through my hair.

"I know, and you'll probably feel like that for a while, but I need you to remember that being angry with yourself isn't going to make the situation better, it'll just stress you out more. You need to let all your emotions about the situation come out and then you need to work on moving on and bettering yourself so that eventually you won't think about him anymore because your life is better off without him."

"Thank you for coming with me and planning this little trip. It means the world to me."

"Anything for you Ellie, it's my job. I just don't want you to be in pain forever. Speaking of, how are you feeling physically?"

"My stomach feels a little tender because of the bruising, but otherwise I'm okay."

"Good. So, you asked about the plan. We're going to do some sight-seeing, I'll take you around to a few of the places that I frequented while I was growing up, it'll be extremely low key and on the opposite side of the country from Jared; just what the doctor ordered."

I stiffened as the plane started to accelerate and I could only hope that I would fall asleep at some point during this flight.

WE WERE ONLY HERE for three days, and suddenly, it was time to head home already. I was laying in the hotel bed while my mother was packing up her things so we could head to the airport when something unexpected came out of my mouth.

"Hey, mom?"

"What's up?"

"Would you mind if I stayed here for a few more days?"

She walked over and sat next to me on the bed. "No, not at all. Not ready to go back yet?"

"No, not yet. I feel some sort of freedom here. Don't worry, I'm not going to move here to keep that freedom. I won't be truly free until I can go back home and feel the same way. This little escape from reality has just been fantastic." I gestured to the room. "It's just so peaceful here."

"I get it, believe me. Unfortunately, I can't stay with you, I have to go back to work. I've been getting texts for the past few days and apparently the hospital's billing department is just falling apart without me." She rolled her eyes. "Are you going to be okay on your own?"

"Yes. I think being alone here will be a good segue to being alone back home. I could use the practice."

"I think it's a good idea, actually. Don't forget to call the airline and see if you can switch your flight last minute. When you have new flight information, please send it to me. You also better keep in touch and answer your phone!" She continued gathering her stuff after she saw what time it was.

"I will. Thank you for understanding."

She came back over to me, hugged me, and kissed my head. "I love you, Ellie. I had a lot of fun this weekend. I'll text you from the airport. Please, be careful and I'll see you when you come home."

"I love you, too, Mom. I'll talk to you in a little bit." I waved as she made her way out the door.

As the door closed behind her, I had to fight the sudden panic that tried to force its way to the surface.

I can do this. I'll be okay for a few more days without her.

THE NEXT DAY, I made my way to the hair salon that we'd passed multiple times on the way back to the hotel. I twirled my blonde hair around my finger while I walked.

I'm sorry, but I can't take any chances.

When I walked in, I was greeted with a salon full of employees, not one of them occupied.

"Hi, I have an unusual request."

"What can we do for you?"

"I'd like to leave here unrecognizable."

One of the hairdressers in the back quirked an eyebrow. "Are you running from the law?"

"Not quite. I live in Seattle and when I go home, I just don't want anyone I know to be able to recognize me at a quick glance."

"Okay, well, I think we can all do a little something to help you with that. How much are you looking to spend?"

I glanced at the board by the register that listed the prices of all their services and was pleasantly surprised with the low prices.

Luck of the draw.

"As much as it takes. I need this done."

"Okay, come on back. Let's see what we can do here."

CHAPTER NINE

DYLAN

"Dyl-Dylan?" I heard a dry, raspy voice call me, and my head shot up towards Natalie.

Her eyes were open, but only slightly.

"Nat? Are you really awake? I'm gonna need you to talk to me again and please don't ever stop because I feel like I'm imagining this." I held eye contact with her while I blindly pressed the button to call the nurse in.

A small smile cracked through her chapped lips and she turned her head towards the cup of water on the table beside her bed. She tried to lift her arm to reach for it, but she was too weak.

I gently pushed her arm back down on the bed. "Don't push yourself, I'll get it. Your nurse says you need all the rest you can get." I reached and tilted her cup of water to her lips until she signaled for me to stop.

"And I meant it!" Denise announced as she made her entrance into the room. She smiled at Natalie, "Hi, honey, I'm your nurse, you can call me Denise. How do you feel?"

"I'm okay. How long was I out?" She spoke softly and winced every time she swallowed.

"Five days," I told her before Denise got the chance.

Natalie's face fell. "I missed graduation." I watched her dwell on that for a moment before she shook herself out of it and changed the subject. "Oh my god, Kathryn. Where is she? Is she okay? Was she hurt?"

She was gaining strength back rather quickly and was now sitting more upright than before and looking at me frantically, waiting for answers.

As if on cue, Kathryn walked through the door and dropped her bag before running over to Natalie's bed. She halted to a stop and looked at Denise. "Can I hug her? Please let me hug her!" She bounced on the balls of her feet like a little kid would when begging for something.

"Yes, gently!" Denise pulled back from checking Natalie's responsiveness to let Kathryn get in there.

She basically just laid on Nat and gently cupped her hands around Natalie's shoulders since she couldn't get her arms around her. "I'm so happy you're okay! I was so worried!" When she pulled away, tears were streaming down Natalie's face.

"You're not mad?" She looked at Kathryn specifically.

"Mad? Why would I be mad at you? I'm just happy you're alive and awake. Nothing else matters. We're both alive and healing and Natalie Rose Fields, this was not your fault. I love you and everything is going to be fine." Kathryn held her hand while she talked, and I watched as Natalie's face relaxed.

She looked towards me as if to ask me the same question and I answered her before she could. "No, Nat. I'm not mad at you either, you didn't do anything wrong. I'm just happy you're still here. I don't know what I would've done if I lost you."

She smiled and I noticed her eyes start to water so she

cleared her throat and changed the subject. "Where's Mom?" her eyebrows knit together.

I felt bad because I know that no matter what, there will just be some things that I can't fill my mother's shoes in, and I suddenly felt like I wasn't fit to take care of her on my own. "I've been texting her, but she hasn't answered. I can try to get her again if you want me to."

A certain disappointment made its way into her expression and she didn't bother trying to hide it. "No, it's okay. Thank you for trying."

My heart instantly bled for her. I often found myself doubting that I really knew what's best for Natalie or that I'd be able to be enough for her when I finally got her out of that toxic house, but at the end of the day, I'd do anything to protect her. The disappointment of my mother's absence was just one of many things that I wouldn't be able to protect her from, even more so now that she's grown up.

I sat and watched as Natalie and Kathryn talked about anything and everything and I truly am so proud of my little sister. She really has grown despite everything she's been through.

I knew if our dad was still alive, she'd want him here. I also knew that he'd be here without her asking. So would Mom. When Mom and Dad were together, they were the best versions of themselves and I really worried about my mom and whether or not she's lost that version entirely. These arbitrary dating habits started to chip little pieces of her away slowly.

Don't get me wrong, I love my mother, but that doesn't mean that I approve of the things that she has done since my father died.

Cancer was the worst thing to happen to this family.

Osteosarcoma was my dad's downfall. One second, he was fine and a few months later he was unrecognizable, and I watched as the life left his eyes. Looking back at pictures that were only a few months before his death, I can't even believe how quickly it took over and took him from us.

After the funeral, my mother didn't come out of her room for days on end. We couldn't get her to talk to us, she barely ate anything and when she finally did come out of her room, more often than not, she would stare off into the distance with a devastatingly glassy look in her eye.

Her responsibilities took the backseat as her grief did the driving.

Part of me thinks that maybe she didn't know how to be a mother without him. Or maybe she just didn't know how to be a person and she had to figure that out all over again. She was the definition of broken.

Then, one day, she just got up, went out and got herself a job after losing the one she had during weeks of heartbreak and just resumed as though nothing had changed.

She never acknowledged what happened or asked me and Natalie how we felt or even talked about it. Nobody pushed the issue out of fear that she would start back at square one. She just plastered on a picture-perfect smile and went about her business. I think part of me has resented her ever since then for how she handled it, but I've never been in love, so I can't judge her if I don't know how I'd handle it.

When we finally made it a year without him, our mom went out and came back with a boyfriend. She introduced him to us and acted as if there was nothing strange about it. I frequently debated with myself whether or not she even remembered what happened or if she blocked it from her memory entirely.

Deciding a year was long enough, Natalie and I would bring it up every now and then and it was like our mother had gone deaf anytime we mentioned it.

While she was grieving, Natalie and I were handling everything in ways of our own.

I ran.

I ran every night after work. Sometimes, I didn't even realize how much of the day I could lose to running until I would notice that the sun had started going down. It got to the point that I lost an unhealthy amount of weight. After a quick visit to the doctor, running very quickly became running and going to the gym so that I could still continue to get the sensation that made me hurt less, but I was also gaining muscle.

Natalie started throwing herself into writing. I think it was to honor our father's memory since he always believed in the author in her. I also think that's why this book that she's putting together means so much to her.

I looked over at her and amazement washed over me. She's as resilient as she is stubborn. When she woke up, rather than resting, she fought me until I agreed to go home to go check and see if the proof of her book had arrived. "It should've gotten there by Tuesday!" she told me. I moaned and groaned but gave in and gathered my belongings to head home; my absolute delight of a sister also demanded that I shower while I'm at home because I stink.

CHAPTER TEN

DYLAN

When I got home and walked up to the front door, sure enough, there was a package waiting. I wondered how long it had been there and whether or not my mother had been sleeping at Chris's since they got back from their trip. If she's been here, she must've stepped over it several times at this point. I promised that I wouldn't open the package because, understandably, Nat wanted to do the honors, so I left it on my bed while I went to take a shower.

After I got dressed, I headed back to the hospital with the box on my lap and as I drove, I started to think about how my prayers were heard and answered and that there's good in the world and I tried to remind myself to see that next time I'm feeling angry and bitter because there's always something to smile about. This whole experience has really brought to light that life is too short, and I wanted to better myself from here on out. I want to make Natalie as proud of me as I am of her.

Arriving at the hospital felt quicker than usual due to my inner conversation. I grabbed the box and locked my car as I headed inside. On the way to her room, I saw Martha walking towards me.

"Hey! What're you doing here? I didn't know you were coming!"

"Hi, Dylan. I just wanted to stop by and see her for a few minutes before I have to be at work. It's so good to see her awake."

"I know, I was starting to go crazy just watching her lay there in that state, it was hard to watch."

She closed the gap between us and hugged me. "I know, but she's okay now. Is that the copy of her book?" She gestured to the box in my hand.

"Yeah, the little witch sent me home to shower and grab this so she can see her pride and joy."

"Well, let's face it, you were a little rank." Martha teased.

"On that note, I'm going to get this to her. Thank you for stopping by, I'm sure it means the world to her. I love you, drive safe and I'll see you later, okay? You have to get to work!"

"Bye, hon. I love you, too. I'll see you later."

We hugged one more time before parting ways and I continued on my path down the hall.

When I reached the room, Natalie and Kathryn were looking at the pictures that they took at prom.

"This one's my favorite, we both look amazing!" Kathryn snorted.

"Are you kidding? Both of our double chins are so prominent!" Natalie tapped the screen for emphasis. They both broke into a fit of giggles.

I cleared my throat, announcing my presence and held the package up next to my head and shook it gently for Natalie to see.

Her eyes lit up and she reached towards me, begging for me to give it to her. She tore through it like an animal and smiled down at it with pride, soaking in her creation before she would even consider showing us. "It's beautiful." She sat with a satisfied look in her eyes as she turned the book to face us.

The matte dark blue cover with the white script and baby's breath flowers on the cover looked so intricate that I knew it was everything that she had envisioned. The back had a little blurb about her and her inspiration for this book. She handed it to me, and I flipped through the pages to find her dedication page which, low and behold, was written out to our father.

"Dad would love it, Nat. You did an amazing job. Now all you have to do is publish, right?" I encouraged her to the best of my ability so that the loss of him wouldn't seep into the cracks of her composure.

"Yeah, more or less. I just have to approve the proof for publication, everything else is done at this point. I'm trying not to get my hopes up, though because poetry books are big right now and there's a lot of them out there to compete with." Not even five minutes after holding a print of her book, she was doubting herself and raining on her own parade.

"Maybe, but you are the only person that can bring this raw emotion to the audience. Nobody has been through the exact same things that you've been through or thinks the same things or feels the same ways or can even come up with the combination of words that you did. This is yours and yours alone and no one can take it from you, don't invalidate it."

"You know I hate to agree with him, but he's right, Nat. It's beautiful, revel in it!" Kathryn added on in an attempt to lift Natalie's spirits.

"When can we read it?"

"When you buy a copy and not a minute sooner!" She

ALYSSA LASTELLA

grabbed her book back and held it protectively close to her chest.

Our conversation was cut short when Denise came back in and asked to speak with me privately, so I excused myself from the conversation with the girls and followed Denise out into the hall, closing the door behind us.

"Now, I don't want to startle you, but I want you to be aware and prepared. She looks great, but sometimes patients show signs of getting better in what could potentially be their final stages. This could be her body's way of processing a final surge of adrenaline which is sometimes called terminal lucidity. Unfortunately, because everybody's different, there is no way to know for sure, but it is a possibility. I want to remind you that this is not meant to be a scare tactic, I really just want you to be prepared, god forbid." She stood in front of me and looked at me, waiting for a response or reaction or... anything.

I felt myself nod slowly, but I wasn't really sure why I did it. I cleared my throat which brought me back to reality completely.

"Understood, thank you for giving me a heads up, Denise. Actually, thank you for everything, you've been incredible, and you've made this so much easier. You've gone above and beyond for us."

"Nonsense, that's my job. You just let me know if you need anything else. I'll keep coming in to monitor her. If you have any questions, you know where to find me."

I couldn't help but feel my fear reappear when she walked away. It reminded me that I'm basically responsible for both of these girls, meanwhile, I don't have anything on them except a few years. My sister might not legitimately be getting better and the thought that this can be a false alarm terrifies me.

I walked back into the room and made sure to plaster a

smile on my face to cover the slight panic that I was actually feeling. "Not to be a big dad, but it's getting late and there was a lot of excitement today. I think you two should get some rest, especially you, Nat. Doctor's orders."

Both of the girls groaned in frustration. "It's only been a few hours, you're no fun!" Natalie said, bringing me back to the night of prom.

I rushed out a response before I was consumed by my thoughts. "I know, I know, I suck. Kathryn, are you staying? I'll see if I can have a nurse bring in a cot for you if you are." I brushed off the complaints and moved on.

"Yes, of course, I'm staying!" Kathryn looked at Natalie longingly and adoringly, but it was gone as quickly as it came. I know that I was not mistaken when I thought I saw it. Natalie wasn't looking at Kathryn and by the time she was, Kathryn just had a friendly smile on her face which Natalie returned.

I nodded and left the room to go bother Denise again and see if she would be able to get a cot for our room. I decided that I would bring her a coffee to thank her for everything since I knew that between my pestering and my sister's varying conditions, she's been working like a dog. And let's face it, she's a nurse; enough said.

After I grabbed a coffee for her, I asked around to find out where she was until I was able to track her down. She was extremely appreciative of the coffee and took it without hesitation. She was also more than willing to look around until she found a cot for Kathryn to stay in Natalie's room. She sent me back to hang out with the girls in the meantime and we stayed there while we patiently waited.

I could tell that Natalie was getting tired, her body was struggling with trying to keep up with her and fix her at the same time. She didn't have much of an appetite but, thankfully, she was drinking a lot of water. Denise already put my mind at ease and assured me that her lack of appetite is not worthy of concern yet. I made sure Natalie was warm and comfortable as I ignored all of her whines about not being able to sleep on her side due to her lack of mobility.

"I'm sorry you're not comfortable, but that's not important right now. Everything that's preventing you from sleeping on your side is only here to help you and it's doing its job so I'm not doing anything about it. We can talk to Denise and see if there's anything we can do for you but please just focus on getting better and stop fussing, you need to relax."

"Fine." She huffed.

Kathryn walked over to try to help the situation. "Why don't you try to close your eyes? I'm sure you're exhausted. We'll both be here when you wake up." She leaned the bed back a little bit, so it was in an easier position to fall asleep in. We each held one of Natalie's hands and she gave us both a squeeze and said she'll talk to us when she wakes up.

Eventually, she finally fell asleep and Denise came in with the cot shortly after. It didn't take Kathryn long to fall asleep, neither of us has really slept, at least not a good night's worth, in a while. At least one of us would get to recharge tonight. I made sure to close the door so it was only cracked, and I turned off the lights so that the girls would be able to sleep without interruption. I pulled out my laptop and started researching surges and rallies before death.

I wasn't even sure how much time had passed when Denise came in one last time, but I had read so much that my eyes were burning, and I felt a headache coming on.

"You know, something told me to pop in here one more time before I left, I had a feeling you'd still be awake. It's past midnight, you should really get some rest."

I closed my laptop and roughly rubbed my hands down my face and tugged at my hair slightly in frustration. "I can't even think about sleeping. I've been researching rallying before death and I'm just consuming so much information that Natalie's actual situation is starting to become fuzzy in my head. I'm worried about her." I whispered.

"It's not certain. Everybody's different, she really might have just bounced back quickly, but I have to say I am glad that you're educating yourself. It's best to be prepared so if you want to run anything by me to fact check it, you are more than welcome." She sat down in the chair next to me.

Denise's warmth and the fact that she opened the door for questions made me feel more comfortable talking to her. "This is more of an opinion or belief question: Do you think it's a spiritual thing or a scientific thing?" I asked, throwing the idea of the two back and forth in my head, unable to decide which one I believed. "I read something that said when organs shut down, they release a compound that's steroid-like and that can cause the body to have a surge of energy which sounds like a real possibility."

"Yes, that's true." Denise looked at me, waiting for me to continue.

"I also read stories that people died when their family was finally united because all of their loved ones were there, or that they waited to die until everyone left the room as if they wanted it to hurt less which I also think I believe." I had to stop to take a breath.

"Well, there's no scientific proof of that, that just depends on what your heart tells you."

"I know, I just can't decide if I want to believe the science side or the fact that she has control over it. Everything was so easy and clear when I was ignorant."

"That's how it always is. Everybody's in a rush to grow up and know everything until they realize how much it sucks. There's so much uncertainty in the world and so much we have no control over." She sighed and looked at me sympathetically.

"Ever since I was a kid, I've gone back and forth between believing in God and then ditching that and choosing science. Now, I want to believe but it's hard. If God really is out there, why is this happening to her? I just feel so lost and helpless and I hate it. I was always able to be everything for her and now I can't." I dragged my hand down my face again.

"I know. But I need you to listen to me, okay? There's no guarantee that this will happen. This doesn't mean that this is her fate. She could be fine, but only time will tell." She sighed.

Denise placed her hand on mine which was resting on my closed laptop. "I know how much you wish I were wrong when I say this, but you don't have any control over this. Science and God both have you beat. This is up to them and your sister at this point. You need rest, too. Try to relax, I'm going home now. I'll be back in the morning. In the meantime, there's another nurse here. Her name is Nicole, she's great, she'll be able to help you if you need me while I'm gone. Again, I know you want to fix your sister, but you need to take care of yourself, too. Have a good night, Dylan. I'll see you in the morning."

With that, she left. I pulled the chair that she was sitting in directly in front of me so I could try to stretch out a little bit more. I took one last glance at the girls before closing my eyes and felt proud of myself.

For someone who kinda just took on the father role, I think I'm doing pretty well. As long as they're comfortable, safe, and healthy, that's all I need.

I just hoped it would continue to be enough for me to get at least a few hours of sleep like it has for the past several nights.

CHAPTER ELEVEN

DYLAN

E ventually, I drifted off to sleep until I heard my name being whispered in the dark. I ignored it the first time, part of me too scared of the voice in the dark after I only woke up partially.

When it happened again, it wasn't as altered by my half-asleep state and it sounded less like a demon after my soul, and more like my little sister.

"Nat?" I whispered back.

"Yeah, it's me." She answered and a paranoid part of me still sighed in relief.

I reached to flick on the light above Natalie's bed.

Kathryn woke up on the other side of Natalie's hospital bed and the cot creaked as she moved to sit up quickly. "Natalie? Are you okay? Do you need anything?"

"Yes, I'm okay," there was a pause. "Actually, can you run and see if you can fill my pitcher with water again? I feel like I'm still sporadically getting dry mouth."

"Dylan, do you want or need anything?" Kathryn shifted her focus to me.

"No, I'm okay, thank you."

"Of course, I'll be right back." She spoke softly and eagerly.

"Thank you," Natalie smiled.

Before Kathryn left, she flicked the light off, probably in hopes that Natalie would still be tired enough to possibly fall back to sleep and closed the door behind her.

"What's wrong, are you okay?" I sat up, facing Natalie even though I couldn't see much. The blinking lights of her machines had helped light up the room only slightly. I waited for my eyes to adjust fully to the darkness.

"I'm scared." Her voice shook when she spoke, and she sniffled.

"What're you scared of?" I asked her.

"I don't want to die." She choked out in a sob.

"You're not dying, Nat. You were in a coma for a while, but your body needed the time to recuperate and it did. Now you're awake and better than you were right before you fell into the coma. A lot better, believe me."

"But what if I'm just rallying? I might die and I won't know when or how long it'll take or if it'll hurt." My eyes widened when she said the word that I'd been centering all my thoughts around for hours before I finally fell asleep.

"What're you talking about?" I asked with a lump in my throat.

"Come on, Dyl. How long did you really think you'd be able to keep it from me for? I heard you talking to Denise when she came in a while ago. I tried to go to sleep and ignore it, but I've been up thinking about it and trying to think my way out of it, but I just keep spiraling into worst-case scenarios and it's scaring me. I don't know what to do or if there's anything I can even do. That's probably the scariest part of all of this for me." She confessed.

"I'm sorry that you overheard all of that, I thought you

were sleeping. I didn't want to tell you because I didn't want you to worry. Which part scares you the most?"

"The part that I haven't had control over anything since I got in the car after Kathryn and I left our prom. I was hit by some other car, which I had no control over because I didn't do anything wrong. Speaking of, do we know how the other driver's doing?" She asked selflessly, even in her time of fear.

I didn't have the heart to tell her the whole truth yet. I knew I couldn't protect her from it forever, but the world is so much worse than I ever wanted her to have to see.

"He's okay as far as I know, but don't worry about that. Worry about yourself and getting better." Truthfully, the cops hadn't gotten in touch with me yet, so my knowledge was limited. My mental justification helped me feel less guilty.

"Good." She wiped her tears from her cheeks and then continued to vent. "Anyway, I didn't have any control over the fact that I went into a coma after or over when I would wake up and now there's this thing looming over my head and I just don't know if it's really going to happen or not and I'm scared. I feel like someone else is behind the wheel of my life and I'm just clinging to the windshield and trying not to get hit by the wipers like some kind of bug." She let out a laugh at her ridiculous analogy in between her sobs.

I got up and sat next to her and pulled her into my side, hugging her, and laughed lightly. "Oh, Nat, you're not a bug. Listen to me," I held her out at arm's length to the best of my ability since we were sideways. "We are going to get through this together just like we do with everything else. Whatever happens, you'll always have me, okay? We'll figure something out, we always do." I wasn't sure if I was reassuring her or myself, but I knew that it helped soothe me a little bit and I felt her exhale and let her shoulders loosen up.

She looked up at me from her lap and nodded with tears in her big hazel eyes. "Okay, I'm gonna hold you to that." She gave me a look that promised me that she wouldn't let me forget about this discussion.

"Hey, I've been meaning to ask you, how did you get the money to almost completely publish a book all by yourself?"

"I've saved the majority of money that I've made from working at the restaurant and babysitting. I also skipped a lot of outings with friends so I wouldn't be tempted to spend. It also kinda helped that I couldn't afford the expensive stuff anytime soon. I keep trying to tell myself that just because I can't afford the best of the best yet, doesn't mean I'll never get there."

"Natalie, that's incredibly impressive, you know that, right? Most kids your age wouldn't be able to resist going out and spending. I think we both got Dad's financial mindset, you know how careful he always was with his money. Speaking of, he would be so proud of you!"

She laughed, but I felt her tears soaking through my shirt as she rested her head on my shoulder. "I just want to make him proud, you know?"

"Of course. I feel the same way, but you've definitely beaten me to actually accomplishing it."

"Your time will come; I know it will. I'm excited to see what the future holds for you." She wiped the remaining tears from her face at the same time as Kathryn opened the door to walk back in with enough water and crackers for all of us. She didn't seem to notice Natalie wiping her eyes, for which I was thankful, and I could tell that Natalie was, too.

"I come bearing hydration!" Kathryn whisper-yelled when she closed the door as quietly as possible using her hip. She winced momentarily when the door clicked shut louder than anticipated.

Natalie patted the bed in front of her and I switched on the lamp above her bed. "Thank god! Come sit." Any evidence of her crying mere moments ago had completely vanished and her infamous smile graced her face once again.

Everything felt normal and it didn't seem to matter how early it was. The silence of the world that surrounded us seemed respectful and peaceful. For the three of us, this was all we needed.

THE NEXT THREE days were filled with a lot of spontaneous 'I love you's, appreciative glances, and warm hugs. Natalie and I weren't very affectionate people in the sense that we don't hug people just for the sake of doing it. I mean, we definitely weren't spending the majority of our childhood hugging one another while our mother cried, it was actually full of a lot of long awkward silences because I didn't know how to communicate with Natalie about serious things at the time.

She was twelve so she was clear on the fact that our dad had died and the impact of it had fully struck her, but every reason that I tried to feed her as to why our mom had stopped talking to us was quickly rejected. Natalie didn't want my explanations, she wanted solutions which I had none of. I couldn't fix it regardless of my age.

The memory of her first day back at school after losing him came flooding back. I called up to her to remind her that the bus would be here in a few minutes and she came downstairs, her brown hair in a big frizzy mess, clearly not brushed. When I told her to go brush her hair and finish getting ready for school, she looked me in the eyes, defiant as ever, and said: "If mom gets to stay home, why do I have to go to school?"

"Mom needs a little more time to mourn Dad. I'm going to work today, you're not alone in this. We need to keep doing what we're supposed to so she can take the time that she needs to get better."

Her eyes filled up with tears almost immediately. "But I'm not better."

That was the first time that I realized how much she needed me. That day, I called her school and told them she wouldn't be coming in and called in sick to work. That was the first time we went to Martha's diner. We spent the day there and abandoned all responsibilities.

From that point on, I stepped up and took care of whatever she needed me to. I wasn't sure what to do, but I knew I wasn't going to neglect her when she needed someone to guide her the most, so I did whatever I thought was right.

It was a pretty bumpy road in the beginning, but I can't imagine our relationship being anything less than what it is today, despite what it took to get here.

Since our mom was so absent, I had a harder time forgiving her than Natalie ever did. She would always tell me, "She had her heart broken, she's allowed to make mistakes and change her life while she tries to figure out how to fix it. Everyone has to heal at their own pace."

Our mother has been acting this way for years now and I resented her for it. I couldn't even mourn my father properly because I've been so stuck in my anger towards her.

I decided on the spot that because of this, the second that Natalie got out of the hospital, we'd pack our things and get an apartment. Our mother is never home anyway, so when we move out, she'll see no point in paying rent there anymore and she'll probably just move in with Chris like she's always wanted.

IT WAS the fifth day that Natalie had been awake. The other days were all great, but today, she was different. She was cold and rude to just about everyone who she came across and was in no mood for conversation.

She said she hadn't been sleeping well, so Kathryn and I both decided that we would make it as dark as possible in her room and then excuse ourselves so she could get some rest. We both went to our separate houses to take showers and grab something to eat.

I was just finishing towel-drying my hair when my phone rang.

"Hello?"

"Dylan? It's Denise. Are you driving?"

"Hi, Denise. No, I'm not, why? Did Natalie have you call me to ask me to grab something she wanted from home?"

"No, honey, she didn't." Her voice sounded shaky at first, but I heard her try to stabilize and recover. She let out a shaky sigh. "I'm so sorry. She didn't make it."

I couldn't help but laugh. "Wait, what?" I laughed again. I honestly never would've thought that these words would hit my ears... but they did, and my life changed forever.

"Natalie's organs shut down and she passed away at 3:52 p.m., I'm so sorry for your loss." She was struggling to get through what she was legally required to tell me.

"We'll be there in ten minutes. Don't let them take my sister, keep fighting for her! She can't die, she's only eighteen. She's so scared, please don't let this be her ending. You need to keep fighting, Denise!" I heard bits and pieces of her telling me not to drive in the state that I was in, but I hung up, not wanting to hear her response, and definitely not taking any advice.

I scrambled to get dressed and get in the car, as I fought to regain control of my shaky hands. My shoes weren't even on completely and I tripped over them as I was running to the car, only infuriating me further.

I called Kathryn with trembling fingers, barely hearing the phone ringing over the pounding of my heart echoing into my ears. "Denise just called me; we need to get to the hospital now. I'll be there in two minutes, be ready."

I paid too little mind to my speed and too much time to my breathing that I couldn't get under control. Turning onto Kathryn's block, I was surprised I made it there in one piece.

When I finally picked Kathryn up, she kept asking questions and when I didn't answer, sobs tore out from her throat and echoed throughout the car.

She kept screaming and sobbing. I kept myself from looking over at her, knowing it would send me into a spiral. It would make it real. I looked down at my knuckles which had gone white from squeezing the steering wheel so tight.

CHAPTER TWELVE

DYLAN

I refused to believe that she was gone, but it's kind of hard to ignore the truth when you see your sister lying flat on her bed, all tubes out and machines off, her eyes closed and her chest still. She wasn't breathing anymore.

Frantic, I ran over and started shaking her. "Do chest compressions or something! Why are you just *standing there?*" I screamed, my voice cracking. My vision was blurred, and I could hardly breathe through my sobs. I knew she was gone at this point, but I couldn't accept it. There's no way that my angel of a baby sister was now just that, an angel.

Kathryn didn't dare even set foot in the room. She stood with her shoulder leaning against the doorway, her hands covering her nose and mouth as she sobbed.

I looked at my baby sister and noticed her skin was paler than when I left.

It was when Denise came in and rubbed circles on my back that I realized that she was gone.

She was still. Too still. I couldn't bear to look at her anymore, I turned to face Denise faster than either of us were expecting and she flinched.

It was when I finally felt the presence of the tears hitting my cheeks that I realized that Natalie and my dad were finally together again, and they would write the best stories together. She's probably so happy and at peace that I can't be upset with her for dying on me.

I collapsed down on Denise's shoulder as I wept. The dramatic height difference made me bend down and I could tell that it was physically uncomfortable for her, but she didn't complain. She just stayed still with her arms wrapped around my back and let me fall apart. Only a few minutes had passed before the sound of Kathryn's hyperventilating brought me out of my blind misery.

I pulled away from Denise and she excused herself. "Take all the time you need. If you need anything, you know where to find me." She covered all the windows that led to the hallway so we could have privacy and then left the room.

I walked over to Kathryn and enveloped her in my arms as she cried into my chest. I placed my chin on top of her head and let my tears fall. I tried to control my breathing, but I couldn't grasp the reins again.

I started getting frustrated with myself for not having more control over my emotions. I could tell that Kathryn was feeling more or less the same sentiment when she kept trying to talk but couldn't get a sentence out before she gasped through her tears or choked out more sobs.

"Why?" was all she could manage.

I took a deep breath to try to calm my breathing before I even attempted speaking. "I don't know, Kat. I just don't know."

I was at a loss. I didn't even want to think about all of the things I would have to take care of from this point on. I didn't want to think about anything. I wanted to crawl into bed, but I couldn't.

I grabbed Kathryn's hand and started walking towards Natalie. When Kathryn realized what I was doing, she dug her heels in and used both hands to start yanking back on my arm. "Dylan, no, stop! Please, I can't do this." She cried.

"Close your eyes, it's okay, I promise." I tried to calm Kathryn down.

She closed her eyes and took a deep breath to calm herself.

Still holding her hand, I led her to Natalie's bed. At this point, everything felt calm and still, aside from the never-ending stream of tears down my cheeks. I pushed Natalie's hair off of her forehead and bent down to kiss her head for one of the last times ever.

Her skin was cold and the reality that this wasn't her usual cold hands and feet sent a shiver down my spine and forced goosebumps to scatter across my body. "I love you, Natalie. I'm so sorry," My throat burned as I tried to finish what I wanted to say. "Send my love to Dad and please take care of each other."

It didn't feel real as I looked at my sister, even more still than when she was in her coma which didn't seem possible as we waited for her to wake up.

I turned to face Kathryn and could barely see her through my blurred eyes. "Do you want to say anything to her?" I asked quietly.

Kathryn shook her head no and then slowly opened her eyes. When she saw Natalie's body up close, I felt her tense as she squeezed my hand. She didn't let go of it until she threw herself on top of Natalie and hugged her, sobbing, and howling into her shoulder. She didn't say anything, she just cried. The sight didn't make it any easier for me to hold myself together. I just couldn't bear to watch. The intensity of her crying rattled my bones and that was all it took for me

73

to understand that she was letting it all out so she could try to pull herself together when she was ready.

She eventually stood up and also kissed Natalie's forehead and grabbed my hand immediately after when she was no longer touching Natalie. As much as it seemed like she needed to hold my hand, I needed to hold hers. It was helping remind me that I wasn't going through this alone. I wasn't the only one losing the best person I knew.

Kathryn buried her face into my chest again, but when she pulled away this time, she was more collected. She wiped her face free of tears and suddenly, the only indications that she was crying were her blotchy face and her red-rimmed eyes.

I followed suit and wiped my face with my sleeves. I pulled out my phone and decided to text my mother.

Dylan: Natalie passed away, I need you...

I immediately realized that Natalie must have rubbed off on me if I'm reaching out to my mother, let alone admitting that I need her.

I decided that I would go find Denise. She was just down the hall from Natalie's room and I remembered that she said she wouldn't stray just in case we needed her. When she saw me coming, she reached under the nurses' station that she was sitting at and pulled out an envelope. As I got closer, I saw that it had my name on it.

"How are you guys doing, do you need anything?" She asked before mentioning anything about the envelope in her hand.

"We're still alive, so that's something." I explained.

"I'm sorry. I just wanted to let you know, I called your mother. Protocol demands that the parents be notified."

"It's okay, I actually tried getting in touch with her myself, but she hasn't answered yet. I've texted her several times in the past few days and I haven't heard back once."

"Maybe you should try to go outside and get some fresh air, it might help. Before you go, I have something for you." She motioned to the envelope. "I'm going to give this to you now, but I don't want you to open it until you are as relaxed as you can be given the circumstances, okay?"

I nodded. "Okay, thank you."

I pulled my phone out of my pocket again and clicked on Martha's contact. I felt a strange sense of déjà vu, only I'd wished that my message would've been the same.

"Martha?"

"Hi, doll, is everything okay?"

"No, it's Natalie, can you get to the hospital?" My throat felt like it was starting to close again as I tried to hold back the waves.

"My car broke down; I might be able to get a taxi or something. Do I want to ask for details?"

"She's gone, Martha... I don't know what to do with myself." My voice was louder than anticipated as I tried to speak through the tears.

The sound of her own sobs flooded through the speaker of my phone.

Kathryn made her presence known by touching my arm. "I just texted Noah a few minutes ago. He said he'll be here asap, but he'll be passing the diner on the way here, I could have him pick Martha up, she should be here."

I nodded at Kathryn. "Martha? Martha, I need you to listen to me for a minute. Noah is on his way here, Kathryn said that he'll be passing you on the way, he's going to come to get you so you can both be here."

"O-okay."

"He'll be there in a few minutes. I love you. I'll talk to you soon."

I walked back into the room and found Kathryn sitting in a chair next to Natalie's bed, staring blankly at the wall on the other side of the bed. She looked lost and broken. I imagined that I didn't look much different. She excused herself before going into the bathroom and closing the door. I heard the flick of the lock and just allowed myself to be consumed by what was happening. I was pacing from one side of the room to the other.

What do I even do at this point? Where do I go from here?

The sound of footsteps pounding down the hall bounced around between the floor, walls, and ceiling and as the footsteps got louder and eventually stopped, Noah came through the door, and Martha followed closely behind him. Their breath had escaped them. Martha still had tears steadily flowing, and Noah's eyes were red and glassy, and his hair looked like he had been tugging at it. "Dylan, I'm so sorry, I came as soon as I got Kathryn's text." His voice was cracking, and he walked over to me and hugged me. His repeated apologies made it significantly more difficult to keep it together.

"Thank you both for coming. It means a lot to me and I know it means a lot to Natalie, too."

"I just can't make any sense of it." He sniffed and cleared his throat.

"Yeah, me neither." I felt like a shell of a person.

"Do we know exactly what happened? She seemed like she was doing great the other day..." Martha was quieter than I'd ever heard her.

"Her injuries took over, there was too much trauma for her body to be able to repair all at once. It was a possibility, but I wasn't sure how much I believed it might actually happen."

It was then that we heard the bathroom door unlock and Kathryn came out. She walked straight to her brother and fell apart all over again.

This is just how it's going to be for a while, an endless loop of pain. We would all cry, collect ourselves and then something would inevitably remind us of reality, and we would fall apart time and time again.

It's going to suck no matter what but thank god misery loves company.

CHAPTER THIRTEEN

ELLIE

Waking up on such a foggy, damp morning made me feel much more at home, only with the added safety of being distanced. I swung my legs over the side of the bed, my feet still not quite reaching the floor. I closed the gap of a few inches and stood to stretch before catching my reflection in the mirror across the room.

I internally jumped at the sight of my hair, forgetting what I had done the day before.

Stepping closer to the reflection staring back at me, I grabbed a chunk of my hair and brought it in front of my eyes. It was still long, but the dirty blonde locks that I was used to for the entirety of my life was now replaced by black.

I hadn't realized what the blonde hair did for my skin tone until with black hair, I quite literally paled in comparison. I pulled it up into a ponytail and took a deep breath, trying to remind myself that I did this for a reason, an important reason.

My safety is more important to me than the comfort of what I'm used to.

In about two days, I'll go home, and I'll work on taking

back my life. For now, I can sit and let my emotions run their course. I should be able to transition back to my old life rather easily.

Nothing has changed, Ellie. Everything is exactly the same, don't make a big deal out of it.

It's almost as if Jared never existed. As long as I don't think about him or give him the time of day, I'll be fine. Carrying on should be easy.

I felt the sudden urge to text Allison and see if she was busy.

Ellie: Hey, what're you up to? Do you have a few minutes?

Allison: Hey, sorry, I'm kind of busy right now. Talk later.

A wave of confusion hit me.

Well, that was weird.

Left with very limited choices, I sat on the bed and clicked on the TV, flicking through the channels until I found something to preoccupy myself.

Not long after, I found myself lost in thoughts surrounding Jared, despite my efforts to distract myself. I knew with every logical fiber of my being that the abuse that I endured wasn't my fault, but there was part of me that just couldn't let it go. I did everything that I possibly could to keep him happy, but nothing worked. Even when everything went perfect in my head, there was something in his that was worth screaming or hitting me.

I got lost in the shameful thoughts of the things that bothered me most, compared to what is the most frowned upon in society. I also couldn't help but beat myself up about the fact that I wasn't leaving the room or even the bed.

Maybe this is what I need, just some quiet, relaxation by myself. Then, maybe I'll be ready to go home.

THE REST of my getaway was spent doing exactly that; relaxing and allowing myself to go through all the emotions that I felt. I decided that it had to be healthier than shoving them deeper inside of me and refusing to let them come out like I would've done back home whether I was with my parents or Jared.

Before I knew it, it was time for me to head to the airport. Nausea settled in the pit of my stomach at the thought of going back home to unknown circumstances.

When I get back home, I'll go straight to my parents' and together we'll go and get all of my stuff from my apartment while I find a new place to live. Or maybe I'll just live at my parents' house for now and let my apartment be. The risk of going back there so soon is too great. He'll be there, I know he will.

I hated the uncertainty of everything at this point in time. I didn't know where I would live, how I would get my belongings, how I would escape my past life. The only thing that I knew for sure was that I wouldn't let *him* run me out of the only city that I've ever called home.

If I have to leave my apartment, I can deal with that, but I will not leave Seattle. Giving him that power over my life is something that I refuse to do. He's taken enough from me; this won't be added to the list.

I grabbed my scattered belongings from every corner of the room and double and triple checked to make sure that I wasn't leaving anything behind. Only after being absolutely certain that I had everything packed, was I willing to leave the hotel and the security of Boston.

I pulled out my phone as I waited for the cab to come get me and pulled up the group chat with my parents.

Ellie: Hi, I'm sure you're still asleep, but I just wanted to let you know I'm leaving for the airport now. I'll text you when I get there, and again when I board. I love you both. Xo

I locked my phone and pulled it close to my heart, getting hit by a wave of how much I missed my parents.

When the cab pulled up to the curb, I couldn't tell if I felt relief or dread, but I got in nonetheless.

"Hi, Logan International, please."

"You got it."

"Thank you." I expected the conversation to fall flat.

"Are you heading home or away for vacation?" The cab driver's kind eyes met mine in the rearview mirror.

"Heading home. Sadly, it's time that my vacation ends." I pulled my lips into a tight line.

"It's always a shame when the fun comes to an end and it's back to reality."

I huffed, "You have no idea."

"Well, I hope you enjoyed your trip here. Did you get to do anything good at least?" He kept his eyes on the road while he spoke this time.

"My mom actually grew up here, she wanted to show me around a little bit, but she had to head back early for work."

"I hope you don't mind my asking, what is your mother's name?" He glanced at me through the mirror again.

"She's Jamie Cowen now, but her maiden name was Carlson, why do you ask?"

I noticed his face shift as he smiled. "Wow, you look just like her. I went to school with your mom when we were kids, how is she?"

"She's good, how long has it been since you saw her last?"

"Last I heard, she was moving to Seattle to be with her long-distance boyfriend... Charlie, if I remember correctly."

I smiled, fond of my parents' love story. "That's my dad."

"Are they still together?"

"Yes. They've been married for twenty-five years. Their anniversary actually just passed not too long ago."

"That's wonderful! I'm happy for her."

The airport came into view quicker than I was expecting. "What's your name?"

"Lucas Hadley."

The name was familiar, and I took a second to figure out what my mother has told me about him. "Oh! My mother has told so many stories about you! You're the one she got stuck in the foyer with back in high school during the lockdown, right?"

"That was me. She was freaking out, being trapped and all, and the only thing that calmed her down was food. Thankfully, there was a vending machine in the foyer, so it was decently easy to control her anxiety."

"It helps that she's easily controlled by food." I laughed.

We pulled up the curb and I found myself sad that I wouldn't get to talk about my mother's adolescence anymore.

"Yes, I'm sure that also makes life easier for Charlie. Tell them I said hello. It was so nice to meet you..." He trailed off and I realized that I never told him my name.

"Ellie. It was nice to meet you, too, Lucas. Thank you for helping put my mind at ease."

I looked at the meter and pulled out my wallet, making sure to tip him generously.

"Thank you, Ellie. Have a safe flight."

I smiled at him before getting out of the cab and heading to my flight. Just as Lucas pulled away, I had gotten a notification that my flight was early, and I only had a half hour to make it through security and get on that plane before the doors closed.

Great.

CHAPTER FOURTEEN

DYLAN

I couldn't tell if the next few days felt like hours or weeks, but I was mentally absent the entire time. Her wake and her funeral were both full of people she had touched. It blew my mind to see how many people she affected in only eighteen years and it really made me wonder what good things she would've done if she had gotten to live her entire life.

I still hadn't opened the envelope that Denise gave me. I wanted to wait until I wasn't so emotional. I wanted to feel calm and centered so I could be prepared for whatever was in it. I tried to tuck it to the back of my head and not think about it too much, but it was proving to be easier said than done. I kept trying to get through things and use it as a reward at the end, but that was another mountain to climb.

Dealing with the loss of my little sister and best friend all in one person was the hardest thing that I ever had to do, and I had to keep convincing myself that everything happens for a reason.

I realized all of these things in the hospital that hit me like a brick wall, but it wasn't until her body was lowered into the ground that it sunk in that I would never even get to see her again.

Despite the ridiculous uphill battle in front of me, I looked over at Noah and Kathryn and for the first time in days, I remembered that I still had things to be grateful for.

After the funeral, I went home but not before exhausting all other options. I bounced around since the day she died, avoiding going home.

I walked into the house for the first time since losing her and immediately got hit in the face with the smell of her favorite air freshener that she insisted on plugging in all around the house and my heart leapt into my throat.

I walked past her room and closed the door without looking in. I continued and walked into my room, changed out of my suit, and got in bed, trying to block out the world. I wasn't sleeping for long by the time I woke myself up with my own screaming. My clothes clung to my damp body.

I had dreamt of the accident. It was bloody and gory and killed my sister on impact. When I woke up, I selfishly wondered if that would've been easier. Sudden, but quick. Final. Her getting better was nothing but a tease and she died anyway. I decided that there wasn't a single scenario that this would've been easy in.

I looked around at my surroundings and couldn't breathe around the weight that was sitting on my chest. *What am I even still doing here? There's no point in me living here anymore, not without Natalie.*

I got up and got dressed before walking to Martha's house. I pulled my hood up and shoved my hands into my hoodie pocket. By the time I had gotten to her house, it had started raining and I was finally able to get out of it under the covering of her porch. I knocked on the door and waited for her to respond.

"Who is it?" She called from the living room as she made her way to the door.

"It's Dylan." I called back.

When she opened the door, she just held her arms open. I buried my face in the crook of her neck, expecting to lose all control over my emotions, but nothing came out.

Her fingers combed through my hair. "How are you doing?"

"As well as can be expected, I guess. I need to talk to you though." I gestured towards the couch.

"Okay, go ahead." Martha took a seat and stared at me with her hands folded in her lap, waiting.

"I really don't even want to say it, I really don't want to hurt you, but I think I need to make a major life change. I'm thinking about moving away from here. As far away from here as possible without leaving the country would be nice... maybe Seattle or something." I kept my eyes averted, terrified to meet Martha's eyes. When I did, my heart continued to break even further than I thought possible.

I saw the tears shaking in her eyes, threatening to fall. "Dylan, I love you, but what are you looking to get from this?"

I sighed and sat next to her, placing a hand over hers. "I don't know, I just can't seem to figure out where to go from here. It just doesn't feel like there's a point in staying here. I promised Natalie that once she graduated, we would get the hell out of here. Technically, she would've graduated by now. Maybe I need to keep my word and leave. Staying without her just doesn't make sense."

"I can't imagine you not living here anymore, let alone being as far as Seattle after all these years. I'm not by any means encouraging you to go, but if you think that this is what you need to do for yourself, you should do it. You know how important it is to take care of yourself and how much I value that. I want the best for you. If this is it, I say go for it."

"Thank you for understanding, I know how hard this must be for you to even hear right now and I'm so sorry, I just feel like this is the right decision. This might not be permanent; I think I just need to go find myself and figure out how to live a life without Natalie. One where I have a different purpose. I'm not sure if that's possible if Natalie's memory is around every corner and practically crippling me every time."

"I say go. Go figure out what your dreams are, chase them, make them happen. If and when you're ready, you'll come back. If not, I might just have to follow you out there." she shrugged playfully despite the tears still drying on her cheeks.

I pulled her into a hug. "Thank you. I love you, too, by the way."

Before she got the chance to say anything, the oven dinged from the kitchen.

"Come, I might have made a few different desserts. Sugar makes everything better ."

"It's worth a shot. Risking a sugar coma is better than feeling this bad." Both of us held our breath for a beat when we realized that the word coma just fell out of my mouth.

Martha laughed uncomfortably and hurried off to the kitchen to escape the tension.

Thankfully, we laughed and ate way too much sugar for a few hours before I got ready to head home.

"Thank you for everything, you've always been nothing short of amazing to us. I love you and I'm going to miss you so much." I hugged her tight and tried to fight the idea that maybe this wasn't the best decision. Leaving the only stable relationships that I have left might make this worse.

No. I need to do this. If I can't take it, I'll just come back home.

"No need to thank me, I've loved having you both so close all the time Thank you for giving me the opportunity to have children." She kissed my cheek before pulling away. "You can do this. God forbid you can't do it, I'm always here. I'll be your home base."

We shared a final tear-filled hug before I turned to walk through the door for the last time in a while. "You better keep in touch or I'll have to start harassing you."

"I will, I promise. I love you."

"I love you right back." She called out to me again just before I made it to the sidewalk. "Hey, Dylan?"

"Yeah?"

"She's always with you. Just like I told you when you first told me you guys lost your dad. If you ever miss them and forget that they're still with you, pick a star and that's where they'll be. Maybe go somewhere where you can see the stars."

I nodded and pulled my lips into a tight line. I looked up into the night sky and found a star in the chaos between the clouds. "I'm gonna miss you, Martha. You've always made everything easier."

"Maybe you'll come back home one day. Either way, I'll always be here." She blew a kiss and waved from her porch.

I wasn't sure when I was planning on moving, but with each nightmare, I couldn't wait to get away.

A few more nights passed where I didn't sleep more than three hours before I'd wake up drenched in sweat. It didn't take long for me to decide that I couldn't take it anymore. Everything in this house reminded me of her. I couldn't look anywhere even in my own room without thinking about her.

I decided that if I was suffering like this, then I should pay Kathryn a visit and check to see how she's doing. I knew that

Noah would be working, so I wouldn't be seeing him. I checked the time and was partially surprised when I saw that it was only 1:00 a.m.

I grabbed my phone off my nightstand and decided to see if Kathryn was awake before I showed up unannounced.

Hey, are you awake? I texted and waited for a reply.

A few minutes later, my phone dinged twice while I was splashing water on my face.

Yes, why? She asked.

Are you okay? She was never able to say everything in one text.

I'm coming over, I'll see you in a few. I never asked anymore, we've passed the formalities and if it wasn't so late, I wouldn't have even texted, but I'd rather not drive there to be greeted by a sleeping house.

I threw on a hoodie and put my sweatpants on over the shorts that I was wearing and stepped into my extremely worn sneakers. Grabbing my keys, my wallet, and my phone, I headed out the door.

I got to Kathryn's and Noah's in only a few minutes and I used my key to let myself in. I whispered Kathryn's name into the almost pitch-black house so that she knew I was here.

There was a soft blue glow in the living room indicating that the TV was on, so I followed it and found Kathryn sitting on the couch in a pile of blankets and tissues. She had comedian specials playing on Netflix, yet she was sitting there staring at the screen with a blank face and she didn't seem to notice when I walked into the room. I sat in the recliner next to the couch and joined her in silence.

Neither of us spoke for several minutes before she broke the silence. "Is everything okay? It's late."

"Yeah, as okay as one can be right now. I just wanted to

check in and see how you're doing." I did my best not to look at her, I was afraid her state would break me.

She didn't break her concentration on the screen when she said, "I was in love with her." so quietly that I just barely heard it. I don't think she meant for me to hear her at all.

I let a few seconds pass before I admitted the truth. "I know you were, I'm sorry."

Her head shot towards me. "What do you mean you know?" Her eyes were wide and glassy, her eyebrows furrowed. She looked so broken.

"I know you were in love with her. You can only hide your real feelings from someone who's known you for your entire life for so long. I saw the way you were looking at her when she was in the hospital. Did she know?"

At this point, Kathryn's tears were flowing freely, and she nodded. "I told her the day before she died."

"And? What did she say?"

"I loved her, and I didn't even realize it. I finally figure it out and gather the courage to tell her, then she makes my life better by saying she loves me back and then she goes and dies. I can't help but feel like if I didn't wait so long things might be different. What do I even do with that? I just feel so lost. How does this make any sense?" She was still crying, perhaps just a little bit less. I think she was just baffled by the situation in general and didn't know what to think or feel. "And before you say anything, I know it's not her fault, I'll be the first to admit that, but I need someone, something to blame. At least that way, it's easier than accepting that I'll never get to see her again."

I moved to sit next to her and hugged her tight. Just like how she didn't know what to think or feel, I didn't either and I definitely didn't know what to do to help someone else who was this lost, so I tried to lighten the mood. "I'm just surprised it took me this long to figure it out."

She huffed and rolled her eyes and I wasn't sure who she was rolling her eyes at until she said, "Imagine how I felt when I didn't realize my feelings for her weren't just platonic until I saw her in her coma. I think I was in denial because I didn't want to ruin anything because she was the best person I've ever known. How do you risk a friendship like that just because of some stupid crush? I guess it was always more than that though. I'm not sure if a crush ever really is just a crush."

I laughed and somewhat dismissed her theory. I've never experienced anything more than a crush.

After a while, the emotions faded away as we turned our attention back towards the comedy specials. Then I had to change the tone again.

"Listen, Kat, there's something I have to tell you and I've been putting it off. I'm leaving. I already know you'll hate the idea and fight me on it, but I've already decided, I'm just letting you know. I'm sorry." I heard the coldness in my voice, and I hated it, but I couldn't get emotional right now because I'd never leave.

Her understanding smile fell. "Wait, I'm sorry, what did you just say?"

"I'm le-" I started before she cut me off.

"Because I *know* you didn't just tell me you're leaving so I'm going to need you to repeat yourself."

"I have to leave. I was waiting for Natalie to graduate before we got our own apartment, but she's gone. There's no reason for me to stay. I can't bear to be surrounded by everything that has to do with Natalie anymore. I can't sleep, I'm barely eating. I already called my boss and quit my job and I'm going to call Noah when he gets out of work. You're the only one I had to tell in person. I wanted to make sure you were okay before I left."

"Okay? My *best* friend for my entire life just *died*, Dylan.

Not all of us get to run away from our problems like you always try to. I can't believe you're leaving because it's hard for you to sleep. Do you really think that moving is going to change the pain that you're feeling? I can't believe you're just going to leave, and I *cannot* believe that you're going to *call* Noah who has been your best friend forever. What kind of person does that?" She was yelling. In my entire existence, I have only seen her yell a few times and this one was by far the worst.

"I do, Kathryn, I do! I came to talk to you in person because I didn't want you to flip out on me like this, but obviously, I can't avoid that!" I stood in front of her and gestured to her.

"You can stop being a coward, that's how you can avoid this!" She mocked me and gestured to herself.

"We can call and text all the time, this isn't that big of a deal." I tried to calm her down.

"Not that big of a deal? I can't believe you would even say that to me, did you just come out here tonight to try to butter me up so this wouldn't be so bad for you? *Get OUT!*" She stood up and immediately started pushing me towards the door until she finally pushed me out onto the stoop and slammed the wooden door shut. The sound echoed back at me from all angles in the silence of the night.

CHAPTER FIFTEEN

DYLAN

When I got home, I stormed up the stairs and flung Natalie's bedroom door open. That hadn't gone how I expected it to at all. I didn't want to hurt Kathryn, or anyone, really, but I needed to do this.

I walked into her room and immediately lost control of my emotions. With angry tears streaming down my face, I left her room and walked into my own to grab my duffle bag and backpack from my closet and then took the duffle back into her room. I grabbed the proof of her book that I had left in here the other day, her laptop and the stuffed alligator that was always on her bed. It was a gift from Dad and she never let the damn thing out of her sight. I decided to grab her journal out from between her mattress and her box spring so nobody else could touch it.

I threw all of her belongings that I had taken into my duffle bag, headed back into my room, and proceeded to throw things of mine in the bag as well. I tossed in my laptop, wiped the bookshelf above my bed clean of all of Dad's books and I made sure to slip on the bracelet that Natalie made for me over a year ago. I pulled one of the ends with my opposite hand and the other with my teeth to tighten it around my wrist. The very ends were frayed at this point and every time I wore it, I feared that it would be the last time; it's already on its last leg.

I loaded up the rest of my luggage with whatever clothing I deemed necessary and took out my phone to buy a plane ticket and call a cab. I made it a point to leave my mother a note in a spot that I'm sure she would see when she got home. Not only did she ignore all of my texts, but she also failed to respond to the multiple calls from Denise.

I'm moving to Seattle. Not sure when I'll be back, but I'm sure it won't be for a while. ~Dylan

When the cab arrived, I grabbed my two bags and got in.

"Logan International." I spoke flatly and felt as though I unintentionally came off as rude. By this point, it was already 4:00 a.m. and I barely had the energy to correct myself. "Please."

I pulled my phone out and pulled up my conversation with Noah. My fingers hovered over the keyboard.

This is wrong, he deserves better.

I swallowed the lump in my throat before giving my fingers permission to text him.

Dylan: Hey, Noah. I'm really not sure how to tell you this and I'm so sorry for the way that I'm doing this, but I'm leaving. I'm moving to Seattle. I need to do this. I can't bear to stay here and see Natalie around every corner. Please try to understand, I'm not sure Kathryn is ever going to talk to me again after this, but I can't say I blame her. Hopefully, I'll talk to you soon. Take care of Kathryn... yourself, too.

I hit send before I could talk myself out of it and shoved my phone into the bottom of my backpack.

After the drive, I made sure to tip the driver generously to make up for the silence and cold vibe. I barely even closed the trunk after grabbing my luggage when he was speeding off to try to pick up passengers further down the sidewalk.

I checked my phone one last time to make sure my flight was still going to be a half-hour delayed and I was pleased to see that it would be. By the time I got through security and everything, I had an extra twenty minutes before boarding started.

Well, at least I thought I did.

The dreadful voice belonging to an employee here blared above me. "Final call for flight 3176, the doors will be closing in two minutes. I repeat, final call for flight 3176, the doors will be closing in two minutes."

I started sprinting at the sound of my flight number and immediately despised that I even had anything to carry.

My heart was pounding in my ears and I felt my bags getting heavier each time my foot connected with the floor. The strap constantly digging into my shoulder was starting to top off my already crappy mood and I aggressively switched shoulders.

Frustration and pure determination fueled me, and I forced myself to push my body just a little bit harder as the gate came into view and I saw the back of the last passenger boarding. The airport employee was walking over to close the doors when she had seen me out of the corner of her eye.

I met her sympathetic look with a pleading one. "Please, tell me I'm not too late!" I begged, spacing out every few words with my deep breaths.

She must have noticed the state that I was in because truthfully, I don't think I've ever been in worse shape. Despite my trying to catch the red-eye flight last minute, I knew my sunken-in, bloodshot eyes weren't due to waking up early and still shaking off the tired feeling. I knew that I looked this way because I was fighting my body probably harder than I ever have to refuse to give my emotions the satisfaction of showing through the exterior that I worked so hard to keep up.

I tried to hold it together to the best of my ability throughout her wake and funeral. I had to relive it more times than I could count as I tried to recall the exact timeline. I told myself that when I was settled and alone in a quiet place, I could let everything out, but until then, I needed to hold on. I knew I looked awful, and quite frankly, it showed in the way that the employee looked at me.

"Go ahead, Sir. Scan your ticket and you may go." She smiled kindly at me, but I sensed a slight irritation in her voice. I don't blame her, she deals with latecomers all the time and at this ungodly hour, I wouldn't want to do it anymore either. I stifled a dry laugh when I heard her call me "Sir" when I've felt like nothing but a helpless kid for the past few weeks.

I did as she said, scanned my ticket and gave her a nod of gratitude as I boarded the plane. When I finally stood in front, I immediately saw all the pissed off faces of passengers that blamed me for the delay. On any other day, I'd probably be one of them, but I wasn't myself today. I desperately wished that I could go back in time and do something, *anything*, to keep this from happening… to keep my life from changing so drastically.

I walked down the aisle quickly and kept my head down except to look up and offer a few apologetic glances. I had to walk all the way to the back where I was supposed to sit, and when I finally got there, someone was already occupying my seat. When our eyes met, she explained that her and her son couldn't get seats with her husband, so they spoke to the passenger that was supposed to be seated in the middle where her son was now seated and she was more than willing to switch.

Not being able to break up a family, especially after

recent events, and honestly, not caring enough to make a fuss, I just nodded and told the family that it was fine before turning to take my seat across the aisle. When I saw the girl who gave up her seat, I realized that it was the final passenger before me. I recognized her long, black hair and the hoodie that she was wearing which was now tucked in a ball in her lap. She was just getting settled in her seat and as I watched, I silently wondered if she'd gotten the same looks of disgust, seeing as she was only a minute or two before me.

I lifted my duffle bag into the overhead compartment and stuffed my backpack under the seat in front of me, trying to get settled as quickly as possible in an attempt to not be any more of a burden. When I got seated, I closed my eyes to relax while the flight attendants went over the safety protocol and the plane started moving. A few moments later, I heard a small voice next to me.

"I'm sorry about the musical chairs, I got talking to the family and they told me that this is their son's first flight. I just know that if I was that kid, I'd want both of my parents next to me on my first flight." She had her head turned towards me as she spoke.

I turned my head slightly to show her that I was listening before I replied. "It's okay, I'm just glad I made the flight. I'd sit in the bathroom for the whole flight if I had to, as long as I'm on it."

Though I didn't voice it, I thought about what she said, and I thought of my dad. Him and my mom did the same thing with me on my first flight. I was in the middle and I felt so protected. I think I was only four or something, my mom wasn't even pregnant with Natalie yet.

My comment made her laugh, but unfortunately for her, I was in no mood to reciprocate.

"Do you live in Seattle or are you just going to visit?" She asked, sounding sincerely curious after a brief pause.

"I used to live here in Boston, but I'm moving to Seattle as of right this second. Yourself?" I was trying my best to be polite since this was going to be a long flight at almost seven hours nonstop.

She looked at me with a cocked eyebrow. "You're moving with just a duffle bag and a backpack?" She then realized what she asked, and her eyes widened before she scrambled to correct herself. "Oh my god, I'm sorry, you don't have to answer that. It's really none of my business, I just happened to notice when you boarded."

It was my turn to be slightly amused, this time, at her expense. "Well, since you asked, yes, this is all I'm taking with me to Seattle. I'm in desperate need of a fresh start."

She nodded understandingly and shifted her gaze towards the TV on the seat in front of her. I think she may have sensed that it wasn't something I was going to willingly talk about, so she decided to leave well enough alone.

Feeling guilty, I stuck my hand out towards her. "I'm Dylan, by the way."

She turned her attention towards me almost as soon as I opened my mouth. "Ellie." She placed her hand in mine and shook it gently. "Nice to meet you." She offered a smile so slight; I wasn't sure if it was really there or if I made it up in my head.

"You, too," I replied.

She turned her body a little bit to face me. "Hey, when I say this, I mean it in the nicest way possible, but you really look like you could use a cup of coffee. That always does wonders for me no matter what the problem is." She was practically whispering as if she feared that speaking any louder would shatter me completely.

"Actually, a cup of coffee sounds incredible right now. You're right, it probably *would* do wonders for me." I appreciated her kindness.

"Well, I don't know if you've ever been to Seattle before, but since I live there, I know all the good spots and I just so happen to know that there's this little cafe on the corner of Pike Street and 7th Avenue and it's *the* best place to get coffee. It's basically all windows and it's right in the middle of the city so you can sit with a cup of coffee and people-watch for hours and not even realize how long you've been there." She rambled passionately.

"Maybe I'll have to check it out one day."

"You should. If you don't, you're only hurting yourself." She playfully raised her eyebrows and shrugged, physically repeating her 'your loss' notion. A few moments of silence passed before she hesitantly spoke again, "If you don't mind me asking, do you have a place waiting for you? Again, no offense, but based on your suspiciously light packing, this seems kind of spur-of-the-moment." I watched as her eyebrows knitted together. She studied me like she was struggling to figure me out, as if I'd stumped her, just by existing.

"Actually, no. I'm going to stay at a motel for a little while until I can get on my own two feet. You're entirely right, this is very spur-of-the-moment and not at all planned, hence why I almost missed the flight. I'm not at all a 'plan' type of person." I gestured to myself as a whole. I stopped abruptly.

Natalie was the planner out of the two of us. She always had everything mapped out. She was very organized and if she weren't organized, she might as well have broken out into hives because each time, she would start scratching.

If I didn't know better, I would think that I was trying to get her to ask more questions and show interest in me, but I knew if I kept going that my emotions would stand a chance at getting the best of me. It really did seem like some kind of line though, something to get a girl hooked on the idea of cracking me open to discover all my mysteries, just like every cliché.

The time seemed to be passing relatively quickly, as a couple hours went by without me noticing. Ellie and I didn't really talk much which I was somewhat thankful for. Although talking to her, even though it was brief, proved to be a good distraction from what was really going on in my life, I needed the silence and I told myself that I wasn't going to let my emotions keep me from living my life anymore after this flight.

My attention was eventually fully invested into the movie that I was watching which made me forget that I was running, and what I was running from. Before I knew it, my eyes were fluttering shut and I was consumed by darkness.

CHAPTER SIXTEEN

DYLAN

I woke up to the plane jolting. We'd hit turbulence. Fortunately, some bumps in the air were the least of my problems. I looked over to the seat next to me and found Ellie squeezing her eyes shut as tight as possible and clutching the armrest on her left side, her right hand gripping my arm.

The middle-aged woman on the other side of her was asleep with her chin resting on her chest, not budging. I wondered how she could sleep through all this movement and not even stir. I also imagined the pain her neck would be in when she woke up and felt a little extra thankful that my head remained upright. Focusing on the more important situation in front of me, I turned my attention towards Ellie and swallowed to get rid of my dry mouth. "Are you okay?" I asked just loud enough for her to hear.

Her right eye opened so she could look at me and cracked an anxious smile. "I'm really not a fan of flying, why? Is it obvious?" She laughed flatly at her own expense, both eyes closed tightly again.

"Well, your nails digging into my arm might have given

you away." I teased, trying to lighten the mood and take her mind off of the situation.

Her eyes shot open for the second time during this flight, this time in horror, and she yanked her hand away as if she'd left it on the hot stovetop. "Oh my *god*," She yelled before clasping a hand over her mouth, realizing her disruptive volume. "I'm so sorry!" She brought her voice back down to a whisper. "I thought I was squeezing the armrest the whole time! Oh god, I'm sorry."

"Honestly, don't worry about it, it's no problem at all. I don't blame you, I usually hate flying, too." I held up my wrist and showed her my motion sickness wristband.

"Ugh, what I would do for one of those right now, you have no idea." She sighed and tilted her head back against the headrest and closed her eyes again, lightly this time, her mind easing after the arm squeezing incident.

I reached down, pulled out my backpack and dug through the front pouch until my hand found the package. I held a pair out towards her and waited for her to take it, forgetting that she had closed her eyes again. I pried her hand off of the armrest that sat between us and put the bracelet on her wrist before guiding her hand back to the armrest it was on and then did the same with the other hand.

Her eyes opened and she looked at me again. "Oh, thank you, you really didn't have to." She said shyly. Her dark hair fell into her face when she looked down to examine the bracelets.

"No, no, I insist. It's no big deal, I mean it." I reassured her.

"So, I'm really freaking out - you know, fear of plummeting to my death and all - so I can really use a distraction. I hope you don't mind but I'm going to put that responsibility on your shoulders since I don't think my other neighbor over here can handle that at the moment." We both glanced over to the woman who was still very much asleep. Ellie let out a snort before her hand flew to her mouth in an attempt to quiet herself again while her shoulders continued to bounce quietly, and I couldn't help but join in on the laughter.

"So, first nosy question: What do you mean you 'usually' hate flying, too?" She looked at me with her head tilted slightly and I noticed that she was counting on her fingers as she inhaled and then again as she exhaled, trying to keep her breathing steady.

For a second, I contemplated lying to her, justifying it in my head that she's just a stranger, what would she know or care if I lied? After all, we only just met, but for some reason, I couldn't bring myself to do it. "I used to fly with my sister. She would keep me distracted, so I wouldn't have time to feel nauseous or worry about the possibilities."

"Ah, okay. Why isn't she with you this time?" She seemed genuine but I couldn't help but notice the stinging behind my eyes and laugh to myself because all I wanted in the world was for Natalie to be with me right now. I reached into the neckline of my shirt and held Martha and Natalie's cross tightly in my hand.

"She passed away about a week ago." I kept it short and sweet for my sake.

The horrified look crossed her face again and she placed a hand on mine. "I'm so sorry for your loss, I can't imagine what you're going through. If you don't mind my asking, why are you moving so far away? Was she your only family in Boston?"

I was impressed. Most people would have expressed their condolences and then stopped talking altogether out of sympathy or embarrassment, but she kept going.

"I think I'm running from her. Everywhere I looked in that house, she was all I could think about and I couldn't bear the fact that I would never see her or hear her laugh or hear her music playing in the morning again. I guess now I'm just lost and alone and I didn't want to be those things in a town that I once called home."

I hadn't realized that tears were racing down my cheeks until I felt the comforting squeeze of Ellie's hand that hadn't yet moved from mine. I wiped my face with the collar of my sweatshirt. "I'm sorry, I didn't mean to dump all my problems into your lap."

"Oh, don't be ridiculous, it doesn't bother me at all." She brushed off my apology as nonsense and apologized again for my loss.

I let out a dry laugh. "I guess you can say I just need a clean slate."

I just thought that it sucked that I could dream about Natalie and remember my favorite memories with her, but it doesn't change the fact that she was ripped from me way before her time.

I kept dreaming about the night that I dropped her off at prom and every time, the sound of my car door slamming shut was also the cue for my body to thrust me back into the harsh reality that was now my life.

I convinced myself that it had something to do with Natalie. That maybe she's forcing me to dream about her. I thought about her and concluded that she'll probably do this to me forever and I saw it clear as day in my head. I would accuse her of torturing me and she would feign cuteness and say "Only for you because you're the bestest brother ever and I just adore you that much!" and I would roll my eyes and she would crack herself up like she always does.

Did.

I felt it immediately; adjusting to the whole "new life" that I was creating was going to be a lot harder than I thought.

I started to miss my little sister even more when I remembered our last trip to the diner.

I squeezed my eyes shut and pinched the bridge of my nose.

"Hey, I'm sorry, I didn't mean to upset you. I know it must be hard to think about her. We can definitely talk about something else." Ellie was honest. She didn't try to nonchalantly switch the subject and not pay it any mind. I appreciated the change of pace. She wasn't just someone polite, she seemed much more... real.

"Thank you. So, what brought you to Boston?" I asked as I finished composing myself again.

"Actually, can we switch to an even lighter subject than that?" She questioned and I couldn't help but notice that she was avoiding making eye contact with me.

"Oh, um... yeah, of course. Is there anything I should know about now that I'm going to be living in Seattle?" I couldn't help but feel curiosity yanking on my pant leg like a little kid. I was intrigued and much too nosy for my own good. I didn't want to let it go, but I could tell how uncomfortable it made her, so I left it alone.

Her whole face changed, and she seemed more bright-eyed and bushy-tailed like before. "Yes! Well, I don't know what you like to do, so you'll have to fill me in on that, but I can totally come up with something for everything, I know all the good spots." She flipped her hair jokingly as she finished her playfully cocky statement.

I cleared my throat and squeezed my fist closed a little tighter. "Movies are good. And music, of course. I like books, too. If you've got any suggestions, lay them on me."

Her eyes widened and she turned to face me even more, her excitement evident and undeniable. "When it comes to books, you've come to the right person! You absolutely *have* to check out that cafe I was telling you about, it's so beautiful and homey there. I'm a big fan of cozy environments with windows and that's exactly what it is. I love it there, it got me through all four years of college!"

And after that, we just got lost in conversation for the next few hours. I learned a lot about Ellie, like the fact that she went to college, unlike myself. Most of the conversation remained mindless except for a few accidental times where sore spots were touched on, for both of us. It was refreshing to notice that there are things that she doesn't want to talk about either. I'm not alone in my suffering.

Eventually, I pulled out my laptop and we watched a movie together. The distraction was a blessing and although I couldn't believe it, I wasn't so tired anymore. Ellie picked some romance-gone-wrong thriller type of movie. It wasn't something I'd normally watch, but to my surprise, it was phenomenal.

Shortly after the movie ended, there was an announcement to put our trays in the upright position and put away our laptops and other belongings.

As we began our descent, I reached to clutch Martha's cross again. I tried to return her cross that she lent Natalie, but she closed my fingers back around it and used both of her hands to try to cup my hand. "Honey, you need this more than I do. I gave it to Natalie to keep and if she can't hold onto it anymore, then I want you to."

I wanted to give Martha the world, she deserved at least that much from me after taking care of the two of us for years. I knew she was struggling financially and wouldn't be able to continuously pour money into fixing her car, and that I wouldn't need my car with me in Seattle, so I made the decision last minute and left it with her. It took a lot of convincing, and I'm still not sure if she'll ever even use it or if she'll feel too guilty, but I got her to accept it.

I haven't decided if I'm going to go back to visit or not

yet, but I think that one day when my healing is finally making progress and my wounds are starting to close, I'll visit.

Kathryn is the only one that I'm worried about, but after our last encounter, I'm not sure she'll ever want to talk to me again.

When the pilot's voice came on and echoed throughout the cabin, I realized that sooner than I thought, we were officially about to land in my new home. I prayed that I would get the fresh start that I was hoping for.

I whispered under my breath, "Go easy on me, Nat. Please. " hoping that she'd hear me and actually listen to me, but if her spirit is anything like she was when she was alive, then this is going to be hell for me anyway.

CHAPTER SEVENTEEN

DYLAN

After we finally landed, I waited for the chaos and commotion to die down. Eventually, the plane emptied out and I grabbed my backpack out from under the seat in front of me and pulled my duffle bag out of the overhead compartment. Ellie was close behind me with her hoodie wrapped in her arms.

She had checked her bag, so we had walked together towards baggage claim since the exit was that way anyway. Most of the walk was quiet, but it wasn't an awkward silence, it felt peaceful. Surrounded by dozens of other people rushing around to wherever it is that they're going, I could feel how irrelevant we were in the grand scheme of things. All the people around us had their own things going on.

Even just looking at Ellie, I didn't know her at all. Our conversation remained shallow and never pressed any sensitive issues. I had no idea who it was that I was walking beside in a city that I knew nothing about, in a life that I wasn't sure how I was going to live or adjust to. Nothing really seemed to matter except for the nagging weight of a certain envelope in my pocket.

I kept telling myself that when I got to the motel, I would go to my room, finally read the letter that I was dreading and anxiously anticipating at the same time.

I just had to get there.

When we reached the baggage claim, I stopped and turned to face Ellie. "It was nice meeting you and talking to you throughout the flight."

"It was my pleasure. It helped me, too. Don't forget to check out that cafe, I think you'll love it!" She smiled and waved as I nodded and promised that I would. I turned around and noticed that my pace was uncharacteristically slow as I walked towards the exit.

Part of me wanted to turn around and ask her for her number or give her mine and I couldn't seem to figure out if it was because I genuinely enjoyed her company or if it was because I was just semi-desperate to have someone, anyone, that I knew in this big state full of unfamiliar surroundings.

I wasn't prepared to feel so lonely here.

While I stood outside waiting for a cab, my thoughts were full of infinite possibilities and contemplations.

I decided to call the motel that I was planning to stay at to double check that they had availability. Fortunately, they did. I booked my room and informed them that I would be arriving shortly.

I had to keep reminding myself on the cab ride there that this is what I wanted. I wanted to move somewhere where nobody knows me, where nobody knows my sister. However, something held me back. I couldn't bring myself to call out to Ellie in the middle of the airport. After all, she was just a stranger to me. Would having her phone number really make a difference? Would it really make me feel less alone?

It was better this way. I had some mending to do and I had to do it alone.

When the cab driver pulled up to the motel, I glanced out the window at what could very well be my home for a while. I dug in my pocket for my wallet and paid the driver. Getting out and grabbing my backpack and duffle bag from the backseat, I thanked him again. Almost the second I closed the door, he drove off.

Taking in my surroundings, I noticed a convenience store right across the street from the motel which was… *convenient* to say the least. I decided that I would go there later to get all the essentials I needed like soap and shampoo rather than harassing the front desk.

When I stepped into the lobby, I was overwhelmed by a musty smell that made my nose crinkle.

I walked up to the front desk and gave my name. The concierge offered a polite smile and handed over my room key.

I walked out, around the building and up the stairs to get to my room. Before I opened the door, I glanced at my watch.

11:07 a.m.

Completely deprived of any kind of relaxation, I trudged into my room.

Closing the door behind me, I locked both locks and dropped my bags on the floor.

I immediately started peeling my clothes off as I realized how disgusting I felt from both the grieving and the traveling. I stepped into the shower and let the hot water beat against my back and my shoulders. This was going to be a lot harder than I thought it would be. Running away got me out of my hometown, but it didn't wipe my memory clean. I knew it wouldn't, but part of me couldn't help but feel disappointed that I didn't feel any better.

I was fumbling with the soap, trying to peel off the

wrapper, but my wet hands kept slipping. Frustrated, I used my teeth to tear the top of the wrapper open.

After what was way harder than it ever should have been to open soap, I scrubbed at my skin, again, left disappointed by the fact that I couldn't just wash away the emptiness that I felt.

"I probably just need to get some sleep," I muttered to myself.

I towel-dried my hair and then wrapped the towel around my waist.

At least I washed the airport off.

I sat on the bed for a few minutes in my towel. *Everything* was harder now. Everything felt draining.

"Alright, come on. Get up." I tried to snap out of it again, but every time, I would get sucked back in before I could even realize it.

I got dressed, barely even realizing that I was moving. When I was done, I left the towel on the floor and got distracted by the envelope sitting in my jacket pocket.

My heart was pounding, and I could feel it in my head, in my ears.

I sat on the bed again and my hands continued to shake as I slid my finger through the top to break the seal that held it shut.

I closed my eyes and took a deep breath as I opened the letter, anxiously anticipating the contents. When I opened my eyes, my breath caught in my throat as my eyes landed on her handwriting.

Dyl,

I'm going to start this off as a little bit of a cliché just because I know you hate them: If you're reading this, I'm dead. Yes, I agree, that was blunt, but I know you hate beating around the bush and I don't want you to hate this letter completely. I know you must be hurting right now; I can't imagine what I would be feeling if I was the one that lost you. Since I know you so well, I know that you're probably finding some crazy, totally irrelevant thing that you could have done differently to prevent this situation. Stop it. I'm serious, Dylan. You did everything right. You have always protected me and taken such good care of me when mom couldn't. Grieving is a crazy thing and I know that watching mom grieve was terrifying to me, so I'm begging you, please don't let this ruin your life. Dad died years ago, and mom is still living a life that isn't hers because she doesn't know how to go on without him. I know you don't believe that she's still grieving at this point and that she's just forever changed, and I know you don't like who she's become, but cut her some slack. She's lost the love of her life, her other half. In a way, I think you feel like that, too, but Dyl, I'm your sister, it's different. When you fall in love, I think you'll understand why she is the way that she is today and maybe you'll be able to forgive her for some of the things that she's done. I hope I can find some way to communicate with you from wherever it is that I am now. I'm gonna haunt the crap out of you! I have some bad news for you even though you've had more than enough for a lifetime: You have to live a life amazing enough for the both of us now. Go after your dreams! If you don't know where to start, try taking a few classes to become a crime scene investigator just like we talked about! If you hate it, try something different. Don't let this hold you back from doing all the things you love or that you've been dying to do. Sorry, too soon? I know I'm not with you anymore, but let life continue to happen anyway. I love you, Dylan, and I am always with you.

Love always,

Nat

I found myself struggling to get through the letter as I cried and two seconds later, I was laughing at her wicked sense of humor with tears flowing freely down my cheeks. Somehow, reading that letter felt like the closure that I needed to get. It felt like we got to say goodbye. I placed the letter on my nightstand and pulled the covers out from under where I was sitting and got under them. Maybe tonight I would be lucky enough to sleep through the night and feel relatively rested in the morning.

CHAPTER EIGHTEEN

ELLIE

I was thankful for the company that Dylan provided on the flight back home. It was a nice distraction and he was really sweet, but it was just that, a distraction. Now that I'm home, I need to buckle down and figure out what I'm going to do to change my life.

Dylan had just walked through the exit when I heard my name being called. I jumped slightly and my heart stopped prematurely before I turned and was met with my dad's eyes across the room.

I relaxed and made my way over to him, dragging my suitcase behind me.

"Hi, Dad." I hugged him.

He returned the hug ten times stronger. "Hi, Ellie, how are you? Did you get what you wanted out of your little getaway?"

"I'll let you know if and when I feel any hint of relief. Right now, I'm just terrified that he'll show up out of nowhere." I looked around the open airport that was now emptying out from the post-flight rush.

"Let's get you home, we'll worry about the rest from there. Sound good?"

"Sound's perfect." We started walking towards the exit again as I followed him to the car. "Where's mom?"

"She got caught up at work, and she had to wrap up a few things, but she'll probably be home when we get there."

"Okay, good. I want to sit down all together and try to come up with a game plan. Since it's the end of the month, I have a week or so to figure out what I want to do before I pay next month's rent."

"That's my girl, already thinking ahead. We'll figure everything out together, try not to worry too much. We're going to figure out what the best way to keep you safe is." He unlocked the car and popped the trunk before taking my luggage from me and putting it in the car.

"Thank you. I really hope you're right about how easy this will be to figure out." I walked over to the passenger side and slid into the seat.

"Yeah, me, too. You're a Cowen, everything is figure-out-able. For now, let's just put on some music and get home."

"Good idea. I'll text mom and let her know we're on our way." I raised the volume on the radio and sent a quick text. I felt surprisingly relaxed being back home considering the potential issues that could arise.

———

WHEN WE GOT HOME, my mom was waiting for us with Chinese takeout and everything felt normal.

A few minutes later, after we all got settled, we sat down for dinner together. I tried to fight the urge to immediately bring up the thing that nobody wanted to talk about, but it didn't work. "Mom, I was talking to Dad about it on the way here, but I wanted to get your input, too. What do you think we should do about my living situation and everything?"

"Well, honey, you can always move back into your old room if that would help you feel safe. But assuming that since you only just got out of here, you probably want your own place, right?" She gave me a knowing look.

"Right. I love you both, but I think I need to be out on my own at this point in my life. You know, get a taste of being an adult without having or needing my parents at my every beck and call." I imagined that this conversation would've been much more difficult if my relationship with my parents wasn't as strong as it always has been.

"I agree. You need to know how to handle yourself out there. God knows you've already been through enough, but you'll never learn anything without experience. Your grandparents always tried to guide us by saying 'Don't make the same mistakes that I did', blah, blah, blah, and I never bought it. We both heard it all the time and neither of us ever bought it. That's the way that everybody is when they're getting to that point in their life. They know x sucked for their parents, but maybe it'll go differently for them. It'd be flawed logic if it wasn't true, but everybody has different experiences." My mom explained in between chews.

"She's right. We decided before we even started trying to get pregnant that the only way that we could protect our future child would be to always be there in case the thing they want to do goes wrong. Within reason, of course. Obviously, we weren't going to condone drinking, drugs, and the works, but when you wanted to go away to school and move out and do your own thing, we had to let it happen. It was hard, but in our minds, we would know that at least we let you spread your wings and we'd always be your safety net." My dad cut in.

"Basically, what we're trying to say is: you tell us what you want to do, and we'll support you." My mom summed up and my dad nodded in agreement.

"My lease is up in around a week, so if we can get a moving truck and get my stuff out of there and into a new apartment before then, then that's what I want." I pushed my food around with my fork, feeling uneasy.

"Okay, now, what's bothering you? You've got a plan, but you're awfully quiet."

"I don't want to go back there. I can't help but think that he's gonna be there waiting for me." My leg started bouncing and my mom put her hand on my knee.

"Ellie, relax. If you don't want to go back there, then you don't have to. We can hire a moving company, and we'll just tell them what to do. You won't have to touch the situation with a ten-foot pole until you move into your new apartment. By then, Jared won't know where you've moved to."

"Are you sure? What if he follows the moving truck?" I picked at my cuticles.

"He might, but if he does, I'll be surprised. If he doesn't see you, he probably won't notice your stuff immediately. If he notices your stuff at all, that is. He's crazy, but he doesn't seem to be too observant of his obsession's possessions. Didn't you tell me he asked you if you got new furniture one day when you definitely didn't?" My dad seemed so calm and steady when I was everything but.

"Yeah, he was waiting for me, so he was sitting in my apartment by himself for a little while, and I don't think his phone was charged so he was extra bored and observant. Plus, we were just about always at his apartment, hardly ever mine. When we were at mine, he was usually too busy on his phone or watching TV."

"So, he probably won't even notice your furniture. To be extra safe, we can ask the movers to box everything and wrap all the furniture with those hideous gray cloths and pads, so it'll all be hidden. There are ways around this. I promise you everything will be okay." I couldn't help but admire how my mother finished my father's thoughts and vice versa.

Jared and I never had that.

"Mom, I forgot to tell you, I saw Lucas Hadley today, he was my cab driver. He asked about you." I tried to distract myself again, remembering my last distraction.

"Lucas Hadley, wow, I haven't heard that name in years. We fell out of touch years ago. How is he?" A certain hint of nostalgia laced her voice.

"He's good, he's happy for you two. I told him that you're still together and just celebrated your 25th anniversary."

She smiled. "It's crazy how much life changes in so little time. Maybe I'll reach out sometime soon. I'm sure I can find him online somewhere."

"He seems really nice; you should reach out! I didn't get to ask him much about his life, but he seemed relatively happy."

"Yeah, maybe I will." She picked up all the containers scattered around the coffee table.

After we finished cleaning up dinner, I couldn't help but keep thinking about all the red flags that popped up in my relationship that I blatantly ignored or disregarded. I watched my parents in awe for the trillionth time, hoping that I can one day be part of a relationship that compares to theirs.

Maybe my parents are right. Maybe you have to have the experiences to learn the lesson and there is no easier way. Maybe you just have to go through the bad to get to the good.

CHAPTER NINETEEN

DYLAN

I woke up and groggily felt around the nightstand for my watch. When my fingertips found it, I went to wrap my fingers around the rest of it but wound up knocking it off the nightstand and onto the floor.

Cursing under my breath, I yanked the sheets off and swung my legs to the side of the bed. Getting up, I checked the time. The small numbers were bigger and brighter than I remembered in my groggy state.

2:52 a.m.

I'd slept much longer than I had imagined I would, but between the exhaustion I was feeling and the time difference, it was earlier than it would be back in Boston. There was absolutely nothing for me to do at this hour.

My stomach grumbled.

Well, maybe there's one thing I can do. I decided to slip on a pair of sneakers and a hoodie and go across the street to that convenience store I saw earlier.

I walked up and down the aisles looking for anything that really caught my eye, but I couldn't find much of anything. I settled for a sandwich and a soda and gave the cashier a ten-dollar bill.

When he gave me my change, I dropped it in his tip jar in front of the register and wished him a good rest of the night.

The sandwich and soda had hit the spot after my days of not having an appetite.

I got back to my room and dug around in my bag until I found melatonin. "Please, just give me a few more hours. Let the rest of the city be awake next time I wake up." I was pretty sure that I was still sleep deprived, but I couldn't get my mind to stop racing. I was hoping that this would help.

As I'd hoped, I fell asleep again and didn't wake up until 7:30. The extra few hours of sleep made a difference and I felt more like myself than I did earlier.

I wanted to try to live today like I would've lived it before Natalie died, so I went for a run when I woke up. I didn't want to go for as long of a run as I usually would, so I decided to compromise and make it short.

At least I went.

I jumped in the shower, determined to make this day work for me and go the way I wanted it to. Today was going to be better. Today was going to be the first step I needed to make in the right direction.

I had begged the concierge to print out a few copies of my resume and then decided that I would wander around the city today and look for a job.

I wandered around to department stores and convenience stores, even hardware stores, and nobody seemed to need any new employees. Getting rejection after rejection was getting tiring and not benefiting my mood or mental state.

I was walking back to the motel when I thought of one last place that I could go before I gave up completely.

The cafe that Ellie had mentioned to me seemed to be the only option that I had left. I walked into the motel lobby and asked the woman at the front desk if she could tell me how to get there. I was relieved when she said it was only about a half mile away from the motel.

When I pushed the door open and stepped into the cafe, I immediately understood what Ellie was ranting and raving about, this place was absolutely gorgeous. The windows that stretched from the floor to the ceiling had caught my eye immediately. I always loved big windows and natural light. The sunrises and sunsets in here must be incredible. I noticed the light fixtures were the kind that I've always been drawn to. The vintage lightbulbs gave the areas that they lit up a soft, orange glow, making the café that much more comforting and inviting.

There was something about the atmosphere that was so charming and peaceful, I loved it. The bustle of all the people getting their coffee before running to continue their day, the hum of the machines, the sight of people who had nowhere else to be sitting and reading book that they could lose themselves in, it was everything Ellie made it out to be and more. I could easily see myself sitting here with a book and a coffee and losing hours without even realizing it, just like she said.

I just so happened to notice a "Now Hiring" sign taped to the front counter and my spirits automatically lifted.

I waited on the line until it was my turn to speak to one of the baristas.

"Hi, I'm interested in applying for a job. Is there someone specific that I should talk to about that?" I was surprised that there weren't any hints of misery lingering in my voice. I sounded fine.

"Hi, yes, you would have to speak to the manager. I'll go get her, hang on one second." She disappeared behind a door and came back a moment later with the manager in tow.

"Andrea, this is the man who is looking for a job." She

offered a kind smile and walked away to go continue taking orders.

"Hi, I'm Dylan, nice to meet you." I extended my hand towards the woman who could potentially be my new boss.

She shook my hand. "The pleasure is mine. So, you're looking for a job?"

I nodded.

She gestured towards an empty table in the back of the cafe, there weren't many people in this corner. "Please, sit. Why are you interested in working here?"

"Well, I'm new to the area and, quite honestly, I'm not necessarily educated for jobs outside of the food industry or retail." It was only the first question and I already felt like I was tanking the interview.

"Brutal honesty, refreshing." She let out a soft chuckle which helped to release some of the tension that sat in my shoulders.

I laughed, too. "Yeah, unfortunately, I'm the worst liar. I hope that isn't a requirement to work here."

"It's not, you should be fine. Back to your brutal honesty, though, what level of education do you have?"

"I finished high school, I just never made it to college." I gave her a copy of my resume.

"Okay, what position are you interested in?"

"Honestly, I was applying for the barista position, but is there a chance that you're looking for someone to help with the library-esque aspect of the cafe? I've always loved books and I volunteered in a library with my sister a year or two ago." I felt a slight pang in my chest at the mention of her.

"Actually, yes, I think I can make that happen, but we are also in need of a barista. Would you be interested in splitting your time? Some shifts you'll be a barista; some shifts you'll be a bookkeeper?" She lit up a little bit at the idea after her contemplation.

"Yes, absolutely!"

She asked me some more general questions that were to be expected from an interview and I was surprised that I had an answer for just about all of them.

"Okay, well you've definitely given me a lot to think about. Thank you for all your time today, Dylan. It was very nice to meet you. You will be getting a call in a day or two that will let you know whether or not you got the job." She stood and extended her hand towards me.

I stood and shook it slightly eagerly, trying to curb my enthusiasm. "Thank you, I look forward to hearing from you. Have a nice day." I smiled and turned to leave.

I felt like that went really well and I was pleased with the way that I handled myself despite my grief. I clutched the cross and decided at that moment that it was my good luck. It was just another way that Natalie would always be with me.

She promised in her letter that she would always be with me and I think that today she was there in my interview. Maybe it wasn't all me that did so well.

I knew I could make the best of my life and live it the way that I should. I could live life amazingly enough for the both of us, just like she wanted me to. Today was the first time that I felt like some of the weight on my heart had been lifted.

I asked her to take it easy on me and I think today was evidence that she heard me and she's listening.

CHAPTER TWENTY

DYLAN

When I was making my way back to the motel, I thought of all the people back home that I loved dearly. All the people that I would immediately want to tell about my interview and how confident my lack of confidence made me. It seemed to work for me for the first time ever in my life. I think Andrea noticed that my slightly self-deprecating tone was putting me at ease rather than doing me any harm.

As I looked around, I realized that I left all those people back in Boston with barely even a heads up. The more I tried to remind myself that this was a good thing and that this is what I needed to do, the less convinced I was.

I decided that I would plug my phone in and reach out to Kathryn, Noah, and Martha. They deserved better than this and I knew that before I even left, but I also needed to get what I deserve: my own peaceful way of coping.

For the first time in my life, I felt free of obligations. It may have just been the slight high that I was left with after the interview, but I felt like I had the world by the balls right now. The only happiness that I wanted to focus on was my own and I was going to do just that. I plugged in my phone and decided to go to the bathroom and change my clothes, I figured I wouldn't be going anywhere else for the day, especially not that requires me to wear the relatively nice clothing that I had thrown on for the interview.

By the time I finished, my phone was turning on, so I grabbed it off the nightstand and waited for it to fully turn on and finish loading. It's only been three days, there probably aren't *that* many messages.

And then the texts started coming in.

Kathryn: Dylan, please come home, this is ridiculous. I'm sorry I yelled at you and kicked you out, this has all just been very hard for me.

Noah: Hey bro, Kathryn's freaking out and honestly, it's kind of weird not having you around. Check in so I know you're alright, okay?

Martha: Dylan, honey, are you okay? I just wanted to check in on you and see how you're adjusting. Your mom has come in a few times. She seems like an emotional wreck, but I don't necessarily buy it. Nothing is the same since you've left.

Kathryn: Stop being stubborn. At least let someone know that you're okay.

Kathryn: You're making everyone worry more than they should have to. We lost Nat, too. This is selfish of you at this point.

Kathryn: Natalie would kill you if you made her worry like this.

Noah: You okay? I'm starting to worry. Maybe even approaching Kathryn-level worry.

Martha: Give me a call when you get a minute, I just want to make sure you're okay. I have something exciting I want to tell you.

Kathryn: Come on, Dylan. This isn't funny anymore.

Martha: Doll?

Noah: Do you need me to come out there? If you need me or someone to be with you right now, I'll either buy myself a plane ticket or pay for whoever you need to get there. If space is what you need, just tell me you're okay and I'll get everyone to leave you alone.

After reading all the messages and listening to voicemails saying basically the same things, I decided to text them all back. I started with Kathryn because I knew that a.) by the time I finished typing out the other two texts, she would have already sent me a reply and b.) she would be the handful because of how high her emotions are. She lost a best friend and someone she loved romantically. If she didn't, I wouldn't tolerate the guilt that she made me feel.

Kat, I'm sorry I made you worry. I'm fine and I'm in Seattle. It's quiet here, it's a nice change of pace. You'd like it. I'm not mad at you for how we left things, it's my fault, I got you riled up. Honestly, I would've been pissed if you were leaving me in a situation like this. It's not fair of me. I'm not ready to come home at least not yet. My phone was off until a few minutes ago. I wasn't ready to talk to anyone especially about what happened and honestly, I still don't think I am, but I realized that I was being selfish, so in that aspect, you're right. But please, do not use Natalie against me. I am the way that I am right now because I lost her, and she'll never be able to threaten me or yell at me again and it sucks. We should be working through this together and I realized that today. I'm sorry that I'm late with this, but I'm here now. We can do this together. Love and miss you tons. I hit send and it immediately felt like a weight was lifted off my shoulders.

I decided that I would call Martha next. I was hoping that I would be able to catch her on her break. The phone rang three times before she picked it up. "Dylan?" Her breathing was shallow, and she sounded frantic.

"Hi, Martha. I'm so sorry it took me this long to call you or get in touch at all. I've been trying to get through most of the tough stuff before I took anyone down with me. I have good news for you, though."

"I almost booked a flight to Seattle! I'm just glad you're okay. It's so nice to hear your voice. I miss seeing your face all the time. What's your good news?" The relief in her voice seeped through the phone and she slowly started to sound more like her warm self.

"Well, you know the cross you gave Natalie for prom night?"

"Yes, what about it?"

"I've been keeping it on my person at all times and it really comforted me on the plane, but today, I think I noticed a little something extra. This might sound crazy, but you know how certain things remind you of those who you've lost? Well, I think somehow, Natalie found her way to be in my life and stay with me through this cross."

"That doesn't sound crazy at all, Dylan. It's something she had close by when she died and now you have it in your possession. It only makes sense that having it with you would feel like having her with you in at least some sense. I'm happy you have a way to stay connected to her, even if it is just her spirit. You'll feel less lonely with her always around your neck."

"Yes, I really think that's what I felt today! I felt more at peace, like my life might eventually get back to normal. I woke up and something just felt different."

"Your heart is healing. Time may not completely heal all wounds, but it does help lessen the sting."

"Thank you so much for understanding, I knew you would, Martha. Anyway, I saw your text mentioned that you have good news, what is it?"

"Well, you know how I've always wanted a child of my own, right?"

"Yes, of course."

"Well, we both know that I can't have my own baby at this point, so I decided that I was going to start the adoption process and I did right before Natalie's prom and there's a woman that's interested in giving me her baby! She's about six months pregnant and she lives close by and she wants to meet with me to get a feel for me and see if I'm a good fit to parent the baby!"

"Martha, I am so happy for you! I know how badly you've wanted this for what seems like forever. I can't believe this is finally happening for you, I had no idea that you even started putting out feelers for opportunities to be a mom."

"I know, I didn't tell anybody at all. I felt like it would unrealistically get my hopes up and I didn't want to be filled with disappointment if things didn't pan out the right way. I just wish Natalie could be here to be around for all of this, too. Don't get me wrong, I am so happy that you're here to go through everything with me, but it's different when there's another woman…"

"I know, Martha. I'm so sorry she isn't here. I absolutely understand that a woman would be more suitable company and I don't take any offense to it. I definitely don't have the instincts and knowledge that she had, just know that I will do anything and everything that I can to help you along the way."

"I do and I wouldn't ask you to come out here in a million years, I know how you feel. I want you to do things at your own pace, don't push yourself too far, too fast, but also try not to stay in the same spot for too long, you'll get comfortable and never move forward."

"I know, I'm planning on coming home eventually, I just know that now is not the time for me. Anyway, before this gets all sad again, I just want to congratulate you again and wish you the very best of luck. Thank you for always being so understanding and always knowing what to say and how to handle me when it comes to situations like this. I should probably call or text Noah now and tell him that I'm alive and doing okay, I love you, I miss you and I'll talk to you later, bye, Martha."

"Thank you, Honey. I love you, too, keep in touch." There was a tinge of sadness in her voice before she hung up the phone. *Maybe Kathryn's right, maybe I am being selfish.*

I was thankful for the conversation that we had, it really made things feel like how they used to be and there was nothing that I wanted more than for things to just go back to what they used to be. How we *all* used to be.

I couldn't decide if I wanted to call or text Noah. I wasn't sure if he was at work today, so I decided to just shoot him a text.

Hey, Noah. I'm sorry if I made you worry in the past few days when I went off the grid, I just wasn't ready for anything that had to do with... well, anything. I just needed to wallow and be alone for a while. Unfortunately, I never learned how to cope in a healthy way, lol. I already texted Kathryn and spoke to Martha, so they know I'm alive. I'm sorry if they've been hounding you about getting in touch with me. Seattle is amazing, I told Kathryn that I think she'd like it here. She probably really would, and I think you would, too. I look forward to hearing from you, it hasn't been the same without you around either. Thank you for checking in on me, love you, man.

Feeling a weight lift off my shoulders yet again, I decided that I could be satisfied with what I had gotten done today and can allow myself to get ready for bed.

Right after I crawled into bed, I got a call from a number that I didn't recognize.

"Hello?"

"Hi, Dylan?" The voice didn't seem recognizable to me in the slightest.

"This is he."

"It's Andrea from the interview earlier today, how are you?"

"Oh, hi, I'm good, how are you?" I sat up from my position on the bed, my attention piqued.

"I'm good, I just wanted to call and let you know that you got the job, congratulations!"

"Really? Thank you so much!" This was the most excited I'd been in a long time. My life felt like it was more on track now than before. I finally had full control over my life, I had my fresh start.

A chuckle came from the other end of the line. "You're welcome, you'll have to go through some training beforehand, of course, so how soon can you start?"

"Um, how does tomorrow sound?" I let out a sheepish laugh, obviously in no rush to hide my excitement.

"That's perfect. I'll see you tomorrow morning at 8:00 a.m.?"

"Great, thank you so much!"

"Have a good night."

"You, too." I hung up the phone and felt the slightest relief. I'm about to have a source of income again.

A wave of exhaustion hit me out of nowhere and I fell asleep faster than I was expecting.

CHAPTER TWENTY-ONE

DYLAN

After a few days of training, shadowing another barista and then having a barista shadow me, I was ready to officially fly solo. Andrea had said I was a quick learner and I was relieved that it came relatively naturally to me, but I had no explanation as to why.

Admittedly, my nerves were starting to get to me. I always had a fear of messing something up and every time I got a new job, I dealt with the same fears and emotions, but thankfully, I realized that messing up someone's coffee order will never be the end of the world. If it were to happen, it'd suck, but it'd be something I can fix.

Fortunately, the day went by rather quickly. I worked the register mostly, only making a few drinks, but the next time I checked the time, I realized that I only had twenty minutes left in my shift.

"Next in line, please," I spoke loud and clear, something Andrea really put an emphasis on during my training. She said something about being polite but also preventing the frustration of customers waiting on the rapidly growing line.

"Hi, can I ha- Dylan?"

I looked up from the register where I let my vision stay while I anticipated the customer's order. There were an awful lot of buttons, I had to try to look at all of them at once to make sure I didn't lose sight of them.

My eyes fell on a familiar head of hair that surrounded soft features and met big gray eyes. "Ellie, hi, how are you?"

"I'm great! I see you took my advice." She laughed and gestured to our location.

"Yes, I did and I'm glad I did. Listen, I get out of here in like fifteen minutes, are you in a rush to be anywhere right now?"

"No, I was just going to head home and do some binge-watching, but I guess I can put it off for a little while." She teased.

"Oh, only if it's not too much of a burden." I joked back "What can I get for you? Choose carefully, this will influence my opinion on you as a person."

"Oh, no, now I'm under pressure *and* holding up the line." Her chuckle echoed slightly. "I'll take a large salted caramel hot chocolate and a brownie."

"You got it." I grabbed a large cup and tried making the drink myself, it couldn't be that hard. When I was done, I grabbed a brownie and walked back towards her.

"Thank you." She handed me seven dollars.

"Oh, wait, you gave me too much, here." I scrambled to slide the necessary coins out of their designated slots and reached out to give her the extra change.

She didn't take her change from me, she just smiled over her shoulder and walked away.

When I finished my shift, I hung my apron in the back room and clocked out before I joined Ellie.

"Hey, what's up?" I slid into the seat that was directly in front of her.

"Hi, nothing, just came to get my coffee fix."

"You *do* know that you didn't even order coffee, yes?" I raised an eyebrow at her.

"Oh, stop, you know what I meant. I wasn't expecting to see you here."

"Yeah, I wasn't expecting to see you either. Unfortunately, I wasn't able to get a job anywhere else, but this place came to mind right before I quit desperately begging for a job for the day."

"Good, I'm glad." There was a moment of silence before she spoke again. "How are you... you know, handling things?"

I cleared my throat, already feeling the sting behind my eyes. I really hope that talking about this makes it hurt a little bit less because if not, it's awfully sadistic. "It's definitely been hard. I keep wanting to text her and tell her things like I'm just away on vacation, but realizing I can't is..." I had to take a minute to clear my throat again and try to calm myself down. "...hard."

"I can't even imagine, I'm so sorry."

"I appreciate it, but you have nothing to be sorry for, this is just the way things were meant to happen, I guess." I shrugged, trying to shake the desperation that I felt to get the chance to hug Nat again or for her to annoy me to the point of me throwing something at her.

"See, I don't really know you from a hole in the wall, but I know for damn sure that you don't believe that your sister was supposed to be taken from you so early. At least, I can't imagine a reason for that." There was a slight fire behind her voice that grabbed my attention.

I'm not sure if I was trying to convince myself or if I was actually succeeding in doing so, and finally believing myself, but I persisted. "Maybe someone on the other side needed her more than we needed her down here. I can't imagine the situation, but I have to believe that there was a reason.

Thinking that she was taken away from me, from all of us, just because of some stupid guy and a drunken accident..."

I turned my attention towards the window, wanting to look anywhere but at the person in front of me. I knew that if she continued to look me in the eyes, it would only speed up the pace at which I fell apart all over again. "It'll just put me in a place that's so dark that I'm not sure if I'll be able to climb my way out." I moved my glance to my hands which were interlocked with one another so tightly that they started to shake.

"I'm not sure how much I believe in there being another side or a life after death or anything like that, but I can understand and respect that you need to believe in something so that you have something to hold onto. I'm sorry you lost her." Ellie placed a hand on mine to keep them from shaking.

"Thank you. I'm sorry I've been rambling both here and on the plane, I'm trying to sort out the way that this whole situation has been making me feel an-"

"Dylan, stop. You're absolutely fine. You *should* be working through this and I'm honored that you are trying to work through it with me. I know you've just moved here and probably don't have anybody to talk to, but if you need to talk to someone or just to be emotional, I'm always pretty easy to reach. Here, I'll give you my phone number and whether you choose to use it or not, that's completely in your hands." She reached into her bag, grabbed a pen, and scrawled her number out on a napkin before she slid it towards me.

I watched as she glanced up and looked behind me right before her face drained of all color. She put on sunglasses that were massive on her small face and pulled her hood up. "I'm sorry, I have to go." She whispered before she ran out of the cafe so fast that she almost tripped over her own feet.

I turned around to look for what could have possibly scared her to the point of leaving and I didn't notice anything out of the ordinary. Everything looked fine. I got up and cleaned up whatever trash was left on the table, pushed in the chairs, and started walking back to what I was currently calling home.

When I got up to my room, I took the napkin with Ellie's number out of my jacket pocket and put it down on the desk in the corner of the room.

I had to get up early, I was basically ready for bed by the time I walked through the door of my room. I was sitting on the bed, exhausted after work when it hit me.

I shouldn't still be in this motel.

I got up, took a shower, and then got into bed with my laptop. I was looking for an apartment that I could afford when I realized that my barista job is just not going to cut it. Even if I work from opening to closing, which Andrea would never allow, my minimum wage wouldn't add up quick enough.

I'm going to have to either quit my job and find a new one that pays more, or I'll have to work two jobs. All I know is that I'm going to have to decide soon because I am draining my savings and pretty soon, I'll have nothing left.

THE NEXT MORNING, I decided that I would text Ellie to check in on her and see how she was doing, but when I looked at the time, I decided that I would wait until later. She's probably not up at 5:30 a.m.

My shift seemed to drag on, but when I got out of work, I was relieved that tomorrow, Andrea didn't want me to come in until 10:00 a.m. rather than 6:00 a.m.

I fell into my daily routine of eating dinner, taking a

shower, and getting into bed. I texted Ellie since it was still early.

Dylan: Hey, Ellie, it's Dylan. I just wanted to check in on you after what happened yesterday. To be honest, I'm really not sure what happened, but it seemed to really make you uncomfortable, so I'm just checking in. Hope all is well.

Shortly after, she responded.

Ellie: Hi, Dylan. I'm sorry about yesterday, but yes, I'm okay now. We'll finish up that conversation at some point, I promise.

Dylan: Sounds good to me. Listen, I hate to end this conversation right after it started, but I'm probably going to fall asleep any minute now. I'm glad you're okay. I'll talk to you tomorrow, okay? Maybe I'll even see you, I'm working from 10-4.

Ellie: That's fine, I need to get some stuff done anyway. Thank you for checking in, I'll talk to you tomorrow.

As I predicted, I fell asleep almost immediately after that.

CHAPTER TWENTY-TWO

ELLIE

As my parents had promised, they helped me find a new apartment and a moving company to hire. The new apartment was beautiful with tons of natural light and a very modern, open-floor plan which I loved. I figured it would be easy to find comfort in an apartment that didn't have many dark corners or hiding spots. If I can't imagine Jared lurking in the corner shadows, maybe I'll be able to sleep.

Today was moving day and the movers started bright and early. By the time dinner rolled around, all of my boxes and furniture were in my new apartment and I no longer had anything to do with my old apartment.

Staying with my parents was proving to be easier than I thought. They were working most of the time, so I basically had the place to myself and Jared never seemed to have any interest in meeting my parents, so he doesn't know where they live. I felt safe.

Well, I felt safe all the way up until I saw him.

I couldn't have possibly known that he would be there, except I couldn't have ruled it out either. As unlikely as it may have seemed, the possibility of dodging someone who knew and dated me for years in the city where our romance lived was even less likely.

The incident at the café gave me an idea of the running that I may have to do until Jared faces the punishment he deserves for his wrongdoings. I wasn't even sure if he saw me or if he recognized me, but I undoubtedly drew an unwanted amount of attention to myself when I ran out of there as fast as I could manage.

This all would've been so much easier if I didn't lie when the beatings sent me to the hospital. I didn't want to lie. I planned out everything that I was going to say, and I was ready to tell the whole story, but when the time came, different words fell out of my mouth.

I told every nurse and doctor that asked that I slipped and fell down the stairs. I was lying through my teeth and apparently, I was convincing. Meanwhile, 'I fell down the stairs' has to be the most common coverup for abuse. Jared helped my story when he came to visit.

Since Allison never knew, and still doesn't know, about the true state of our relationship, when Jared called asking where I was, she told him. Jared's a lot of things, but stupid isn't one of them. He knows exactly who to go to so that he can get the information that he wants.

Every time I would 'disappear', he knew that my best friend would be his best option for a right answer. He was right every time. You'd think I would've learned to lie to her, too. Unfortunately, you'd be overestimating my intelligence.

When he got to the hospital, he played the concerned boyfriend card every time, despite the environment that I chose to hide out in. When he got to the hospital, that was his most convincing act. He told the nurses and doctors that I was always so stubborn and clumsy and that he hadn't been home to help me down the stairs with the box of decorations from the attic.

They ate it up. Usually the fake story of how the injuries came to be doesn't get backed up by a supportive boyfriend. After I was taken care of, they told Jared what to do to help me heal easier and faster at home and he sat there, listening attentively. He held my hand and kissed my head, and I held back my winces every time. I wanted someone to hear the internal screams coming through my eyes, but I'm almost positive that it was all just dismissed as part of a concussion.

Being sent home with him that night before my parents could get to me was devastating. Once I recovered, I decided that he would never get the chance to hurt me to that extent again. I'd been plotting my escape since then, calculating when he would be gone, when he'd come home, how big of a window I'd have.

Things were different now that I finally got the escape route that I've been desperate for. In a few hours, I'll be safe in a place where he can't find me. He can't touch me anymore.

MY PARENTS CAME with me to the new apartment to help me unpack some of my things and settle in. It would drive me nuts if there were boxes piled in the corners, I just wanted this to feel like my normal life. A smooth transition was all I could hope for at this point.

When we walked in, I was greeted with a wall of boxes and the white walls were muted by the chaos.

I immediately started sorting the boxes based on what room they belong in and had my parents start unpacking the kitchen first, while I started in the bedroom. Having them stay here was probably the best decision I could've made, otherwise moving the furniture, and unpacking everything would've taken three times as long.

"Are you gonna be okay here on your own tonight? Do you want us to stay here just for tonight to help ease the transition?" My mom sat on the floor next to me while I worked to reassemble the coffee table.

"No, I'll be okay." I kept my focus on the screwdriver that I was using, feeling my eyes start to well up with tears.

"Ellie."

"Yeah?"

"I'm gonna need you to look at me and say that. Your staring at the ground isn't too convincing." She put her hand on the screwdriver to stop me from twisting it and waited for my eyes to meet hers.

I turned my head to look at her. "Did I say I'll be okay? What I meant to say was that I'm terrified and I need you to stay with me for the night."

"You got it. I'll have your dad run home and grab some clothes for us so we can just head to work from here in the morning." She kissed my head. "Charlie!"

"Yes, dear?" My dad came out from around the corner of the kitchen.

"Can you run home and grab us some clothes and toiletries for tonight and work tomorrow? We're gonna stay with our girl tonight and christen her apartment." She turned to look at me and smiled.

"Yeah, I'll head out in a few, I just want to finish what I'm doing in here real quick." He nodded and wiped his hands on his jeans.

"Thank you both for everything you've been doing for me. I can't imagine going through all of this without you guys."

They both offered loving and supportive smiles and I stopped to take a minute and appreciate that I have a strong relationship with not one, but both of my parents and how rare that is.

My mind drifted back to Dylan briefly and I wondered what his story was. He said he lost his sister who seemed to be everything to him, but what about his parents? Are they alive? Are they in the picture? Someone had to raise him right if checking on me after I fled the café even crossed his mind.

Maybe tomorrow I'll reach out to him and clear things up. I'm definitely going to need something to distract me while I'm on my way to work.

CHAPTER TWENTY-THREE

DYLAN

Suddenly, I was back in the house that Nat and I grew up in. I was in my old bedroom.

Everything looked exactly like it did before I left.

My mind immediately shifted to Natalie. I ran down the hall and grabbed the edge of the entrance to the kitchen to slow myself down enough to swing into the room. To my delight, my eyes landed on Nat, who was covered in flour, her eyebrows knitted together in frustration as she looked down at the recipe book in front of her.

"Hey! What're you doing?"

"I'm trying to make some dessert that I found the recipe for online and I can't seem to get the dough to stop being so sticky no matter how much flour I use." She slammed the ball of dough down on the countertop and rested her head on the heels of her hands. When she pulled her hands away, there were two dabs of flour in their place.

"Maybe you should leave the baking to the pros, look at the mess you made." I teased her playfully, but she huffed at me. "So, where's mom?"

"I don't know, out with Chris or something." She kept her focus on the dough as she continued to knead it.

"Surprise, surprise. Some things never change." I opened the fridge to grab a drink, but my attention was pulled back towards Natalie as I heard bowls clattering together.

She tore off her apron, threw it on the counter and slammed the recipe book shut before she opened the door to the back deck and stormed out, closing the door behind her. She slammed that, too.

I had no idea what I did that made her so upset, but I knew I needed to fix it. I decided to neaten up some of the mess in the kitchen so she would have some time to calm down and I noticed that she had somehow managed to get flour in every nook and cranny in the tile countertop.

When I finished, I opened the door to the backyard and found her sitting on the edge of the deck with her back to me and her legs dangling.

"Natalie?" I spoke gently, trying not to anger her any further.

Her voice was quiet but firm. "Go away."

I ignored her wishes and walked towards the edge to sit right next to her. "Please, talk to me."

"I just don't understand why you don't appreciate the things that I do for you. Or why hating mom makes your life easier or whatever. I was trying to bake for you to congratulate you on finally getting the raise you deserve, but you come in and all you have to say is that I made a mess of the kitchen and that mom's never home. It's like you always forget that you're not the only one that lost dad. We all did, so stop being so angry all the time because it's not our fault and we are suffering just as much as you are, if not, more. You weren't close to him like we were, so I guess it's almost like you've never lost anyone that was truly significant to you. Just figure out your issues and why you're so mad all the time because if you keep acting like this, you won't have anybody left." Tears were racing down her cheeks, something that I've seen happen more times that I care to admit, but this time it was worse.

This time, I was the reason.

I pulled her into my side and hugged her. "I'm sorry, I'll work on it. Maybe I wasn't married to dad or his favorite kid, but I did always look up to him. I lost my dad and my role model. I have no other male figure in my life to look up to so now I kinda just have to figure out the rest on my own. He can't help me figure things out or make decisions anymore. It's killing me, too. It sucks and I wish he were still here, but in a way, I'm glad he's finally moved on from the pain and the suffering that he couldn't escape. He's better now."

Before I realized it, the sun was setting and it was just me and my little sister sitting on the back deck in silence as we both remembered the same person in extremely different ways.

———

WHEN I WOKE UP, I couldn't bring myself to move. I was just laying on my side, the blackout curtains drawn, leaving the room almost pitch black, tangled up in blankets.

My dream left me with nothing but pure confusion. I dreamt something that happened a few years ago, but everything about the dream screamed that it was much more recent than that. The actual memory brought comfort; it was something that strengthened my relationship with Nat. She was always the person that kept me in check. She was right, I wasn't the only one going through stuff. That rang true then and now.

There I was, laying in the dark, motionless, when my phone started vibrating. Someone was calling me. I figured that it was either the middle of the night or still early, so I mentally dismissed it as a spam call and allowed myself to go back to sleep.

I woke up again after what felt like twenty minutes later and moved my head just enough to see the alarm clock on the dresser.

2:00 p.m.

I was supposed to be at work hours ago.

I was sure that it was Andrea that called me to see where I was. I rolled over and buried myself under the blankets even further. I already dug my grave when it comes to work, I might as well just lay in it.

I DRAGGED myself out of bed when I couldn't wait to go to the bathroom any longer. When I was making my way back to the bed, I noticed that Ellie was calling me.

I sighed and picked up the phone, sliding to answer. "Hello?"

"Dylan, hey. Just out of curiosity, where are you staying?"

"A motel by the airport, why?"

"The one on Pacific Highway South?"

"Yes, why?"

"Just wondering, thanks, bye!" Before I even knew what was happening, she hung up.

Huh, that was weird. I stared at my reflection in the black screen and saw my hair sticking up in every direction.

I crawled back into bed under the blankets for a maximum of ten minutes before there was a knock on my door.

I groaned and kicked the blankets off me and got up again.

I know for a fact that I put that damn 'Do Not Disturb' sign on the doorknob.

On my walk over to the door, one of my toes caught the edge of the bed frame as I passed around the other side.

"Damnit!" I slammed my fist against the TV stand.

I reached for the door handle, more fed up now than I was five seconds ago and swung the door open.

My eyes met a pair of wide, slightly concerned eyes which I realized was probably a result of my hasty behavior. "Um, hi, I hope it's okay that I'm here, I just noticed you weren't at work and I wanted to check up on you. I come bearing Chinese food." She brushed past me, walking to the desk in the corner to set the food down before opening the blinds, allowing sunlight to flood into the room. "It's so dark in here! The sun will set shortly, Dracula, you only have to deal with the light for a little while."

I cocked my eyebrow, ignoring her teasing. "How did you know I was supposed to be at work today?"

"You told me last night while we were texting. Now, are we gonna eat or are you gonna stand here and keep trying to make me sound like a little bit of a stalker?" She shifted her weight to one leg and crossed her arms for a second before taking the food out of the bag.

I let go of the door and waited to hear it click shut before excusing myself. "I'll be out in a minute."

I walked into the bathroom and washed my hands and face to freshen up a little bit. When I walked out, Ellie was awkwardly resting against the bed, not standing, or sitting, she just seemed uncomfortable and distracted.

"You can make yourself comfortable, sit wherever you'd like." I gestured to her options: the bed, the chair that was questionably stained, or the floor.

She turned to look at me but didn't move. I made my way back to where I had spent my entire day, but this time, I sat up and on top of the blankets that I sloppily fixed, so they weren't in a ball anymore. I sat with my legs crossed, facing the other half of the bed where I expected she'd sit. A few moments later, she did exactly what I expected and sat in front of me, almost mirroring my actions.

I left it to her to hand out the food which she did almost the second she sat down. "I don't have any idea what you like so I just got you sesame chicken. I figured it's something most people are familiar with and usually like so it's a safer bet than some random option. If you don't want that you can have my meal which is just rice with a side of steamed shrimp and vegetables."

I nodded and picked the sesame chicken. It was quiet while we ate, the room almost silent except for the little noise coming from the TV. I looked up at Ellie, "Thank you, I really appreciate you doing this,"

"It's no big deal, I figured you could use a friend," She shrugged, she wouldn't look up at me.

"I wouldn't have asked you to come, or even admitted that I wanted the company, but it's helping me a lot. I just hope next time you need a friend, you'll let me be there for you."

Her head shot up towards me, "Next time?" Her eyebrows knit together.

Deciding to take over the role that she just gave up, I looked down at my food. "Mhm."

"Care to elaborate, or do I have to guess?"

"Well, since you've admitted that you really don't know anything about me, allow me to bring you in the loop: I'm fairly observant. I know the other day something triggered you. I don't know what it was or what has happened to you in the past, but I know something set you off and I know that it's easier to come back from stuff if you have someone by your side. I'm not going to push you to tell me, but I hope you know that when you're comfortable enough with me, I'm all ears."

"You're right." She was practically whispering, and she seemed lost in her own head.

After a few moments of silence, I realized that she wasn't going to tell me, and it seemed as if she was just done talking about it. Not wanting to make her uncomfortable, I cleaned up after we finished eating. I use the term "cleaned up" lightly, seeing as how I only moved the empty containers off the bed.

I sat with my legs stretched out and stared forward at the TV. I wasn't sure what I was watching, but Ellie put it on, so I didn't ask, I just let it get rid of the silence that felt too heavy.

CHAPTER TWENTY-FOUR

DYLAN

I woke up, not realizing I fell asleep, and glanced at the clock. It was 1:15 a.m. Much to my surprise, I looked at the other side of the bed and there was Ellie, laying on her right side, facing the other way. Seeing the Chinese food containers litter the table around the TV, I remembered last night. Silence filled the air most of the time, neither of us knowing what to say or how to act.

Me, still haunted by my nightmares from the night before, and Ellie, well, I don't really know what's going on in her life. I got up as quietly as I could to turn off the TV, trying not to wake her.

I failed.

When I got up, the bed shifted and so did she. She moved to roll onto her other side, her eyes opened slightly. Taking in her surroundings, she shot upright, her eyes bigger than usual, like a deer in headlights.

Her eyes landed on me and she calmed a little bit, but it was too late, her panicking got the best of her and her eyes welled up with tears.

I moved from where I was back to next to her on the bed.

She buried her face in her hands and choked out a sob. I sat and watched from a comfortable distance, unsure of how to approach the situation, while I waited for her to calm down again.

She wiped her face, but some of her hair, now wet with tears, clung to her skin. She looked at me with red eyes and a blotchy face, completely different from the person that I've met on the past two occasions. I was unsure of who this person sitting in front of me was, but I knew that there was something inside of her that was scared and broken despite the facade that she wore so gracefully.

"I'm sorry." She sounded mad at herself, frustrated.

"You have nothing to apologize for. It's okay to fall apart, especially considering I've been doing it constantly since we've met. You've never even seen me put-together and let me tell you, if I was the normal me when we first met, you would not be able to resist me, I am a catch!" I made sure to kick up one of my eyebrows semi-suggestively and I got the exact reaction that I was hoping for, the exact one Natalie would've given me in a situation like this.

Ellie rolled her eyes at me and laughed as she pushed me playfully. "If that was a sneak peek of who you usually are, I don't know what I'm gonna do with you when you're all better and healed." She laughed again, but less this time, like she was being dragged down again by what haunts her.

Seeing no harm in making my statement at this point since I was already losing her again, I took a chance. "I can't wait to see who you are when you're better and healed." Neither of us laughed this time, I just looked at her seriously and she looked at me, something dull and sad behind her eyes, they were dark and empty.

"What if we both confess something so that we're even?" I proposed.

"Depends on what you're expecting me to reveal, I still

don't know you." Her walls were back up again, she was colder now than she was before, her responses short.

"I'm not going to screw around with you, life is too short for games, so I'm going to be nice and blunt. I want to know what's going on with you. I want to know what scared you in the coffee shop, I want to know why you freaked out when you woke up, I want to know what happened to you that made you build up these walls that you hide behind." I tried to throw in everything I could think of so that she was left with nothing to question, nothing to find her way around or get out of.

"You have no right to ask me any of that, but if we're going to continue being friends, it'll be easier for both of us if I just tell you. But just so you know, I am going to grill you after I'm done because you'll owe me at least that much." She got up and walked over to the jacket that she had left on the questionable chair and dug around in the pockets. "I really don't even know why I'm doing this, seeing how I would never ask you to do this, except I know I would for the same reasons that you're doing it... you're concerned. I'm sorry, it's just hard for me to talk about, none of this is your fault." She turned back towards me with a piece of paper in her hand and extended it towards me.

I took the paper from her, only to learn that it was a picture. There was a girl on it who looked a lot like Ellie. I looked up at Ellie and then back at the picture a few times, noticing more similarities each time. Their eyes looked identical along with their noses and their mouths. From the few times I've seen Ellie genuinely smile, I remembered it looked a lot like the girl's. I opened my mouth to ask if this was her sister, but she beat me to it.

"That's me. Just about six months ago." She looked uncomfortable already, her right hand placed across her torso, cupping her left bicep while she stared at the floor. She turned around so she was facing the window and continued. "I dyed my hair, obviously, and I wear a lot of makeup now, and I dress a lot more... comfortably." I studied the picture in my hand, unable to imagine her like this.

The girl in the picture had blonde hair, her face completely bare of any noticeable makeup, her clothing much more feminine and less conservative than how she looks now. Her floral top seemed uncharacteristic; it didn't match the personality that I'd seen so far. She was laughing, she looked so happy. I'd for sure never seen her that happy. The girl in the picture seemed to match the girl I met on the plane the most out of the few times I've been with her. She seemed playful and sincere in everything that she does.

A few feet away from me stood the same girl, with black hair now, and lots of makeup that looked like it altered the shape of her face. Her cheeks were more sunken in now, but I couldn't tell if that was due to the makeup or if she had lost weight. Her clothes were a lot baggier now, but they were different. She wore sweatpants and either a t-shirt or a hoodie now, replacing the floral top.

"That's my ex-boyfriend with me, his best friend actually took the picture." She turned away from me, looking out the window.

"You look really happy here."

"I thought I was. I was blinded by how much I loved him or how much I thought he loved me. It took me getting hit seven times to realize that my friends, my parents, they were all right; he didn't love me. Once, I ordered take out and his order came wrong. He insisted it was my fault and that I did it just to screw with him. Some of his other justifications varied from him just coming home drunk, to him accusing me of being too flirty with other guys, to him punishing me for trying to leave him. The worst time was when I finally found my voice in an argument and yelled back. So, I flew to

Boston and I tried to change everything about myself that I think could be recognizable from a distance, and then I came back here, back home. I will not let that bastard scare me away from my home." She turned to look at me.

"Is that what freaked you out the other day? You saw him?"

"Yeah, he was at the cafe. Usually, when I would leave, he would harass me and everyone in my life until I answered, but I haven't heard from him recently. Not since I left. He used to try any means to contact me and I would just ignore him. I don't know if he's biding his time or if he just gave up, but I don't want to take the chance of his frenzy starting all over again if he sees me."

I watched as she took a deep breath to gather herself.

"I thought he was the love of my life, but he just wanted to control someone. I guess I just happened to be in the wrong place at the wrong time. He charmed me and made me feel so special and like he would love me forever, but he didn't. He hit me instead, so that's always fun." Sarcasm dripped from her voice as she huffed and sat down next to me. Sighing, she continued, "So, that's my story. You still wanna hang around me, even with all my damage?" She looked at me, her face covered in smudged makeup, waiting for me to respond.

"Well, I hate to play this card, except I don't really hate it too much because I'm going to play it anyway: You've got some competition in the sad game." I shrugged dramatically, bringing my hands up in line with my chin on either side of my face.

She playfully looked at me in disbelief and scoffed. "You're unreal, my life is much worse."

We laughed with a heaviness.

I turned my body to face her, "I really am sorry to hear about all of that. As much as you women drive me crazy, my mother and sister included, I could never imagine laying a hand on a woman. Is he ill?" I felt awkward asking her that, as if it wasn't my place to ask such a question, rather, I knew it wasn't.

"It's funny, he always refused to go talk to someone like a therapist or something so technically, no, he's never been diagnosed with any kind of mental illness or any explanation of why he's so violent, but then again, it was kind of my own little secret for a long time. You know how sometimes, when you talk to someone about something, you leave out some parts because you know that person will probably pass along some kind of judgement? I never told anyone when he hit me for the first time because I knew that it was bad and that they'd all say that he's just going to do it again and it'd escalate to something much worse. Maybe I tried to protect him because I thought that I could get him to change or that he really loved me so he wouldn't do any *'real'* damage. As if emotional damage wasn't valid enough, I had to wait for a whole bunch of actual physical blows. But to answer your question, I believe he is mentally ill, but how could anyone know for sure? Aren't we all at least a little mentally ill?"

She was fiddling with her hands in her lap again, refusing to look up at me and I could tell that her previous decisions and the time that she lost being in that relationship really took a toll on her.

"I have anxiety, and I'm definitely suffering from some kind of emotional damage after losing my sister. Most likely depression, but I think just about everyone on the planet experiences both of those things at some point in their lives, it's just a part of life. Unless your life is somehow miraculously fantastic and problem free, you can't get out unscathed, it's physically impossible. I'm really glad that you got out of that relationship, I'm just sorry you had to go through it at all."

Before I got the chance to continue, she interrupted: "No, no, no, there's no reason for you to be apologizing. Having said that, I have to agree with you, I'm glad that I'm finally out of it, too. I just wish that I didn't have to always watch my back, but I've lived here for my entire life. I grew up here. In the park a few blocks away, I learned how to ride my bike. Twenty minutes from here, I started playing softball and absolutely fell in love and stuck with it all the way throughout high school. I went to college at Washington State University for four years. That poor excuse of a man will not run me out of the only home that I have ever known."

I watched her, in awe of her strength and her determination to keep what was hers. "You're incredibly brave." was all I could manage.

She huffed, "Or just incredibly stupid."

"Either way, you're going after what you want, and it doesn't seem like you're going to let anything get in your way."

"I'm not. I contemplated leaving and just letting him win, but I wouldn't have been able to live with myself if I did. It took me a really long time to see what was wrong with my relationship with him, but once I did, I was furious with myself for being so blind to it. I used to roll my eyes whenever someone would use the excuse that love makes a person blind to all the negativity that they're surrounded by in their relationship. Imagine how hard I rolled my eyes when I realized that I did the *exact* thing that I don't believe in." She cracked a smile and somehow, I was able to tell that she sincerely was able to find humor in a seemingly humorless situation.

Deciding to try her tactics, I joined in. "I continued to live with my mother even after I didn't have to anymore just so Natalie would always have someone there for her and on her side. Right before she graduates, which would've set us both free from the figurative chains that bound us, she died. We were supposed to move out together. I can practically feel the universe laughing at my misfortune. Sadistic, I tell you." I laughed and didn't realize how unsuccessful my attempt at being easy breezy was until Ellie came and sat next to me again, staring at me.

She grabbed a tissue from the box on the nightstand and balled it up while she moved to get closer to me. I had no idea what she was doing until she was wiping underneath my eyes with the crumbled tissue.

"I guess I'm just not ready to be as strong and healed as you yet." I laughed.

"Being able to joke about the things that happened to you that are most definitely not funny takes time, patience, and a lot of letting your wounds just bleed rather than trying to slap some miracle tape on it and making light of it. Let yourself hurt, Dylan. Something terrible happened to you, let yourself grieve." Her tone was light and joking when she started talking, but somewhere in the middle, she got serious and I could tell that she was speaking from experience.

Little did she know, she had opened the floodgates even more than they were already opened and I was having a hard time catching my breath. "It just feels like it will never stop hurting. I'm trying to keep myself occupied, but I jus-"

She didn't say anything, but the way that she looked at me and my surroundings disapprovingly cut me off. "That explains the fact that it was pitch black in here, and you didn't get out of bed, let alone go to work today." Sarcasm flooded her voice.

"Okay, fine. I've been trying to keep myself occupied for the most part, but I moved myself to a new place where there's no one for me to hang out with rather than sitting home alone after my work shift. I'm basically on a strict work and sleep schedule at this point and now even when I sleep, she's there and it just haunts me. I've been laying here, trying to sleep the day away but also dreading falling asleep because last night I had a dream and she was there and she was so mad at me, so disappointed. I haven't been able to stop my mind from racing. I just feel like I'm failing her." My words were coming out rushed as I tried to keep my sentences coherent while my emotions got the best of me.

"Dylan, please calm down, breathe with me. Come on, in for three seconds, out for three seconds. Deep breaths." She grabbed my hand and started to take a deep breath and held her hand up while she counted the seconds on her fingers. I didn't join her until she inhaled for the second time and gave my hand a squeeze.

I struggled to keep my breathing steady, but eventually, I was able to keep up with her, no faster and no slower.

We kept breathing for a minute until she was sure that I was calmer now before she broke the silence. "Much better. I need you to listen to me, okay? I know that it's hard to stay calm when you think about her, but you need to try, for your own good. Is there anything that you have of hers that will remind you of her, but not so much that you'll spiral?"

I nodded and got up from the bed. I dug through my backpack for a minute so that I could find where one of her most prized possessions ended up. My fingertips grazed the matte cover that felt so familiar. I moved the clothes that were surrounding it out of the way and then my eyes fell on the proof of her book. I sat on the edge of the bed with it. "This is her book. She got the proof while she was in the hospital."

"Are you sure you'll be okay with this?"

I nodded hesitantly, "I think this is what I need."

A moment of silence passed as Ellie allowed me to do this at my own pace.

"She would absolutely kill me if she knew I was doing this." I held the closed book on my lap, unable to bring myself to flip through the pages.

"Dylan, I know you're trying to respect her wishes, but your sister unwillingly left you out of nowhere and you need closure." She took the book from my hands and held it on her lap. I watched hesitantly while she opened the cover and flipped through the first few pages.

"I can't look, you have to do it." I stood up and faced Ellie so I could no longer read the pages. I know for a fact that I wouldn't be able to keep myself from looking. Plus, better Ellie facing my sister's wrath than me.

A few minutes went by and all I could do was stand there and watch Ellie's eyes brush through the words as she flipped from one page to the next.

I was about to interrupt her and ask what she found when she beat me to it. "Dylan, this stuff is incredible. Your sister was so talented. I just want to read everything she has in here." She looked up at me and I rushed to her side.

She pointed to the page, "Here, start here and read this line." She handed the book to me.

"And soon, running from my problems was the only way that I could catch my breath."

I couldn't help myself, I flipped through a few of the pages so I could satisfy my curiosity. I just wanted to know everything, and I felt like having this window into Natalie's brain was something that I may never have gotten while she was alive.

I felt closer to her just about as much as I felt further away from her. What was my baby sister going through that she felt this way? Her poems and prose were semi-dark, and I could sense the pain behind a lot of it.

Regardless, I wished she would have shared this stuff with

me, it was incredible and our father would've been so proud of her.

Scratch that; wherever they may be, they're together and Natalie is flipping out that I have my eyes on her work and my father is holding her still and trying to keep her calm, telling her that her work is good and deserves to be seen.

My vision got blurry as my eyes teared up, I missed my family more than I ever imagined possible and I wanted nothing more than to be able to see them and hear them and talk to them. This didn't feel like the pain from earlier did, I was crying again, but this time I felt at peace. I knew Natalie was keeping our dad company now and that they were watching over me together.

CHAPTER TWENTY-FIVE

DYLAN

Ellie and I quickly got used to keeping each other company and started spending more time together. It was easy being around her. When we were together in public and I would see someone do something that reminded me of Natalie, I would feel a pang in my chest that was all too familiar and each time, Ellie helped me work my way through it.

I went through phases of putting on a tough guy act and she would call me out every time.

"Stop acting like you don't have feelings, it doesn't make you any less of a man." Her frequent reprimanding rang through my head.

We saw each other most days, whether we met up for a quick bite or had a movie night and ordered some takeout. Whenever she was around, the weight of my grief didn't sit so heavy on my shoulders.

It was all bearable with her.

In my eyes, it wasn't worth trying to pinpoint what I felt for her because there were undoubtedly crossed wires in my brain. I told myself that once I fully recovered from losing

Natalie, everything in my head would most likely get sorted out, I just had to push through until then.

My phone chimed from the nightstand.

Ellie: Hey, I'm running late, but I'm on my way. See you soon!

I put my phone back down without answering. It barely connected with the surface before it chimed again.

Ellie: You better leave the door open because it's pouring, and I'm drenched!

I laughed and put my phone down.

I walked over to the door and made sure that it was unlocked before I sat down on the bed and turned on the TV.

I was mindlessly clicking through the channels for mere moments when the door swung open.

She wasn't wrong about being drenched.

She dropped her backpack by the door with a soggy thud.

Her hair was up in a ponytail but there were stray wet hairs that clung to her forehead and her neck as she fought to get out of her hoodie, getting stuck halfway. Eventually, after she won the battle, she huffed and took her hair down.

She looked different than she usually did. She didn't have her usual makeup on, her face bare and her hair a wet curly mess.

"So, I'm kind of tired of eating complete crap, so I made dinner for us tonight." She dug through the backpack that she had with her and pulled out Tupperware containers full of food. "I didn't feel like going to the store to get something to make, so I made whatever I had laying around."

I smiled to myself.

"What are you smiling about? Are you making fun of me in your head? I will eat all of this on my own and you can chew on your tap water for dinner." She crossed her arms and glared at me.

"No, I'm not making fun of you, it all looks and smells great and you know I appreciate it more than anything. You just made mashed potatoes, it made me think of Kathryn, she's a mashed potato vacuum."

"Do you miss everyone back home?" She stopped what she was doing and sat to look at me when she asked.

"Absolutely. I grew up with those people and saw them just about every day. It's hard to go so long without seeing them. It's weird, it feels like I'm on vacation or something. I'll go home one day, when I'm ready. I'm not sure when that will be, but I know it's not any time soon."

I had no idea how wrong I was.

WE FINISHED EATING and Ellie laid back on the bed and whispered my name. "Dylan?"

"Yes?"

"Not it."

"What?"

"Not it. As in, I cooked, so I'm not cleaning up dinner."

I groaned but didn't put up a fight, I just got up and cleaned up what I could.

My phone rang while I was in the bathroom cleaning out the containers Ellie brought over.

"Ellie, can you check and see who that is?" I yelled over the sound of the sink and the TV that Ellie had on louder than usual.

"It's Noah, do you want me to bring it to you?"

I had just finished cleaning out the last container and shut off the water as I walked out of the bathroom drying my hands. "No need, I'm coming. Thank you."

"Noah? Hey, man, what's up? How are you?"

Ellie was grabbing her stuff and mouthing to me that she was going to run home but would see me tomorrow.

"Hey, Dylan. You know how all the houses around yours used to always look almost exactly like yours?"

"Small and dingy? Yeah, what about it?"

"Well, I was just driving past your house and noticed a sign out up front. It says something about new construction that's supposed to start soon. Apparently, your house is getting knocked down within the next two weeks so that they can rebuild it to be bigger like the other ones around it."

I've known our landlord for a long time, and I can't imagine that he would just kick my mom out of that house after so many years of paying rent there, something was up.

I immediately assumed that she hadn't paid the bills in a while.

"Oh, wow. Thank you for giving me a heads up. I guess I'll have to make my way back in a couple of days."

"No problem. Just let me know when you're going to come back, and I'll see if I can get a day or two off from work. If you need help packing or anything or just want to hang out, I'm in. Kathryn, too, she just doesn't know it yet."

"She'll get over it, she always does. I'll let you know when I book something, looking forward to catching up. Love you, talk to you soon."

"Love you, too."

I rubbed my hand down my face after we hung up, unsure of how to approach the situation.

I'm not ready to go back there, it's too soon.

I felt conflicted and had no idea what I was going to do. I threw on my jacket and grabbed my phone and my wallet before heading out of the motel room. I decided I was going to walk to Ellie's apartment so I could have some time to clear my head before I got there.

As I walked to her apartment, I thought about how much I missed having my own car like I did in Boston, but honestly, walking everywhere here in Seattle has its benefits. It's nice that everything is within walking distance here.

I got to Ellie's apartment within fifteen minutes of hanging up with Noah and texted her to let her know I was here since she didn't have a bell to ring. She came down less than a minute later and opened the door for me.

"Hey! Wait, what's wrong? Did the conversation with Noah not go well? You're wearing your tense, stressed out face."

As we walked up to her apartment, I explained the situation to her, and she took a minute to think about it before she offered any opinions.

"Honestly, I think you should go. I think you really need the closure and maybe you should use this trip to patch things up with your mom. I know she infuriates you, but she's still your mom and you only get one of those. I could just be being kinda biased since my mom is basically my favorite person in the entire world. Plus, maybe all the grieving and mourning changed her and snapped a sense of reality into her, just like you've always wanted." She was sure and confident in her answer.

I laid on my back on her couch and groaned in response. "Do you really think that's possible? Grieving sent her into this facade to begin with, what if this just pushes her further down the spiral?"

"Try giving her the benefit of the doubt, Dylan. People can change."

"I'm going to sue you for emotional distress one day." I said, my arm thrown over my eyes.

She walked over to me and lifted my arm off of my face. "My ass you're going to sue me, I'm the best, no, scratch that, I'm the only friend you have here which automatically deems me your best friend. Suing me would be nothing but a mistake." She dropped my arm back down over my eyes, earning a painful grunt from me when the unexpected weight of my arm whacked me in the face. I heard her fiddling with something on her dresser for a moment while she was quiet. "Plus, if you sue me, how am I going to afford a ticket to go back to Boston with you?"

I lifted my arm off my eyes slowly and peeked over at her. I sighed in defeat and covered my face again, with a throw pillow this time, muffling my voice slightly. "You know, it's really not nice to screw with someone like that. It kinda sucks that my alleged best friend is nothing but pure evil."

She swatted my feet off the couch so she could sit where they were. "I'm not screwing with you, I'll do it. I'll go back with you."

I sat up to look as deep in her eyes as possible, searching for any indication that she was lying. I came up with nothing. "You're being serious...?"

"Yes, Dylan, I'm being serious. I know you don't want to go even though we both know that you should go and I know I've only been back home for a little while, but I miss Boston, it's beautiful there. Let me come, I'll try to make you laugh through the pain the whole time."

I laughed and stood to hug her, probably tighter than I should've considering the squeak that came out of her. "Thank you! I'll make it up to you, promise."

"Yes, you will. I'll determine your level of debt at a later date. For now, we should probably check online and see when the next couple of flights go out and see which is the cheapest. I know you're good for it, so I'll cover whatever you can't pay for the flights and you can pay me back later when you can, deal?"

"Deal. Hey, thank you for being my only- no, scratch that, my very best friend." I sent an appreciative smile.

For the next few hours, we looked up all the airlines that we could think of, flights with and without layovers, red-eye flights, weekend flights, middle of the week flights, any variation of flights that you can think of, we looked it up and compared prices. By the time we finally booked something, I only owed Ellie $200 and I was dead tired.

I was thankful that I owed her a small amount, I can get that to her in less than a month.

After my whole skipping work stunt that I pulled, I spoke to Andrea the next day and thankfully she was incredibly understanding, but she warned me that I'm only getting one last chance.

Ellie's always nagging, telling me I should start looking for a new job, one that pays better than being a barista, especially since I have to eventually pay rent and Natalie's hospital bills, but I haven't brought myself to start making any actual moves. *"Yeah, yeah, I'll do it eventually."* I always told her. I doubt this little vacation will go over well with Andrea being that it's last minute, so maybe I should just give her a call and quit now. This way, when I come back, I can start seriously looking at my future and figure out what I want from it.

Times like this made me even more grateful for the fact that Ellie really has stuck by my side. I think our traumas really helped us get a jumpstart on our friendship. I dug myself a pretty deep grave after my sister died.

Hey, look at that, I can make dark jokes about my trauma now!

After I moved away, I had no idea which way was up, and Ellie was consistently right there to somehow inspire me to get my life back on track. I decided a few weeks ago that my grief wasn't going to rule my life and I meant it. I'd been doing pretty well with it so far, but I knew for a fact that if she wasn't coming on this trip with me, I wouldn't be able to do it on my own.

Hopefully, with her, I'll be fine.

CHAPTER TWENTY-SIX

DYLAN

A few days later, we were sitting in the airport with our luggage and my palms were sweating non-stop. "I really don't think this is a good idea, maybe we should just leave and go back to our lives."

"Nope, you're not going to chicken out on me now, it's too late. You're already here, we made it through security and now you're committed. I know you're nervous about going back, but we're going to get through this together. I promised that I would be there for you the entire time and I intend to keep that promise."

"Okay, fine. Can I at least take a pill or something so I can sleep through the flight? I'd rather not make myself sick by overthinking the whole time. I have sleep aid pills in my bag." I knew that she would most likely hate the idea, not wanting to be on her own for the whole flight, otherwise, I wouldn't have asked.

"You know what? I think that's a great idea. We should both probably take some." She wiped her palms on her jeans.

"Good. That way, the whole experience will be a lot less painful for everyone."

I got up from where I was sitting and walked over to the closest store in the airport to buy the drinks we wanted. By the time I got back to Ellie, passengers were being called to start boarding.

I took a seat next to Ellie while we waited for our boarding group to be called.

"I think the thing that I'm most nervous about is seeing everybody. I haven't seen any of them since I picked up and left. I don't know how they'll react... or how *I'll* react if I'm being honest." I confessed, looking down at the floor.

"I can only imagine. Have you spoken to any of them since then?" She tilted her head at me.

"Yeah, I reached out to all of them a few weeks ago. I guess I just realized how wrong I was for trying to heal myself like that. It was selfish and I shouldn't have tried to outrun my problems. Look how well that worked out for me."

"Hey! You got me out of your bad decisions, and you know that's a good thing because I'm a blessing." She huffed and dramatically turned her head away from me, her arms crossed.

"Yes, I know, I know. You're right, I'm sorry. You're the best thing that came out of my bad decision, please forgive me, I'm begging you!" I played along with her game.

"Okay, all is forgiven. Anyway, how did it go?" She dropped the act and jumped right back into the previous topic.

And so, I told her.

"I was making my way back to the motel on the day of my interview and I started looking around and I realized that the reason that none of those people were around was all because of me. It kept getting harder to convince myself that this was the right thing for me to do. The more I tried to convince myself, the less I believed it." The guilt set in again.

Ellie sat with her undivided attention on me as she patiently waited for me to continue.

"My phone was dead for three days at this point, so I plugged it in when I got to the motel. They were my support system and I was part of theirs and I just left. It took longer than it should have, but I realized that they all deserved better than this. Actually, scratch that, it didn't take me a long time to realize it at all. I knew it as I was leaving, I guess if I didn't, I wouldn't have felt so guilty. By the time my phone came on, I knew it had been a while, but I wasn't expecting there to be so many texts."

"I'm sorry, your phone was dead for three days right after the person that you loved most in the world died and you decided to run off to a state on the opposite side of the country and you didn't think there were going to be so many messages? Are you insane or just oblivious?" The disbelief was dripping from her voice.

I laughed at how right she probably was, a pattern that I had come to accept. I decided it would be easier if I just handed my phone over to her so she could read through all the messages. I started her off on the messages from Martha.

"This is my conversation with Martha, start here." I offered the phone to her.

Ellie smiled at me, "She seems to really care about you. It sounds like she's trying to lift the mood, I respect that."

"You two would probably get along well, you're both a major pain in my ass and refuse to let me suffer alone. These next ones are from Noah, my best friend for as long as I can remember." I reached over to switch the messages from one contact to the other as she tilted the screen towards me for easier access.

"That's sweet. I feel like I can imagine your relationship with Noah. It's like a less mushy, gushy, version of girl best friends! I love how he's putting his worrying in by saying that it's his sister that's worrying, such a guy."

I tilted my head, "What do you mean? I don't understand what that has to do with being a guy."

"Of course, you don't." She rolled her eyes. "So that just leaves Kathryn, right?"

"Yeah, when I decided to text them all back, I started with Kathryn because I figured she would be the one that needed the most apologizing. She lost her favorite person, too, and I just abandoned her."

"Your sister died. It was unexpected and devastating. I'm not necessarily saying that I agree with the way that you dealt with your emotions around the topic, but I understand why you did it and honestly, who am I to talk about how to cope?" She gestured to her hair and huffed.

"I look at the situation now with a more level head than before and I can see how awful what I did was. Keep reading, you'll see my apology. She took a couple days to answer which is unlike her, which I'm assuming is because of how mad she was at me, but when she did..." I slid my finger up the screen so Ellie could see Kathryn's response.

Kathryn: As much as I want to stay mad at you, I've done it for long enough... I know how you feel about facing the things you've done wrong and I appreciate your apology. I'd rather go through this healing or whatever with you rather than without. I haven't been doing well, Dyl. I don't know how to keep myself preoccupied so that I'm not thinking about her. How are you doing it?

"I called her, and we spoke for a few hours that night, all about the memories we had with Natalie and how she impacted our lives. It almost felt like everything was okay again. Something was undeniably different, obviously, but it was as normal as I think it could be." I sighed as my pain rushed to the surface. "I'm still not even sure that it's real, but I keep waking up and going about my life and I'm not coming out of a dream, she's never there when I wake up. I just have to figure out how to accept the fact that she's gone."

"Well, it doesn't sound like it went terribly, which is good. I think you're overthinking it; everything will probably be just fine. If you want complete forgiveness from them, you need to forgive yourself, too."

"Yeah, you're probably right." I dug around in my bag for the melatonin before opening it and handing Ellie her pills and her drink. "Here, take these."

"Okay, now let's go, they called our group a few minutes ago. We should go now; the line is nice and short."

"Are we always going to be the last ones on the plane when we travel together?" I raised an eyebrow at her, and she laughed.

"Yeah, probably. If you're gonna do it, do it right, right?"

"I guess so."

When we finally sat down, I felt the medicine start to kick in and my eyelids felt heavier by the minute.

"Is it hot in here, or is it just me?" Ellie was yanking her arms out of her sweatshirt and trying to open the air vent above her at the same time.

"No, you just hate flying." I grabbed her hand and pulled it down to her armrest. "Relax, let yourself fall asleep."

"Okay, you're right. I can do this." She sighed and folded her hands in her lap.

She gripped my hand tighter as the plane took off. Once we reached the desired altitude, we both relaxed as the medicine took over.

"I'm about to fall asleep, are you going to be okay if I do?" I asked Ellie as I rested my eyes, leaning my head back against the seat.

When she didn't answer, I opened my eyes and looked at her to see that she was already asleep, her head slumped to the side. I nudged her gently to wake her up.

She hummed in response.

"Bring your head this way so your neck isn't sore later." I tapped my shoulder.

"Mmkay." was the only response that I got as she shifted in her seat.

I was thankful that we would both be asleep for the flight.

I was less thankful when the turbulence before we landed had shaken me awake. I glanced over to look at Ellie.

"How long have you been awake?" I asked her quietly.

"Just a few minutes, the bumping around woke me."

"Are you doing okay?"

She didn't respond, she just tightened her grip which I hadn't even noticed was around my forearm, squeezing whenever the turbulence picked up.

I left it alone and just placed my other hand on top of hers in an attempt to comfort her and she offered a sheepish smile in response.

I sat with my head back against the headrest and my eyes closed lightly, feeling occasional squeezes on my arm, waiting for the flight to be over completely. When we finally screeched to a halt, I felt nothing but relief. Unfortunately, I realized that it was relief that would be replaced with dread all over again in a few days when we got back on another plane to go back home.

One thing at a time.

CHAPTER TWENTY-SEVEN

DYLAN

After we got off the plane, we walked towards the exit. Right outside the doors, by the curb, my eyes caught those that belonged to someone that I've loved for years.

Martha.

I smiled and placed my hand on the middle of Ellie's back and guided her towards Martha.

I took my arm back from around Ellie and closed the gap between Martha and me. I bent over slightly and kissed her cheek before I wrapped my arms around her. She hugged me tighter than she ever had before.

I pulled back and gestured for Ellie to come towards us. She stepped forward and I'd never seen her look so shy.

"Ellie, this is Martha. Martha, Ellie."

Ellie tucked her hair behind her ear and stuck out her hand, waiting for Martha to shake it.

Martha kindly pushed Ellie's hand away and hugged her instead.

A small laugh came out of Ellie, unexpectant of the sign of affection and acceptance.

Martha pulled away and held Ellie at an arm's length. "I've

heard so much about you! Including that I owe you for keeping Dylan sane, thank you!" She pulled Ellie back in and Ellie responded by wrapping her arms around Martha.

My heart warmed at the sight in front of me. Martha accepted Ellie, but then again, I don't think I've ever met someone that Martha disliked without reason. The sadness crept back in slowly as I wondered what Natalie would've thought of Ellie.

I shook my head to snap myself out of it. "Come on, ladies. Let's go, we're holding up traffic." I tried to offer a playful smile, but I could tell by the pitying look in Ellie's eyes that I wasn't as successful as I'd hoped.

WHEN WE GOT BACK to the house, I was relieved when I saw my mother and Chris weren't here.

After realizing how unkempt the property was, my eyes fell on Noah's car. As we were pulling up, Kathryn was getting out of the passenger seat. Noah climbed out of the car quickly and jogged over to hug me.

"Dude, I can't believe you left me here with... her!" He whispered and not-so-nonchalantly pointed at Kathryn.

"Shut up, I'm not that bad." Kathryn rolled her eyes.

Noah laughed and pointed at her directly. "Aha! You admit you're at least a little bad!"

"Ugh, shut up, Noah. Hi, Dylan." She turned her attention towards me but kept her distance.

"Hello, Kathryn." I stiffened and looked away from her before I turned back towards her. "Now that that's over, can we be normal?" I teased. "Get over here." I laughed and held my arms open.

She walked over and hugged me, her frame smaller than it used to be, something I would definitely be asking

173

someone about later. I figured I would let some time pass and some pleasant conversations happen before I potentially make people uncomfortable.

"Guys, this is Ellie." I encased her small wrist in my hand and pulled her towards us gently.

Everyone introduced themselves to her and got to know her briefly. The women of the group asked some nosy questions that they probably shouldn't have, like if Ellie had a boyfriend, but Ellie held her own and handled it like a champ.

After about an hour of talking outside, I realized that I can't put this off any longer. I have to go inside and face this again.

I unlocked the front door and walked in only to immediately be greeted by her keys hanging on the hook. They haven't been moved. Her lanyard and her plethora of key chains remained untouched. I used to tease her and tell her that by the time she's able to find her house key in that mess, she would already be dead in literally any horror movie.

I forced myself to step in the house and pass the key hooks, I knew this was just the beginning.

This is gonna hurt.

I tried not to look at all the pictures of us on the walls as I walked towards our bedrooms. Me, Natalie, the two of us together, us with our parents. Just all one big happy family. It blew my mind how we were once so put together. Once our dad died, everything blew up in our faces. My mother dug herself pretty deep and left me and Natalie on our own. Natalie's frequent excuses rang through my ears.

She's heartbroken, she'll get better.

She never did.

Needless to say, when she walked in through the front door and asked me how I was doing, I wasn't exactly in the mood to talk. I completely ignored her question and moved on with the conversation.

"Have you paid the rent?"

"Hi, Dylan. I'm well, thank you for asking. No, I haven't, what's it to you? You don't even live here anymore."

"That doesn't mean you get to just throw your life away. I worked my ass off to help you pay these bills and now you're just throwing in the towel?"

"Dylan, there is no reason for me to be in this house anymore. I'm moving in with Chris anyway. He loves me, you know. At least someone does." She made little digs, looking for pity, crying herself a river of such depths that even *I* was impressed.

"*Chris?*" I rolled my eyes.

"Yes, why? Not everyone finds me unlovable."

"Chris is toxic and if you can't see that, then I'm sincerely sorry for you. If you're moving in with him, then what are you doing with all of this stuff?"

"Selling it."

"Everything?"

"Yup." She popped the 'p' and I was instantly taken back to when she would argue with my dad. This was how she always insisted on ending it.

"Even Natalie's stuff?"

"Yes, Dylan. She won't be using it anymore and Chris doesn't have much storage space."

"I can't believe you're really that much of a selfish bitch." I scoffed.

"Dylan…." I heard a new voice in the conversation and looked over to the doorway to find Ellie standing there, her face sad as she shook her head, signaling me to stop. I didn't even know she was in the room.

I looked into Ellie's eyes, sighed, and looked back towards my mother. "I'm sorry, I shouldn't have said that, but I don't agree with you selling everything, *especially* Natalie's stuff. You realize she's never coming back, right?"

It was too late for apologies. Her eyes were narrowed at me in anger. "Why don't you follow her lead?"

"Get out."

"Excuse me?" She took a threatening step forward, not caring that she was more than a foot shorter than me.

"I said 'Get out.' I will do what I have to do and then I will be on my merry way and you will never see me again. Just get out so I can do this and not say something that Natalie would have me sent to Hell for."

"You really think that you can kick me out of my own house?"

"Do you really want to play this game? I paid the rent for a year and a half with zero help from you. Since I left, you haven't spent a penny on this house. As far as I'm concerned, it's my house at least enough to get a day or two to myself." I internally winced. I promised Natalie that I would never throw anything financially related in my mother's face, but I couldn't help myself.

"Fine. I'm going to Chris'. I will be back in two days. Everything that is still here by then is going into the driveway for the garage sale. Goodbye."

I didn't answer her, I couldn't. I couldn't believe the situation, the conversation that just took place. Even more so, I couldn't believe that my mother, one of the most stubborn women that I know, gave up so easily. She just did a 180 and decided to leave. It's been years at this point, but her instability and unreliability never fail to baffle me.

Considering that conversation went the way that it did, I think Natalie would've been proud of me for biting my tongue... for the most part, at least.

CHAPTER TWENTY-EIGHT

DYLAN

I was rummaging through all of Natalie's belongings for hours by the time my thoughts surrounding her started to subside and become bearable. Noah and Kathryn went to a few stores to get stuff for tonight and tomorrow so they could stay with us. Martha left once my mother showed up, which, who can blame her? She told Ellie to pass the message along that she would be back later.

While we were waiting for the three of them to come back, I could tell that Ellie was trying to give me my space. I appreciated it beyond belief, but I didn't know what I wanted. I couldn't decide between a distracting conversation or the deafening silence. Neither really seemed too enjoyable at the moment. She just stayed in Natalie's room with me and helped me dig through all of her stuff, trying to sift out what's important and what wasn't.

"Dylan?" Her voice was somewhat muffled since she was completely sitting in the closet.

I got up and walked over to her. "Yeah?"

"I'm not sure what this is, but I'd say it's pretty important." She pulled a wooden box out of the closet.

"I don't recognize it. Is there anything else with it?" I took the box from Ellie's hands and held it, looking for a way to open it.

"No, but look at the bottom, there's a note." She said.

I read the note and quickly realized what I was holding.

"What is it?" Ellie asked curiously.

"A note from my dad to Nat. He was always pretty skeptical so he would keep the majority of his money in his possession. I guess this box is where he kept all of her college money and wanted her to keep adding. It makes sense why there's just a tiny little slot that's barely noticeable."

"You didn't have a college fund?"

"I did, my father was not at all discriminatory when it came to his children. He made sure that no matter what, he provided for us both equally. He put in a certain amount of money and then handed us our designated box. When we reach 16 years old, we're expected to start adding to it ourselves. He must've gotten more paranoid towards the end of his life because my box was just a shoebox rather than this homemade wooden creation. Anyway, when he died, my mother blew through the money that he left quickly so I had to empty my box to keep us afloat."

"God, Dylan, I'm sorry."

"No, it's really not a big deal, I wasn't planning on going to college anyway, so it wasn't some major loss on my part. Nat would've gone though."

"Take it." Ellie stated, not an ounce of hesitation in her voice.

"What?" I tilted my head at her.

"Take it. Your mother shouldn't have it. She shouldn't even know about it. It's not for her."

"It's not for me, either."

"I know, but it'll be safer in your hands than in your

mother's. From what you've told me and what I saw today, I already know that she'll use it for selfish reasons only."

"El, I have an idea. A really good idea!" I got excited and was practically ready to leave the rest of the stuff and head back home to Seattle.

"Well? Tell me." She encouraged.

"Not yet, I want to talk to everyone about this together during dinner."

She seemed slightly annoyed that she had to wait, but she nodded regardless. "This better be good."

As painful as it was to go through all of Natalie's things, I managed to get through it, and I owe it all to this idea. I couldn't wait to share it with everyone when we sat down to eat dinner.

Ellie kept glancing over at me and I know she was resisting the urge to ask about my idea again and I saw relief flood her features when she heard the front door open and Noah call out for us.

The smell of the pizza that they brought had immediately filled my senses and made me realize how hungry I was.

Ellie came out of her shell faster than I expected and ran to the front door to help rush Kathryn, Noah, and Martha in so they can sit down, and Ellie's curiosity can be cured.

I followed them to the kitchen and got ready for dinner. We all sat down, and Ellie interlocked her fingers before resting her chin on her joined hands. Her eyes were wide as she waited for me to start talking.

"Okay, if you haven't already noticed that Ellie is absolutely losing her mind, it's because we found Natalie's college fund in her closet. I'm going to be taking it, but I want to get your opinions on what I'm planning to do with it."

Ellie's eyes continued to bore into my soul as I caught everyone else up on the situation.

"Trust me, we've noticed, she's got crazy eyes." Noah laughed from the other side of the table.

Ellie whipped her head towards Noah and glared briefly, making everyone laugh.

"So, Nat got her book's proof while she was in the hospital and we know that it's always been her dream to publish. If you all agree that it's a good idea, I want to use the money to publish her book and try to get it the attention that it deserves. I don't know how much it'll run to go through the whole publishing process but since she did the majority of it on her own, I think the hard part is over. Thoughts?" I looked at Ellie first, knowing that she's probably bursting at the seams.

"I think it's a beautiful idea and that you'd be the best person to do it. I don't really know anything about this, and I don't want to overstep, but I say do it." She looked towards the other end of the table and we both waited for someone else to offer their input.

I hadn't realized that Kathryn's eyes were filled to the brim until she looked up at me.

"Do it. It's exactly what she would want. You saw her face the day that she opened that book, I've never seen her so proud. I'll help you in any way that I can." Kathryn grabbed my hand and looked at me with supportive eyes.

"I agree. She was always so secretive about it, but I think the world should see her work." Noah chimed in.

"I have to say, I read through the book, and I agree. This needs to be out in the world."

Martha cleared her throat from her seat, and she looked at me with approving eyes. "I've actually read it before, too. She swore me to secrecy, but I don't have to tell you that, you know her well enough. But I agree, her writing is beautiful and it should be published."

"I'm not surprised that she let you see it at all. I'm glad she had someone supporting her while it mattered. So, it sounds like we're all in agreement?" I looked around at everyone one last time just in case anyone wanted the chance to change their mind.

"Yes." echoed back at me in unison and the tension in my shoulders released.

The rest of the night was spent laughing and catching up and a few hours later, we all fell asleep, scattered on the living room floor and couches.

I was actually able to sleep and I give the credit for that to the fact that for the first time in a long time, I had a goal and there was a light at the end of the tunnel.

CHAPTER TWENTY-NINE

DYLAN

The following afternoon, Martha gave me my car back for the day so I could get some running around done. I told her I would drop it off at her house later on and take a taxi to the airport, but as she usually does, she refused and insisted that she drive us.

I spent most of the day bringing the boxes of Natalie's stuff that I was keeping to the post office so it could be shipped back to Seattle and dropping all of her old clothes and stuffed animals in a donation bin. There wasn't a doubt in my mind that this is what she would've wanted, but tears pricked at the corners of my eyes as I did it, nonetheless.

I sat in the car on the way to Kathryn and Noah's house with Ellie in silence until she broke it.

"Are you sure you're ready to go home today?" She kept her eyes forward.

"Yes, it's been great seeing everybody, but I feel like I've been holding my breath since we got here."

"What do you mean?"

"I think we're all doing a little bit of putting on an act. I don't know when everyone's going to start to feel better, but I know it's not now. Also, leaving made this even less of a home than it was, I'm having a hard time getting comfortable."

"Okay, well we're going to the airport in a few hours, then you can go back to the new normal and we can throw ourselves down the publishing hole if that's what you want."

"I think that's a good idea."

"Me, too. You just have to make it through these few goodbye-for-nows and then we can sleep through the whole flight again." She reassured me, but the thought of saying goodbye again put a lump in my throat.

Ellie's right, it's just for now.

When we walked into Kathryn and Noah's house, we found them watching TV in the living room.

"Hey, guys. We're going to be leaving for Martha's soon so we can give the car back, I just wanted to pop in again."

The sadness in Kathryn's eyes was more evident than in Noah's, but neither of them hid it completely which made me abandon all hope that I could conceal my own feelings.

Kathryn didn't fight her emotions for long and let them run rampant while she hugged me. "It was so good seeing you again, I've missed you."

I decided against talking to keep myself from choking on a sob and I just nodded in her hair and hugged her tighter.

Noah came over and hugged us both but also kept quiet.

Kathryn's small frame pulled out from between Noah and I as she turned to reach out for Ellie. "Come over here, I owe you so much for taking care of him. I've been trying not to say anything to avoid the sappiness, but to hell with that."

Ellie's own glassy gray eyes smiled as she walked over and got pulled into the group hug.

Shortly after we pulled away from each other, I made the

decision that now was the best time to ask any last-minute questions.

"Kat, can I talk to you alone for a minute?"

"Absolutely." She walked out into the front yard and sat on the concrete.

I walked past her and over to the car to grab something from my bag before joining her.

"I want you to have this." I held out Nat's first copy of her new book towards her.

"Jesus, Dylan, what are you doing to me?" She laughed through her fresh tears after she just stopped crying.

"I know, I'm sorry. Since I've understood your relationship with her on a different level, I bookmarked the pages that I think she wrote about you. She would want you to have it. This way, you'll always have the first piece of her vulnerability."

She looked at the book and slid her fingers across the cover before throwing her arms around my neck. "I love you, Dylan. Thank you for this."

"You're welcome. I love you, too, by the way. I don't want you forgetting that."

"Also, I'm sorry for judging your way of coping so harshly. It sucked, but I get that you gotta do whatcha gotta do to heal. I kept going to her grave and tried watering the seed so the grass would come in faster. I guess I thought if her grave wasn't so freshly dug, my wounds wouldn't be either."

"That makes sense… kinda."

She laughed and it echoed slightly down the block. "No, it doesn't, not at all, but it helped. I cried out all my tears and didn't laugh at any of those comedy specials. Standup comedy might just be ruined for me now, but you live, and you learn." She laughed at her own misery.

"Is Noah staying for long?" I looked at her.

"No, he's leaving in a few days, but honestly, I think I might follow your lead and get the hell out of here. I should go to college like I planned to and I should chase after my dreams. If Noah can do it and Nat can make her dreams happen from Heaven, why can't I make my own come true?"

"I think that's a great idea, where are you going to go?"

"I got into a school in California so maybe I'll move there? If I'm really lucky, I'll be able to convince Noah to come with me. I know his job has locations in California that will probably pay better, but he's tried to stay close to us. This might be the new beginning that we've all been needing. Plus, I don't have anything here by myself either. What's the point of staying? Our parents moved to Texas which hardly makes a difference since they were always traveling or something anyway."

"I think you should do it. Then you'll be closer to me, too."

"Yes, that's the one bad thing, who wants to be near you, yuck." She scrunched up her nose.

"Oh, stop. You love me, I know you do. We'll get to see each other more if you move to Cali."

"It's just an idea for now, but maybe."

"That's better than nothing!" I stood and held my hand out towards her to help her up. "I have one more question that I want to ask you. Promise me you won't get mad."

"Hm... Okay, fine. I promise." She stood with her weight shifted to one leg and crossed her arms.

"Are you eating?"

"What're you talking about? You've seen me eat since you've been here."

"No, I've seen you push your food around your plate and pretend to eat or eat incredibly small portions. I felt how small you were when I first got here, and I don't want to leave knowing that you're not taking care of yourself."

"Damn you for being so observant, Nat taught you too well. I'm trying. I'm working on building it up slowly, my appetite just isn't what it used to be anymore. I already went to my doctor and we're working on it together. Thank you for looking out."

"Always. I'm glad you're taking the necessary steps to take care of yourself. She taught you well, too."

I glanced at my watch and realized that our time was running out and we should probably get going. I walked back into the house behind Kathryn with my hands on her shoulder. "Noah, good luck with this one!"

He laughed. "You're telling me."

Ellie looked up at me. "We should probably get going, it's getting late, we have to be at the airport soon."

"Yeah, I didn't realize the time, are you ready to go?"

"Yes, I'll go wait in the car." She told me before getting up and hugging Noah and Kathryn, saying goodbye once more.

After Ellie walked out through the front door, my attention turned to Kathryn. "I'm not saying goodbye to you again, I'm just gonna hug you and that's it, no crying, got it?"

She laughed and promised there would be no tears this time.

I turned to Noah and threatened the same thing. "I better not hear any sniffles or feel any tears come out of you either, you hear me?"

"Nah, I don't cry, man. I have no idea what you're talking about." He rolled his eyes.

"Yeah, sure you don't." I hugged him but tried to keep the conversation light. "You need to keep an eye on that rascal over there, she's gonna give you a real run for your money."

"I know, she's already driving me nuts." He groaned.

Just before I was fully outside, I stopped, looked at the two of them and said, "See you in Cali!" before closing the door and running to the car and driving away immediately.

Kathryn's going to kill me for sure. I know she wanted to tell him on her own terms which I just threw way off balance.

Whoops.

On the drive to Martha's I thought about how satisfied I was with the terms that I'm leaving Boston on this time around.

By the time we pulled up to her house, she was already waiting outside, and I got into the backseat so she could drive.

"Thank you again for taking us to the airport, you really didn't have to." Ellie said before Martha even got her seatbelt on.

"Nonsense, of course I did."

The drive was quick, but we had some time to talk about the publishing idea.

"So, Kathryn and Noah might move to California, when are you gonna come over to the dark side?"

"Who knows, maybe I'll make my way over when I get a baby." She joked. I know she can't leave Boston; her whole life is here. She has the diner and she might have a newborn to take care of soon, there's no way she'll move in the middle of that chaos.

After we grabbed our luggage from the car, I hugged Martha. "I love you, thank you for everything. I'll text you the second we land."

"You better! I love you, too." She pulled away and shifted towards Ellie. "Hon, it's been delightful meeting you. Don't be afraid to keep him in check, he needs it every once in a while, okay?" Martha has always been a terrible whisperer, but this time, she was definitely doing it on purpose.

"Always. Thank you for giving him someone to go to for all these years." Ellie hugged her tight before assuming her position beside me.

"You two have a safe flight and I'll talk to you later. I love you!" She yelled as she slid back into the driver's seat.

We waved from the curb and watched as she pulled away before heading inside to make our way through security all over again. Last time I left from this airport, I was in a very different mental state, but I found myself reaching for Ellie's hand for comfort anyway.

CHAPTER THIRTY

DYLAN

The flight back home was relatively painless, we stayed awake this time and allowed the conversation to distract us for the most part.

When we finally landed, I was stuck in my thoughts as I shot Martha a quick text to tell her that we landed safely. I'd been spending so much time with Ellie the past couple of days that it'd be weird to part ways.

After getting off of the plane, Ellie was walking directly in front of me and stopped abruptly. Unexpectant and distracted, I walked right into her and immediately grabbed her by the shoulders to keep her from falling over. Thankfully, I was able to stabilize us both.

"Yes?" I questioned, crouching slightly so our eyes were level, my hands still on her shoulders.

She offered a sheepish smile as she apologized, "I'm sorry, I have a thought though."

"What is it?" I straightened out and let my arms fall to my sides.

"Come back to my place with me. There's no point in unnecessarily wasting more of your money on staying in the motel while you look for your own apartment. I think you should just stay at my place until you find your footing... on the couch, of course, but it's very comfortable. I should know, I fall asleep on it all the time. What do you think?" She was looking up at me while she pitched her idea until she asked for my opinion, that's when she picked a floor tile to stare at.

"You'd really do that for me? It's not too much constantly having me in your space?" I grabbed her attention and her head shot up and her snarky personality came back.

"Do what for you? All I have to do is go home. It's not like you're going to be hogging all my closet space, you've only got so much stuff. I wasn't sure if you would want to extend the trip, so I took tomorrow off from work, too. If you want, we can go look at some apartments for rent in the area for you. Seattle isn't the cheapest place to live, but you'd have your own apartment and your own space! Until then, you should know that I'm a fantastic roommate, you'd be lucky to stay with someone as fun as me. But, if you can't handle the fun, you could always just go stay in the same creepy motel again." She made a cocky face and shrugged before she turned and walked away, leaving the ball in my court.

I strode to get next to her and matched her pace. "I'm in. But I insist that you figure out a way that I can make it up to you." I negotiated.

"I'll consider it, but I make no promises, I really don't think you owe me anything. What're friends for?"

We agreed and got into the first taxi we saw and had it bring us to Ellie's apartment. I paid the fare, still feeling guilty that I was invading her space.

The best part of me not having a lot of stuff in Seattle with me, is that I can bring it around fairly easily. I'm also thankful that I just took all my stuff with me to go back home, otherwise I would've had to pay for those two nights at the motel while my few possessions had the room to themselves.

That night, she laid a twin sized sheet out on the couch for me, tossed me a pillow from her bed with a fresh case on it and brought a blanket down from the closet. "If you need anything else, let me know. Help yourself to whatever and make yourself at home."

"Thank you, Ellie."

She winked playfully at me and walked into her bedroom.

OVER THE NEXT TWO WEEKS, we started apartment hunting and worked our asses off to try to get this book published. Ellie turned into a drill sergeant throughout the entire publication process.

Natalie did everything on her own and even went as far to look through the proof that she ordered, so all we had to do was approve the book for publication. She had everything set up so that the book can be found everywhere in both stores and online.

I even heard from Kathryn at one point and she told me that she's been posting the link to buy Nat's book all over the internet. Hopefully hyping up the book for a few days got people excited. I want Nat to be able to see the success that she deserves, wherever she may be.

Ellie and I got closer with each passing day and I wasn't sure what to make of it. I've never been friends with a girl like this before aside from Kathryn, but Kathryn was always like a little sister to me. Somehow, I feel closer with Ellie but there's an attraction that I felt for her that I never felt for Kathryn, a simplicity. All I knew was that this feeling that I had for Ellie was completely new to me and I never felt like this about anyone before. Afraid to act on my feelings, I kept them to myself and decided to continue doing so until I'm in a better place to be able to decipher my feelings.

I don't want to act on anything until I know that it's sincere rather than just because she's been here for me throughout all of this.

She deserves something real.

IT WAS OFFICIALLY a month since we published Nat's book and we found an apartment for me to move into that seems perfect. It was small, but it'd just be me living there anyway. I'd get to move in within the next few days. Thankfully, I've been building credit for just about as long as I legally could, so I was easily approved.

I was sitting on the couch, watching TV at Ellie's when I heard her scream. I got up and ran into her bedroom before I could register what was happening.

"Guess *what!*" She turned to me, her laptop resting on her forearm as she paced around the room.

"God, Ellie, you scared the crap out of me, what's going on?"

"I just saw the date; I didn't even realize what day it was! We can finally check how Natalie's book did during its first month!"

I immediately understood why she was screaming, but I hesitantly joined her in her excitement. "And? How did it do?"

"I'm gonna need a drumroll." Ellie stood with her hand on her hip as if she were disappointed that she even needed to tell me.

"*Ellie!*"

She just looked at me, her eyebrow cocked.

I rolled my eyes and drummed on my thighs in anticipation.

"Five hundred copies!" She screeched.

"*Oh my god!* Ellie, if you're screwing with me, I'm gonna lose it."

"I swear on my life, look!" She thrusted the computer in front of me and I couldn't believe my eyes. She was right.

I immediately took her laptop from her hands and dropped it on her bed.

I closed the gap between us, picked her up and spun her, "I cannot believe this! I couldn't have done this without you, this is unreal!"

"This was all you and your sister! I'm so happy it's doing so well!"

I put her down gently and held her face in my hands. "I couldn't have done this without you. You were a massive pain in my ass, but you made sure that it got done, and that it got done right. You did this just as much as we did." My voice was much lower now.

She stared up at me and visibly swallowed.

I was relieved that we shared the same sentiment.

This proximity wasn't something we'd ever encountered before. I was noticing for the first time how stunning she actually was. Taking in her appearance in the moment, she was so relaxed after work. Being this close, I was able to fully appreciate the barely-there lines in her face. I watched her forehead crinkle every time she was stressed or worried. Her long, dark hair always fell gracefully down her back, but seemed impossible to contain. Her eyes were always quick to laugh before her mouth could make a sound.

Taking this all in, I suddenly couldn't help myself as I stroked her cheek with my thumb. "Can I?" I lifted my gaze from her lips to her eyes and there were only seconds between her nodding and me granting myself the satisfaction of allowing my lips to touch hers for the very first time.

When we separated, I kept my forehead on hers. "You've helped me heal more than I ever could've imagined. You've helped me realize that life doesn't have to be so serious all the time. You have changed my life."

She shushed me sweetly, "Dylan, please, just shut up and kiss me."

I refused to let her slip away from me. I wanted to hold onto her and this moment for as long as I could.

Maybe telling myself that I was only just starting to develop feelings for her was downplaying it. Just a smidge.

Something has always felt so different when it comes to her. From the first time we met, I felt some sort of security. Despite the walls that we both had built up from all the unrelated trauma we'd been through, I felt like I could trust her.

"Why are you looking at me like that?" She smiled with her head tilted.

"Looking at you like what?" I cocked an eyebrow.

"Like you're thinking about me intensely. Hopefully in a good way and not a murdery way. But! If you *are* thinking about me in a murdery way, I'll do anything to persuade you to let me live as long as it's legal."

"Oh, really? *Anything* legal, huh? Be very careful, Ellie, there are lots of loopholes to laws." I teased. I could've described the exact face she was making before she even made it. I saw it in my head before I finished speaking the words; her eyes wide, her jaw dropped, slipping into the shape of her infamous smile.

"Yeah, like you have a single, solitary bad bone in your entire body. You wouldn't hurt a fly, let alone me." She laid down on the couch with her knees up, threw on a bored look and fake yawned at me.

"Yeah, mhm. I'm a real danger. Nobody's safe. But on a serious note, I want to talk to you." I sat on the couch and tapped her knee in an attempt to get her to sit up and look at me.

She obliged immediately. "Okay, what's up?"

"I really don't know how I'm even going to talk to you about this, just for your information. So, we've been spending a lot of time together basically since I've moved here and we've gotten to know each other a lot and I think, and yes, I mean *think* that I might've started developing feelings for you. Maybe. Kinda."

Ellie opened her mouth to say something, but I kept talking before she could get anything out.

"I just want to get this last thing out before you say something. I didn't even want to tell you yet because I want to get to the point where I can be sure that I mean this sincerely and that it's not just the grief and the fact that you're always around that's tricking me into thinking that I'm feeling this when I'm not. That sounds awful, hang on, let me rephrase. I want to make sure that my feelings for you are actually romantic rather than something that will go away when we both heal more. Nope, that doesn't sound right either, I'm sorry, I'm pretty shitty at this."

"Dylan, do us both a favor and stop talking, you're just tripping over your own tongue and making a fool of yourself." Her tone was teasing, as she kept the topic light. "To be honest with you, I think I might have feelings for you, too. I understand wanting to make sure that your feelings are authentic, and I appreciate that almost as much as you telling me how you feel even though you're not sure. What do you think we should do?"

"I dunno, maybe make out for like ten minutes and see if we feel anything?" I shrugged at her.

"You're incapable of being serious about anything for more than five minutes, aren't you?" She swatted my arm.

"Yes, especially when the situation is as uncomfortable for me as this is. I've never been in a serious relationship before, I'm not sure what to do. I think you have more experience in this type of field than I do, so if anyone would have an idea where to start, it would be you."

"Okay, well, judging by how my last, and only serious, relationship went, I can safely say that I didn't have much control over that situation, but I've watched a ton of romance movies and stuff so I guess we can just wait for the moment where we just have to have each other right there in the middle of the field of daisies and then we'll go from there?" She tilted her head, waiting for my response.

I sat with my chin resting on the heel of my palm as I tapped my chin with my finger. We both busted into a fit of laughter before I recomposed myself. "We're never gonna figure out a solution to this, are we? Neither of us are being serious enough." I laughed.

This may not be super productive, but it's still a lot easier than I thought it was going to be.

This is one of the reasons that I was attracted to her. She does plenty of stressing, but not over the things that don't matter.

"Okay, come on. Game faces. I think we should just keep hanging out and going about our relationship the way that we have up to this point. If things progress naturally, then we go from there. If we kiss, we kiss. If we give each other high fives instead, we'll know where we stand. Since we both know about the other's feelings, let's set some ground rules. One, there will be no sex, not until we know what we feel. I don't do the whole 'meaningless sex' thing so if it's gonna happen, it's gonna be really important."

I laughed and raked my hand across the back of my neck. "No beating around the bush with you, huh?"

"No, you know this by now. Two, we'll start small, but I don't need to tell you that. Three, if we decide we are into each other enough to be in a relationship, we are to keep it under wraps until we are both ready to tell people. Mind you, both of us probably never will be ready because I doubt you'll want to tell your mother and I'm still terrified of Jared, my ex, and that will probably always be the case until he's either locked up or dead. Any thoughts, comments, requests, or needs for clarification?"

"I think you've covered all the bases. Very well thought out, we'll approach this as it comes. Deal?" I extended my hand towards her.

"Deal." She took my hand and gave it a firm shake.

"Excellent. Wanna go get a cup of coffee?"

"More than anything! I'll go grab my jacket."

I wouldn't have suggested going to get coffee if I knew what was going to come of it.

The last thing that I wanted to do was damage her further.

CHAPTER THIRTY-ONE

ELLIE

I was people-watching while I waited for Dylan to come back with our drinks when my worst nightmare became a reality. My eyes met Jared's across the room, and I watched as the realization crept across his face forcing my whole body to become rigid and cold.

I walked up to Dylan as fast as I could without drawing everyone else's attention to me on top of the one crippling gaze from the wrong person. I tugged on his arm. "We need to go... *now*."

Without hesitation, he threw an arm around my shoulders and pulled me in close to his chest while he stood tall and kept his head on a constant swivel.

As terrified as I was, I was able to tell the difference between how my heart was pounding because of how loved Dylan made me feel and how terrified Jared made me feel. I couldn't pinpoint or name the fear that Jared instilled in me. I always shoved it down and pretended it didn't exist and then it would rear its ugly head at the worst times possible.

The more abusive he became, the more I realized that I knew what he was capable of from the start. I always told myself *'He'd never do that to you. He would never hurt you; he loves you!',* but eventually, he just proved me wrong too many times for me to ignore.

'He'll never hurt me' quickly became *'When is he going to hurt me next?' 'Will he hit me this time or call me names?' 'How am I going to hide the next bruise?'*

With Dylan, I never thought any of that. I never really thought of what cute moment we were going to have next, either. That wasn't nearly as important to me as living in the moment that we were in, and that's the way that I liked it to be. Being afraid of the future or scarred by the past is no way to live.

I know how easy it would be for me to just walk away from Dylan at this moment. I wouldn't have to fear for my safety, I know he would respect my decision and leave me alone. I could just leave. I never felt that comfort when I was with Jared, I was terrified to go to the store without telling him, let alone leaving him and the relationship that I was locked into.

Maybe I shouldn't be so stubborn. Trying to live here even though I'm terrified on a constant basis can't be healthy. I should probably just move to a different state and change my name just like you see in the movies. Don't the girls like me usually end up dead anyway? I don't want to die; I just want what's mine.

The thought of ever leaving Dylan didn't feel good at all. Quicker than I thought, the idea of my life without his protectiveness and sense of humor became unimaginable. He had me crushed into his side so tight that all I could hear was the sound of his heart pounding and the cars driving past us. He only walked us a block or two before he slipped us into an alley and tucked us securely into a corner.

Goosebumps covered every inch of my body as I heard Jared's voice. He walked past the alley that we were in. He was on the phone when he passed. "You'll never guess who I just saw. She's still here." His voice trailed off as he got further away.

Dylan was still using his body to shield me and anyone who walked through the alley probably couldn't even see me behind him. He had his right elbow propped against the building, his jacket almost making a curtain to cover me, even though everything on me from the waist down was still exposed. His left hand was wrapped around my neck, holding my face to his chest while he shushed me quietly.

My breathing was ragged. I was trying to focus on something to calm myself down, but the silence was deafening.

We stayed there for a few minutes to make sure that he was gone. After Dylan felt enough time had passed, I felt his body relax under my cheek and he dropped his arm.

He cradled my face in his hands and searched my eyes frantically as he looked for any signs that I wasn't okay. I knew I wasn't, but I tried to act fine. The way he looked at me told me that he knew I wasn't okay, but he didn't press the issue. When I was ready to talk about it, he knew I would.

He took his jacket off and handed it to me before shrugging out of his hoodie. He took his jacket back and put it back on and gestured for me to put his hoodie on.

I went to take off my jacket and hand it to him before he stopped me. "No, I'm assuming he knows how you look in big sweatshirts. Put it on over your coat and put the hoods up. He won't recognize you from behind if you look heavier."

I needed his help getting his hoodie over my puffy jacket and I'm almost sure that I looked ridiculous. I looked up at him and let out a nervous laugh.

Dylan offered the weakest of smiles and then wrapped his arm around me. "Come on, let's get you home."

The whole walk back to my apartment, I was more aware

of the way that I carried myself than ever. I didn't want Jared to notice the familiarity of my walk. By the time we got home, I had no idea how we got there.

I took a shower and decided to just climb into bed early.

"I'll take the couch; I just need a blanket." He called from down the hall as he walked into the bathroom to take a shower.

I could already tell it was going to be a long night.

Dylan

After I got out of the shower, we sat on the couch for an hour or so before Ellie said goodnight and went into her room for the night. I had just finished curling up under the blanket and finally got comfortable when I heard it.

"Hey, Dylan?" She sang sweetly from her bed.

"Yes, Ellie?"

"Can you come in here for a minute?"

I was already up before she finished her question, figuring I would either have to get her something or do something for her. As she finished her question, I appeared in her doorway.

"What's up?"

"Okay, so I lied a little bit, it's not just for a minute. I need you to stay in here with me."

I turned and walked away as she called after me asking where I was going. I returned seconds later, holding my makeshift bed in a ball in my arms. I tossed the blanket on the bed and was flapping out the sheet to lay it on the floor when she stopped me.

"Oh, don't be ridiculous. This bed is plenty big and if I'm gonna force you to stay in here with me, it's the least I could do." She patted the bed.

I climbed in and used my blanket to cover me, all but clinging to the edge, trying to keep my respectful distance.

She turned onto her left side, leaving us facing away from one another. I really wanted to be there for her in every way that I could and part of me wanted her closer to comfort her again, but the other part of me knew that she didn't need it.

I could already tell that I was going to be up all night.

A FEW DAYS had passed since we saw him last. Ellie seemed to be more at ease with each passing day which I was more than thankful for. I know she's still on high alert, but I don't want her fear to hold her hostage and keep her from living her life.

Since we knew better than to assume that he had just given up, we were still careful if and when we left the house. We went to a diner that was just outside of Seattle in hopes that we would be able to just relax and enjoy our time out, rather than being on edge the entire time. Thankfully, nothing out of the ordinary happened and we were able to eat peacefully. I had just asked for the bill when Ellie said she was going to run out to the car to let it warm up before we left.

I should've either gone for her or with her; we still weren't safe, and I knew that. Wishful thinking, I suppose.

CHAPTER THIRTY-TWO

ELLIE

When I pushed through the first set of doors to leave the foyer of the diner, I was greeted by a thick sheet of rain and pulled my hood up. I planned to just run to the car to try to stay as dry as possible.

Planned.

Once I turned the corner at the bottom of the steps to walk around to the side of the diner, I felt a strong arm around my waist and before I knew what was happening, there was a hand clamped over my mouth.

I was immediately enveloped in a smell that was all too familiar. My nose filled with the sharp and slightly nauseating scent of Jared's favorite cologne and my heart dropped.

I didn't try to fight him. I'd been in this situation too many times to make the same stupid decisions. I tried to will my hammering heart to shut up before Jared would hear it be fueled by it. I attempted to steady my shaking hands by squeezing my fists closed tight. I resisted the urge to let out a bloodcurdling scream, it'd be no use.

First, I don't get myself out of an abusive relationship until I have to, and then I don't even fight back when he grabs me.

When I first started dating Jared, we were just kids and we used to wrestle all the time and I always thought it was a cute teenage-couple-y thing to do, except every time we would wrestle, I would get hurt one way or another and I never stood a chance at winning. I would fight so hard and I could never push him off of me. It became a competition to him, and he *hated* losing. Every time I almost got out of his hold; he'd only get more aggressive.

I knew that I deserved better and I came up with a plan to get myself out of this.

I tried to keep my plan on loop in my head as he was dragging me to a part of the diner that wasn't lit up.

I thought of this scenario plenty of times before, so my escape plan had been in my head for a long time at this point.

I must've been going over it for the fourth or fifth time before my thoughts were interrupted by a piercing pain in the back of my skull that followed Jared slamming me against the brick building.

I squeezed my eyes shut and dug my nails into my palms to try to distract myself from the throbbing in my head. When I opened my eyes, the beautiful blue eyes that I once fell in love with were staring back at me. I took advantage of the silence and watched as the storms behind his eyes started to roll in.

I've seen it all happen before.

"You've been pretty difficult to catch," he chuckled, "I guess it's a good thing that I *love* the excitement of a good chase, but you already knew that didn't you?" He licked his lips and grinned at me.

I resisted the urge to spit in his face, but in the same breath, my heart broke as I watched the monster that I once had so many reasons to fall in love with look at and speak to me with such disgust.

"Answer me!" His hand slammed into the building right next to my head, his thumb grazing my hair.

I winced and nodded, not wanting to upset him further. The back of my head felt warm and wet.

Every time he opened his mouth, the scent of liquor was unmistakable.

"Yeah, of course you knew that. After all, you made me chase you for a long ass time before you finally gave in to me. You were worth every minute. Something's telling me that you're not really worth it anymore, but I had to find out for myself. You know, baby, I really liked you better before this 'makeover' you gave yourself. You've ruined yourself."

"What the hell happened to you?" My eyes widened in surprise as I heard my voice come out steady despite the fear coursing through my veins and my shaking knees.

I felt something press into my stomach and I was immediately disgusted because based on our proximity, I made an assumption.

Compared to the reality, I would've preferred if being a dick to me gave him a hard-on.

I glanced down to see a gun pressed into my stomach. Letting out a gasp, I looked up at him and he looked... hungry.

"I'd watch what you say if I were you." He warned, "I might just decide right here and right now that you're not worth the chase." He whispered in my ear and I felt the goosebumps run down my spine.

Where's Dylan? He has to have noticed I've been gone for a while at this point.

"You won't do it." I resented the fire that burned inside of me and my own terrible timing.

"Don't challenge me, Ellie. You don't know what I'm capable of." He moved the gun up to the side of my head.

I didn't move or make a single noise.

I closed my eyes and held my breath as I waited for the death that I imagined inevitable.

"I swear to god, I'll do it, don't *fucking* push me, Ellie."

His threats were ringing in my ears so loud that I had to remind myself that nobody could hear him.

Nobody's coming to save me this time.

"Please, don't." I opened my eyes and broke my silence but kept my glance up at the sky, trying to hold back my tears. He has hit me and abused me verbally, but he has never held a gun to me. He has never threatened to kill me and honestly, I wouldn't put it past him.

"Maybe I'll consider letting you live if you can come up with a good enough reason."

"I still love you." I whispered, fighting back the bile rising in the back of my throat.

"What?" I locked eyes with him again and his eyes were back to being the ones that I fell in love with. Soft. Gentle. Kind.

"I do. I know I shouldn't, but I do. I'm sorry I keep running and hiding from you, but I can't be in a relationship where all you do is hurt me. It's too much. I never wanted to leave you, I just wanted you to stop hitting me. I could've loved you forever, but you kept breaking and taking parts of me away that I can never get back." I saw no point in holding my tears back at this point since I couldn't even distinguish the truth from what I was saying just to get myself out of this situation. "Can I ask you a question?"

"Go ahead." He let his arm drop, the gun no longer pressed to my head, as he shifted his weight.

I didn't expect him to cooperate so easily, I thought I would've had to put up more of a fight.

"If you really loved me so much, why did you hurt me?"

"The way I felt- *feel* about you is just so intense that I can't bear it. Then you go and do these things that make me *furious* and then when I hit you... it's like scratching an itch that's been driving you crazy for days. It's addicting. It just felt so good seeing you so vulnerable like that, begging me to stop." He closed his eyes, reliving the feeling. He jabbed the barrel of the gun against the side of my head again. "You needed to be punished, I never wanted to hurt you, I've just always known that I want to be able to keep my women in line. You made it easy."

He smashed his lips into mine, trying to shove his tongue into my mouth, attempting to fight his way through my clenched teeth. I kissed him back lightly but kept my jaw shut.

"Always such a tease." He spat.

"What do you want with me?"

"Come home, stop playing these games with me. If you really wanted to leave, you would've left the state or at least the city."

"You're telling me that you wouldn't hunt me down if I left? This is my home; you know I'm never leaving here." I challenged him which probably wasn't my best move.

"Like I said, you're fun to chase." He smirked at me. "If you ever want to see your parents alive again, you'll come with me. If not, I'll have to go home and take care of them. Just in case you needed a little bit of an incentive."

"What are you talking about?" I stepped towards him for barely a second before he shoved me back into the wall.

"I figured you'd put up a fight and I needed insurance. If you come with me, get your parents to calm down and give you their word that they won't go to the cops, then I'll let them go." His other forearm was pressed against my throat until he finished talking.

"Fine." I placed my hand on top of the gun and gently pushed it down, so it was facing the ground at his side. "I'll come home. I just forgot my bag inside. Go get your car and I will be right back."

I turned to walk back the way that we came but he abruptly grabbed my wrist and spun me back to face him.

"Promise you'll come back?" He questioned, squeezing my wrist way too tight.

"Mhm." I swallowed.

"I know your rule about promises. Say you promise and I know you won't break it. If you're lying to me, I will make your life more of a living hell than I ever have."

"I promise." It was childish, but I found comfort in the fact that he didn't know that my fingers were crossed behind my back.

"Go. If you're not back in two minutes, I'm coming in to get you." His voice was one step away from a growl.

I knew what I had to do.

I walked back into the diner with tears steadily flowing down my cheeks. I tried to keep my composure as strong as possible.

I walked up to the front counter where I found Dylan and I grabbed his hand and whispered to the cashier that I needed her to call the police. I couldn't keep myself from glancing out through the window, waiting for Jared to come into view.

Relax, Ellie, you have two minutes. He's probably just getting in the car now to pull it around to the front.

"Ellie?! What happened to you?" He touched the back of my head tenderly and then pulled his bloody hand into both of our views.

I shushed him and pushed his hand down and out of sight. "I can't worry about that right now, I'm okay, I promise."

"Tell me what happened."

I pulled Dylan to the side to talk to him as privately as possible. "Dylan, he's here. He said if I don't go with him, he'll make my life a living hell. Worse than usual. He has my parents; I have to go with him. Take out your phone, I will share my location with you. When the cops get here, please come get me."

"No, absolutely not! *Have you lost your mind?* There's no way in hell I'm letting you go with him, he's a lunatic, Ellie, come on. Does this sound like a good idea to you in even the slightest?"

"Dylan, these are my *parents* we're talking about, this is not up for discussion. Plus, I'm more afraid of what he'll do if I don't go than if I do. I've survived before, I'll survive again. I know you'll come get me and then we'll be safe together, it's okay. I'll be fine, I promise, but I really have to go before he comes in. I'll see you soon." I went up on my toes to kiss his cheek and I gave his hand one last squeeze as I was walking away. I grabbed my bag from him, making sure to keep my story in line.

I didn't dare look back and see whatever reaction I just left him with.

It's okay, Ellie. Dylan will come get you and everything will be fine.

Everything's going to be fine, just keep yourself alive until then.

When I walked out, Jared was leaning against his car, looking at his watch, counting the seconds, I'm sure.

"Sorry, I had to run to the bathroom before we left." I played innocent to the best of my ability.

"Wow, not a second too soon, cutting it kinda close, aren't we?"

"I'm here, aren't I?" I shot back.

"Get in the car."

I got in, shared my location with Dylan and made sure my

phone was out of sight before Jared was able to walk around the car and get into the driver's seat. I knew that if he'd seen it, he would've taken my phone and destroyed it by now. Now all I have to do is stay alive until Dylan can get to me and hope that Jared's drunken state doesn't wear off. I can outsmart him this way, but not when he's soberly obsessed.

CHAPTER THIRTY-THREE

DYLAN

I stood in the corner where I was just talking to Ellie, barely able to move. I didn't know what to do. Of course, I knew what to do, I just didn't know how all of a sudden, I ended up in this situation.

I heard sirens faintly in the distance and got a notification on my phone letting me know that Ellie shared her location with me.

I ran out into the parking lot to meet the cops, trying to use every second of time we have rather than wasting it. My heart pounding in my ears was distracting and it was getting increasingly more difficult to focus. The sooner I get to Ellie and can make sure she's safe and sound, the less time Jared will have to do more damage than he already has.

I ran up to the first cop car that pulled up and asked him if I could get in and he gave me permission quicker than I was expecting.

With an anxious, bouncing leg, I explained the whole situation to him as fast as I could, considering that there were holes in my story because Ellie didn't have time to tell me the whole thing. I told him everything that I knew and just like that, we were following my GPS, racing to save the woman that I was too afraid to decipher my feelings for. All I know is that I feel the need to protect her at all costs and I will stop at nothing to make sure that she's safe.

The entire ride there, I was terrified as I imagined the things that he could be capable of and all the ways that he has and still could hurt her.

I was ready to go into the house when we pulled up to the curb, the squad car and the one behind us completely dark, but I was told to stay put.

Of course, I didn't listen.

The cops noticed me almost immediately and tried to silently get my attention, but I ignored them, something I figured I'd pay for later.

With my impeccable luck, I stumbled into a room where Jared had a man and a woman tied to the banister, then my eyes landed on Ellie who was sitting on the couch. Her leg was bouncing frantically as she looked around the whole room with wide eyes, her hands tied behind her back, and the cloth that was tied around her head was also keeping her from speaking. My heart ached at the sight, but I forced myself into action.

There's gotta be something I can do.

When I saw that Jared was nowhere to be seen, I ran over to Ellie, pried the cloth from her mouth and glanced at the ties that were holding her. *Maybe I can get her out of here before he comes back.* "I cannot believe you did this; this was such a stupid plan. I'm here, the cops are here, we're gonna get out of this, okay?" I tried to keep my voice as quiet as possible, and Ellie kept her eyes on the hallway while I tried to work out the knots.

"You gotta get out of here, he'll be back at any second and he'll kill you if he sees you here!" She whispered frantically.

She nodded me in the direction of another room and the

second I was out of view, I heard him coming down the hallway.

Taking in how distraught Ellie was, I gathered that the people tied to the banister were indeed her parents. I looked at them again while I was hiding in the room and noticed all the similarities, surprised I didn't catch that sooner.

I tried to get her attention without getting Jared's, but when I took a step forward, the floorboards beneath me gave me away.

My breath caught in my throat. There's no way he didn't hear me. I looked up and met his eyes for the first time.

He lifted his arm and held his gun aimed at me from across the room. I could've sworn my heart stopped and time no longer existed. Everything was so still as this one person who deserved nothing good, contemplated my fate.

"Really, Ellie? I thought you were better than this." His eyes remained locked on me.

I watched as she frantically searched her brain for anything to say to him that would make this situation better. "JJ! Please, just put the gun down, this doesn't need to get any messier than it already is. Please." Her voice shook but fell on deaf ears.

Jared lessened the gap between us before pistol whipping me. The blow to my head led to my collapse and I felt as the warm drip of blood made its way from the gash on my forehead, into my hair. I wanted to scream, partially because of the pain, and partially because of the fact that I couldn't get to Ellie. I couldn't help her. He disregarded me from that point on because he knew as well as I did, I was not going to be getting up any time soon. I was just about useless as long as my head kept spinning.

I think being pistol whipped was less painful than realizing that I had to just sit there and watch while Jared caressed Ellie's face. Both her and I were powerless. All four of us were sitting here, unable to do anything to stop what was happening. One person somehow managed to pull this whole thing off and my mind was blown.

The last thing I remember was hearing Ellie scream my name, and the cops running into the room. After that, the voices faded into indistinct chatter. I got to see the cops tackle Jared to the ground and cuff him before untying Ellie and her parents. Ellie ran over and knelt beside me,

"Dylan, are you okay?" She inspected the wound on my forehead.

"Yeah, I'm fantastic. A real hero tonight, aren't I?"

"I could never thank you enough or repay you for this." She closed the gap between us and pressed her lips to mine.

Ellie ran to check on her parents before coming back to me where she held my hand as we waited for the ambulance. The cops tried to offer any medical assistance that they could manage, but even the slightest pressure on my forehead made the pain nauseating. Once they were able to clean up the blood around the wound and keep an eye on how much blood I was losing, they were willing to let me wait until the ambulance arrived. I'm going to need stitches for sure.

I glanced over at Ellie and realized that if it weren't for her, I would probably be sleeping right now, rather than sitting up against a wall in her psycho abusive ex-boyfriend's apartment. The situation might not have been perfect, but maybe dealing with the little bit of drama together was worth it if the reward was having this woman by my side every day.

My impeccable luck might be changing.

CHAPTER THIRTY-FOUR

DYLAN

I didn't even realize I passed out until I woke up in the hospital, bright lights and sterility overwhelming all my senses. Once I realized where I was and remembered everything that happened, I immediately looked around the room to see if Ellie was anywhere to be found. I was relieved when my eyes fell on her, but I felt a pang in my chest at the sight of her bandaged head.

"I'm here, Dylan, it's okay." I felt her hand in mine. Her touch and her voice have never felt so good.

She was sitting in a chair next to my bed.

"What happened? Did they arrest him? They had to; he committed a hell of a lot of crimes. Please tell me we don't have to worry about him anymore."

Ellie walked over to the side of my bed and ran her fingers through my hair and kissed my forehead. "You're an idiot, you know that? I cannot believe you put yourself in that kind of danger. I just wanted you to bring the cops, I didn't want you to try to *be* the cops."

"Look at the pot! Has the audacity to call the kettle black!" I lectured her. "Just tell me, are you okay?"

"Yes. I feel fine. The doctor's fixed me up as best they can, and I'm ready to go home whenever you are."

I watched her anxiously as I tried to figure out if she was okay or not. She looked just about ready to start pacing laps around the room, but she seemed to be trying to hold herself steady in an attempt not to freak me out or put me on edge.

As if getting hit with pure metal didn't effectively put me on edge.

"I'm sorry." She said quietly with her eyes averted elsewhere.

"For what?"

"I got you into this mess. I was selfish and somehow, it landed you in the hospital, and it was all because of my damn pride. I should've just let him run me out of the state where I could start over. He even brought it up himself and asked me why I didn't just run." She gave in and let herself start pacing around the tiny hospital room, walking from one side of my bed to the other.

"El, sit down, you shouldn't even be out of bed." I waited for her to be seated before I continued. "Honestly, he seems pretty invested in hunting you down to just give up once you cross the state line. I doubt he'd give up that easily." I closed my eyes, the fluorescent lighting too much for my head to take and rested my head on the poor excuse for a pillow that I was given.

She huffed, "Yeah, that's what I said. He didn't deny that he would probably still try to find me. I shouldn't even say try, seeing as how he's plenty capable."

"Ellie, you were right outside the town that you two both lived in, I'm sure it wasn't hard to find you. Don't give him credit that he doesn't deserve, it's not like he's proved to be some sort of criminal mastermind."

"How are you so calm?"

"What?" I opened my eyes and lifted my head to look at her.

"I asked you how you're so calm. You literally got hit in the face with a gun and here you are just chillin. I don't understand. I'm more worked up than you are. Quite frankly, it's driving me insane that you're so calm right now when you should be totally freaking out." She rambled at me.

"First, I would like to remind you that I am on pain killers so right now, *nothing* is going to bother me. Second, this hurts a hell of a lot less than Natalie dying and me not being able to do anything about it." I shrugged and went back to resting my head with my eyes closed.

There was a light knock on the door.

"Do you want me to send whoever that is away so you can rest?" Ellie grabbed my hand gently.

"No, it's okay, you can let them in. It's probably just a nurse coming to check on me." I gave her hand a squeeze to reassure her, sensing how tense she was.

When she opened the door, I quickly realized that the cop on the other side of the door probably wasn't even here to talk to me since I knew just about nothing. Whatever I did know, I told the cop that I was riding with and everything else was pretty fuzzy afterwards. If anyone knows anything about the situation at hand, it's Ellie.

"Hi, officer, what can I do for you?" Her voice was higher than usual, something I quickly learned that she did on the phone and when she was talking to strangers.

"Good evening. I just want to talk to you and ask you a few questions regarding the events that took place late last night. Do you have a moment?"

"Yes, of course, come on in." Ellie stepped backward still holding the door, opening it further and gesturing for the officer to come in.

"Thank you." He walked over to the area next to the bed

217

where there were two chairs and a small table. "Hey, Dylan. How are you feeling?"

I quickly recognized the officer as the same one that I rode in the squad car with. I cracked a small smile. "Hi, Officer Gonzalez. I'm okay, thank you for asking."

"It was a stupid thing that you did, kid."

"Yeah. It was." Ellie piped up from where she had just taken her seat.

"Yeah, I got hospitalized for my stupid thing, to try to keep you from getting hospitalized for yours. I stand by my opinion that my thing wasn't all that stupid since you came out close to unscathed." I narrowed my eyes at Ellie.

"I can respect that." Officer Gonzalez nodded at me in understanding and then turned his attention towards Ellie. "So, who is the suspect, and what is his relation to you?"

"He was my boyfriend once upon a time."

"And his name?"

"Oh, sorry. Jared Jenkins."

"Wait, what's his name?" I interjected.

"Jared Jenkins," Ellie repeated herself.

Every hair on my body stood and I got the chills as his full name fell on my ears for the second and third time in my entire life and felt bile rising in my throat.

I shoved the bedside table out of my way, making it hit the wall as I tried to get up but because I was weaker and slower, Ellie noticed and stopped me before I could get anywhere.

"Dylan, what's wrong?"

"I need some fresh air. I can't be in here. Let me out of here!" I kept trying to get up, yanking out my IV, but Ellie was persistent in not letting me.

"You are not going anywhere. You are in no shape to get out of this bed. Officer Gonzalez, do you mind if we take this into the hall so Dylan can have the room?" She proposed.

"Sure thing, I'll be outside when you're ready." He nodded at her and then got up and left the room.

She sat on the bed and looked at me, holding my hands in her much smaller hands. "Do you want to talk about this now or do you want me to go take care of that first?"

"You can go. I'm not ready to talk about it yet, I need a few minutes." I refused to look at her.

She didn't say another word, she just brushed my hair back with her hand and kissed my forehead again before making sure my blanket was still covering me and then leaving the room.

A nurse came into the room to put my IV back in. Ellie must have asked someone to come in.

A few minutes had passed before Ellie came back into the room.

"Hey, are you okay? Do you need more time?" She asked cautiously, trying not to stir the pot.

"No, it's okay, come on in." I patted the bed, inviting her to come to sit next to me so we could address the dreaded elephant in the room.

She came and sat next to me again and just looked at me, waiting for me to open about what had me so freaked out.

"I've heard the name Jared Jenkins before, and I don't necessarily tie it to fond memories."

"What do you mean? How could you have heard of him on the other side of the country?" Her eyebrows knit together in confusion.

I exhaled and cracked my knuckles. "Remember how I said that he doesn't deserve all that credit because he's not a criminal mastermind or anything?"

She nodded.

"Well, I may have been mistaken. He might be smarter than I originally gave him credit for. I think he followed you to Boston. I think he might have followed you and when you got your makeover, he might've lost track of you. If he did, I imagine that would've upset him a great deal. Maybe it would've driven him straight towards drinking himself into an oblivion? Maybe some drug use? Has he ever shown any signs of that type of behavior?"

"Yeah, I guess so, but I'm still not understanding where you're going with this." She looked at me, her confusion was evident on her face, so I decided to just come out with it.

"It was him that caused the car accident that killed my sister." I said in a voice low enough for me to be able to get my sentence out without my voice cracking.

"*What?!* How did this never come up before? You knew his first name was Jared all along, how come you never said anything?"

"Ellie, do you know how many kids named Jared I went to school with growing up? It's not a rare name. I figured 'Wow, that kind of sucks that he also has the same first name as the guy that crashed into my sister but there's no way it's the same person on the opposite side of the country.' but clearly, I was mistaken."

"What are you feeling?"

My face felt hot and I clenched my jaw, grinding my teeth and cracking my knuckles.

I could kill him.

"Rage. I'm not sure if it's more directed towards him or the fact that I can't go and do something about how much I hate him because I'm stuck here. I just hope that they lock him away for good. I don't even know how he wound up getting out of jail after the accident. His blood test threw him under the bus and considering other people were injured or killed due to his shitty decision making, he should be locked up by now but instead he's out roaming about, hitting me with the same gun he had held up to you. Funny how that works, huh?"

"Listen, Officer Gonzalez gave me his card so you can give him a call and tell him whatever you want or need to when you're ready. I'm not going to pressure you into calling him because it's so not my business or my place to do so, but I think you should and I'm going to leave this card with you just in case. We all want the same thing; to see Jared locked up for all of the crimes he's committed and from the sound of it, that'll probably wind up being for the rest of his life. If you decide to call, great, if not, I'll respect that decision anyway. I'm here no matter what."

"Thank you." I smiled at her and she returned the smile before turning to pour me some more water. "Hey, Ellie?"

"Yeah?" She kept her back to me, continuing what she was doing.

"I'm sorry." My voice came out quieter than I was expecting.

"For what?" She handed me the cup of water.

"I know you loved him at one point. I can't imagine what it must feel like for you to sit and see what he has become and wonder where the person that you fell in love with went."

She gave me a small smile that failed miserably at hiding the sadness behind her eyes. "Yeah, it's not a great feeling, but I know that nothing I did made him this way. Whatever his damage is, it isn't my fault."

"I'm just really glad you know that. I used to watch Natalie think that everything was her fault and somehow connected to her, but always in a negative way. You amaze me sometimes, El."

She offered a more sincere smile this time. "I know, I am pretty amazing, aren't I?"

"You're definitely one of the strongest women I know, and I admire that. You're a badass."

She didn't say anything in response, she just walked over

to me and stroked my cheek. "You're not so bad yourself. You know, coming to save me and everything is pretty badass, too."

"All in a day's work, babe." I winked at her, making her throw her head back in laughter.

"We should probably run through the care directions that I was given at some point within the next few days, and make sure we don't have any questions for the doctor before you get discharged. It sounds like we just have to keep you calm, hydrated, fed, away from screens and visually straining things, etc."

I zoned out of what she was saying and just watched her as she continued giving me the rundown. She was looking down at the packet in her lap which she had already marked up with a highlighter that she undoubtedly borrowed from a nurse. While she looked down, she tucked her hair behind her ear to keep it from blocking her view.

Something about moments like these just always reminded me that we're going to be okay and that maybe not everything has to be so damn serious all the time. We made it through this, and we'll continue to make it through whatever life throws at us.

CHAPTER THIRTY-FIVE

DYLAN

I made the decision to call Gonzalez two days after we left the hospital. I couldn't bear to sit and watch Ellie continue to live in fear. Eventually, I realized that by hiding from the darkest parts of my life, I was making her face hers. I figured if we teamed up together, we could get Jared locked up and then we'd both be free to live without worry that he is going to be around the next corner we turned.

Gonzalez wasn't in on the day that I called, so I left a message. I was told he would be back in the next day so he would give me a call then.

Every night I would make myself a bed on the couch and every night Ellie would call me to sleep in bed with her, except tonight. Tonight, she got to me before I could get the couch ready. "Why do you keep setting yourself up out there in the living room if I keep inviting you to sleep in here with me? I'm obviously okay with it."

"Well, to be honest with you, we don't really know what we are yet when it comes to a potential romantic relationship and I don't think we're going to figure anything out until after Jared gets locked away and it's not polite for a gentleman to assume. I figure if you want me in your bed, you'll tell me. And every night you do." I kicked my way under the covers and got comfortable in bed next to Ellie just like the last few nights before this.

"Gentleman, huh? Interesting. Sounds to me like someone raised you right. Listen, I'm kinda unstable and it's very nice to have another warm body in the bed. Especially one who's bigger and stronger than me. I feel safe when you're here. Whenever you're around me actually. So, from now on, as long as you're comfortable with it, you are to come straight in here instead of the living room, okay?"

"Yeah, I guess I could do that."

"Oh, and while I'm telling you what to do like the bossy woman that I am, stop sleeping on the edge of the bed before you fall off in the middle of the night. Come sleep in the middle. We don't have to *cuddle* or anything if you're not okay with it, but seriously, you're going to fall off the bed and scare the crap out of me because you were the thing that went bump in the night and then I'll probably end up swinging at you." She took a deep breath to make up for the rambling. "So, to avoid all of that, just sleep in the middle so I don't have to swing at you, okay?" Her voice was sweet and playful as the moonlight flooded in from the window and shined on her face. I could see her looking at me with her big, beautiful eyes.

"You've got yourself a deal. I have a confession to make though, I think it'll make everything really make sense to you once I tell you." Surprisingly enough, I didn't feel nervous to tell her this, I wasn't worried at all.

"Ooo, finally, some answers to the mystery that is Dylan Fields, do tell." She sat up excitedly.

"I've never been in a relationship, at least not a serious

one that went beyond middle school childishness, so I've never slept in a bed with someone else, let alone someone I'm attracted to. I'm sure from this you can connect the dots to the fact that-"

"You're a virgin?!" She sat up abruptly and looked at me.

"Yes."

"Wow. I, um... I have to say I'm surprised." She combed her hair back with her fingers.

"Is that a bad thing?" I propped myself up on my elbows and looked at her curiously.

"No, not at all!" She cupped my face with her hands. "That's never a bad thing. Especially not to me. Honestly, I wish I could say the same."

I cocked my eyebrow at her. "Why's that?"

She nodded sheepishly. "It took me a long time to realize that what I'm about to say actually isn't selfish, but it was never about me. Jared is the only person that I've ever slept with and it was always about pleasing him and making sure he was content, but my pleasure was never a concern. My gut instinct was to just be like 'It's okay, I don't need anything in return.' But now that I know better, I'm kinda furious about it. It just wasn't enjoyable for me and especially at that age when it's fresh and new, I should be decently pleased. You know, I feel like every time I talk to you about my relationship with him, I realize how stupid and blind I must've been to have stayed with him for that long."

"I'm sorry, Ellie. I can't imagine having something that special just... ruined for you. I know I've said it before, but I'm really happy you're finally out of the relationship. We're gonna make sure that he'll never be a threat to you again and I'll keep you safe. Even if nothing romantic comes of this," I gestured between us, "I'll be your own personal bodyguard. Sound good?"

"Sounds perfect. Do you care if we touch throughout the night or should I build a pillow wall?" She joked, lightening the mood.

"You can be as close or as far as you want, how about that? I'll do as I was told and lay right in the middle and you do whatever you want." I shifted over and laid in the middle but tried to ensure that Ellie would have room to move around.

"Okay!" She laid in her spot and curled up but wrapped her hands around my arm.

I was more than okay with this being taken at a slow and steady pace; I didn't want to rush this. We both have decently large things keeping us preoccupied, and if we're going to be in a relationship at one point, I want us to be all in, not half mentally absent.

I rolled over on my side, facing her now so she can continue holding onto my arm. She fell asleep within minutes and I just watched and admired how peaceful she looked in her sleep despite the chaos that was constantly wreaking havoc on her mind.

I WOKE up and clicked on my phone to see what time it was. It was 4:00 a.m. and Ellie wasn't in bed anymore. I got up groggily and stumbled into the living room to look for her and sure enough, there she was, sitting on the couch with a blanket and a big bowl of popcorn while she watched a movie. When she saw me, she extended the popcorn in my direction, offering me some, so I grabbed a handful and picked at it one at a time.

"Couldn't sleep?" I asked her, both of us now focused on the movie that was playing.

"No, I'm just so aware of the fact that he's still out there. He could be right outside the building right now, you never know. I just can't wait for him to no longer be a concern." She sighed and rubbed her forehead. "Did I wake you with the movie or the microwave or something?"

"No, no, I'm not really sure what woke me, but I saw you weren't in bed, and I wanted to make sure you were okay."

"Oh, I'm sorry. Why don't you go back to bed? I'll be there in an hour or so." She lowered the volume on the TV.

"Or you could just come with me now and we can finish the movie in the morning. I'll keep you safe. I promised and I meant it."

I watched her as she contemplated her options for a few moments and then she got up, turned off the TV, took the popcorn into the kitchen, stood in her bedroom doorway and looked at me. "You coming?"

I got up and followed her in, climbing into bed together. "What can I do to make you feel safer?"

She hesitated before she spoke. "Nothing, you're doing great."

"Okay, now the truth, please."

"Can you just hold onto me? I think it'll help."

"Absolutely. Come here." I patted the bed and she turned to face away from me but scooched her back against my chest. I wrapped my arm around her with the blanket in my fist. "Blankets protect you, too."

She giggled and pulled the blanket up to her chin. "Thank you for everything that you've done for me, Dylan. You've changed my world."

I lifted my head off the pillow to kiss her head. "Goodnight, Ellie."

She hummed in agreement.

WHEN I WOKE up the next morning, she was facing me, her face right under my chin, our legs tangled together. The sun was just coming up and the sky was beautiful colors. I didn't move, I just took in the moment and all of my surroundings and the smell of Ellie's shampoo so close to my nose. I wished that my life would always be that peaceful.

I felt her shift as she started to wake up and I tried not to move her. When I heard her sigh after she finished stretching, I whispered to her. "How did you sleep?"

She nuzzled into my chest further and let out a content sigh. That was all the answer that I needed.

Then, when she realized where she was and who she was with, I think it freaked her out a little bit. She pulled away really quickly and apologized.

"Ellie, what are you apologizing for? Everything's fine, I promise. I slept really well actually. We should do that more." I smirked at her and she rolled her eyes at me.

"I'm sorry, I just felt disoriented. I was *really* comfortable though; I might just have to crawl back into that little space."

I held my arms open for her and she did exactly that. We laid there for a while, completely silent, and treasured it.

When we finally got out of bed and went about our day, I got a call back from Gonzalez. He was ready for me to come in and talk to him and I couldn't tell how I felt about it.

Ellie had to go to work, so I'd be alone today anyway.

She was busy running around the apartment while she got ready for work when I got the call from Gonzalez.

"Hey, I'm gonna run down to the station today and try to help Gonzalez with any information he might need. I'm actually gonna head out now so I can stop home before you get out of work. Have a good day, I'll see you later." I pulled her forward gently by the back of her neck so I could kiss her forehead.

"Okay, I'll see you later. Be safe." She reminded me as I walked towards the door.

"You be safe, too. Call me if you need anything." I scrunched my nose at her as a sign of affection before closing the door behind me.

CHAPTER THIRTY-SIX

DYLAN

On the way to the station, I thought about Jared. I wished there were a way for me to ensure that he got the punishment that he deserved.

I swore to myself that I wouldn't stop until he's put away.

My phone started vibrating in my pocket and I pulled it out to see who was calling me. To my surprise, it was Kathryn.

I hadn't gotten the chance to speak to her much since we got back from Boston since the world basically decided to set itself on fire when we did.

I talked to her the whole walk to the police station and it was nice to catch up on all the little things. It brought me back to how things used to feel before Natalie died.

When I walked up to the station, I let Kathryn finish what she was saying before I said anything. "Hey, listen Kat, there's something really important that I have to take care of, can I give you a call back in an hour or two? Maybe we can get Noah in on that call?"

"Yes, absolutely. I'll text him now and ask him if he'll be free to talk. Then you can explain to both of us what the hell you're doing in Seattle that's so important that you're ending a call with *me* of all people!"

"Yeah, yeah, yeah. I'll talk to you later. Love you."

"Love you, too. Talk to you later."

I jogged up the steps and in through the door, stopping at the front desk. "Hi, I'm here to speak to Officer Gonzalez."

"Name?"

"Dylan Fields."

"Yes, I see it here. Have a seat and I'll have him come bring you back to his office."

"Great, thank you."

I wasn't seated for long before Gonzalez came into view.

"Hi, Dylan. How are you doing?" He gestured towards my head as we walked back to his office.

"I'm recovering well, sir, thank you for asking."

"That's good to hear. Have a seat. I have to say I'm half surprised that you took this long to contact me. From what I can tell, you'd do anything to protect your girl and, in this situation, that includes ensuring that Jenkins faces the proper punishment."

"When I realized that I could help her and take part in protecting her, it was a no brainer. I have a feeling that besides her, there aren't many people in her corner that can really keep her safe." I shrugged.

If I can be the one to help her feel safe, then everything is right in the world. If not, then I know that our paths weren't meant to pass in a way that was more than just friends.

"You're very respectable, Dylan. How long have you two known each other?"

"A few months now. I just moved here from Boston which brings me to how I know Jared. On the night of my sister's senior prom, she was taking her best friend home. Some guy ran a red light because he was drunk and high and now my sister's dead. I thought 'JJ' was just some cringey nickname Ellie had for him while they dated, I didn't realize it was his initials until you came into the hospital room and asked."

"I'm sorry for your loss."

"Thank you. My sister said she forgave him before she died. She begged me not to do anything to hurt him and to find it within myself to forgive him, so I did. I left it alone. I was told he was taken into custody, but I guess he somehow got himself out. I really thought he wouldn't see daylight again for at least ten years, but I guess the kids in jail for possession are more harmful." There was a pissed off kick to my voice, and I realized it a little too late.

When I looked up, Gonzalez had an eyebrow raised at my sudden outburst.

"Sorry, touchy subject." I huffed.

"It's alright, I get it. I lost my wife a year ago because of someone else's stupid, reckless decisions. Now, I just try to make it my mission to protect everyone that I can from losing someone so important to them, I definitely have a different perspective on the whole thing now. I know I'm not a god or anything, but if I can do something, anything to prevent people from feeling that kind of pain, I'll do it. Sounds like you know that song and dance all too well if you ask me."

I nodded.

"I already spoke with Ellie's parents and I have all the notes from them. Is there any chance that you could get Ellie to come on down here so I can talk to her a little bit more? I have a few questions that I want to ask her."

"Yes, I can probably get her to come, but she most likely won't be too happy about it, she's really trying her hardest to just leave all this behind her and I don't really blame her. How soon can you see her?"

"She can come whenever she's ready and available. Tell

you what, you call me when she wants to come and I'll clear a spot in my schedule for her, it should be relatively quick and painless." I could feel that he was trying to reassure me, but I worried anyway. I wanted her to come out of this situation with minimal negative outcomes.

I nodded, appreciative of how understanding Gonzalez was being about the situation. I'm sure it wasn't easy dealing with so many different people and their cases, not to mention all of their feelings. I knew for a fact that I would be overwhelmed, and he seemed fine despite the mess of papers and files that littered his desk leaving only a few inches of clear space. "Thank you, I'll talk to her later today and I'll give you a call afterwards."

"Talk to you then." He nodded at me and then turned to tend to the papers on his desk.

AFTER I WALKED out of the police station, I decided to text Ellie and see what time she would be home so we could talk about when she'd want to come in to talk to Gonzalez.

Dylan: Hey, when you have an idea of what time you'll be getting home today, shoot me a text

Ellie: I'll be home by 4:30. What's up?

Dylan: Nothing major, we'll talk about it later. Have a good rest of your day and I'll see you later, okay?"

Ellie: You got it. See you then.

I called Kathryn back and as promised, she answered immediately.

"Hey! How'd your super important top-secret mission go?" She answered before I could speak.

"I promise there was nothing top secret about it. Maybe if there was it would've been more fun for me. Did you get in touch with Noah?" I decided that I would stop at the park on the way back to Ellie's apartment or maybe take the long route and enjoy the sunshine.

"Wow, Dylan. And here I was thinking you wanted to talk to me." There was a playful teasing in Kathryn's voice, something I went from hearing every single day to not at all for a few months. She sounded more like herself than she has since we lost Natalie.

"Oh, stop. He's my best friend, too. I love you both equally."

"Unacceptable. Say you love me more." She huffed from the other line.

"Fine, I love you more than I love Noah. Now call him in." I rolled my eyes at her, forgetting she can't see me.

"Much better. Alright, calling him now."

We waited for a few seconds before his voice poured through the speakers of my phone.

"Hey, Dylan, what's going on out there in Seattle? I hear there's some top-secret mission?"

I laughed, knowing that Kathryn put that idea in his head at some point while I was inside. "You two are going to be very disappointed when I tell you the truth."

"Well, that's not the way to get someone excited about a story." Kathryn sounded like she was getting further away from the phone as her voice continued to get quieter.

"Okay, fine. I had a top-secret mission to take care of, are you ready to hear all about it?" I mocked enthusiasm, earning a snort from Kathryn.

"You could never be an elementary school teacher, you're too serious." Noah chimed in.

"Yes! Thank you, that's what I'm saying!" Kathryn laughed and I heard her car turn on and the door slam shut. "Listen, Dylan. I have a decent drive ahead of me, so you gotta keep me entertained. Can you handle that?"

"Okay, if you two are going to just team up on me and

tease me, I'll just keep my super interesting story to myself and you'll have to just deal with the curiosity."

"Okay, we'll be nice now, we're sorry. Please tell us your story, grandpa!" Noah had his infamous whiny voice on.

"Don't make me come back home just to beat your ass, Noah, I'll do it! Anyway, when I first met Ellie, we were sitting next to each other on the plane. Turns out we had more in common than I thought, and she was dealing with her own stuff. Her ex-boyfriend was super abusive, and she left Seattle to go to Boston, got a makeover and went back home. Long story short, she couldn't hide from him forever, he went after her and took her parents as hostages. I had to go to the police station and talk to one of the officers that was there that night. That's all, nothing too exciting."

"Wait, what? I'm so confused, what do you have to do with any of this?" Kathryn was the first to speak.

"Yeah, I was wondering the same thing." Noah waited for me to explain further.

"I left out a tiny detail. Not only have I been around Ellie *a lot*, but I got pistol whipped by her ex who also happens to be the one from your accident."

"WHAT?!" Kathryn screamed, forcing me to yank my phone away from my ear.

"Damn, Kathryn, shut the hell up, you're gonna make us go deaf." Noah grumbled.

"Sorry, but can you blame me? 'By the way, I got pistol whipped by the guy that killed Natalie.' *Are you kidding me?*"

"Dylan, elaborate." Noah demanded in his older-brother voice.

"I needed to get to her and know that she was okay, so I snuck into the house, and I just happened to get to her before the cops did. He wasn't in the room, so I talked to her for a few seconds before she heard him coming down the hallway and she told me to hide, so I did. Then I accidentally drew attention to myself and he got pissed obviously and did a number on me. I'm fine, there's really nothing to worry about. Ellie called him JJ and I didn't make the connection until the cop came to talk to her while we were in the hospital."

"Dylan, how could you not tell us this?" He continued to lecture me, something that I would've expected from Kathryn rather than him.

"I know, I'm sorry. I really thought that Kathryn was going freak out and I didn't want to worry you guys because I really am fine, I swear and I'm going to have his ass sent away for a long time, we're working on it."

"Yeah, Kathryn, you're being uncharacteristically quiet, especially considering the bomb that he just dropped on us, are you still there?"

She didn't answer Noah's question, instead, she asked me one of her own. "Does Martha know?"

"No, I haven't spoken to her in a few days."

"Well, I suggest you wait until I can be with her in case you give her a heart attack or something because I really can't believe you. And how could you just stop talking to her? After everything she did for you and Natalie, the least you could do is check in every once in a while, and let her know that you're okay, especially *after you find out something like this!*" The Kathryn that I was expecting had finally come out. "Swear on my life that you're okay?"

"Kathryn, you know I don't do that, but yes, I promise that I'm okay. If I'm lying, you can kill me yourself, I promise that, too." I tried to lighten the mood to no avail.

"Okay, as long as you're okay we can move on. What happened at the police station, any news? How is Ellie? I'm sure she's all shaken up." Kathryn's tone changed and she sounded legitimately concerned.

"Rightfully so." Noah added.

"She's trying to get through it all, it's been hard on her and she's not sleeping well. I'll usually wake up and she won't be there-"

"Excuse me?!" Kathryn got loud again. I walked right into that one though so I couldn't blame her.

"Oh shiiiiiiit!" Noah laughed.

"Oh, god, I really make it too easy for you, don't I?" I groaned.

"Sometimes!" They said in unison.

"I started staying with her like two weeks ago. She was scared so I laid out a sheet and blanket on the couch and then she told me she wanted me to sleep next to her, so we share a bed now. Making her feel safe is the least I could do. She's done so much to help my healing process along since... you know."

"Do you love her?" Kathryn asked. I wasn't prepared for the conversation to take this turn.

"I'm not sure yet. I think so, but I want to make sure that I really love her before I make any decisions that could potentially change my life. We've kissed and it was incredible, but I want to be sure." I explained, feeling vulnerable.

"Well, good. At least you're not being a total ass about the whole thing." Kathryn responded.

"I'm happy for you and your maybe-feelings for Ellie. I like you two together."

"Me, too." Kathryn agreed with her brother.

"Thank you, guys. I do, too." I laughed and took a deep breath in as I contemplated what the future may possibly hold for Ellie and myself.

In that moment, it felt like the possibilities were endless and she wasn't even physically with me.

We ended our call shortly after that. Saying our goodbyes before hanging up didn't seem sad this time, but the fire burning inside of me to get Jared thrown away for the rest of his miserable life was stronger than ever. I knew that we were falling back into our usual relationship. Things felt more natural today and I wasn't sure if it was just the dynamic of the group call or if I was getting better or if maybe we all just subconsciously decided that it was time to stop blaming ourselves for things that we can't control.

CHAPTER THIRTY-SEVEN

DYLAN

I felt like things were falling back into place. The dust and rubble were finally settling. Maybe we were never really broken. Maybe just a little bruised or scratched up. I know that a part of me will always ache when I think about Natalie and what I really lost when I lost my sister, but I also know that it doesn't have to make me any less of a person.

I'm still breathing.

We're all still here.

I am still me.

Fortunately, I felt considerably lighter considering all the chaos going on around all of us and I decided not to try to shut it out. I welcomed it instead.

After glancing at the clock, I realized that I had about a half hour to forty-five minutes before Ellie would get out of work, so I decided to go back to my apartment. I sat on the couch and allowed my fingers to dance over the keyboard as I wrote out a text to send to Martha.

I must've gotten really lost in my head and all the things I wanted to say and tried desperately not to forget before my fingers got the chance to catch up to my brain because my thoughts were interrupted by Ellie's voice on the other side of the apartment door.

"Dylan, it's me, open up." She knocked lightly and tried to project her voice and keep it relatively quiet at the same time trying not to disturb the neighbors.

I got up and walked over to unlock the door and greeted her before almost immediately turning on my heels to get back to what I was doing.

"Whatcha doing over there? You look like you've got a mission." She followed behind me but kept her own pace.

"I'm planning a text to send to Martha. She's going to kill me for sure, so I decided not to tell her in person next time I go back to Boston." I tried to continue typing while I talked to Ellie, but I quickly realized that I do not have the mental capacity to do those two things at the same time.

"Why would she kill you?" She questioned as she shrugged out of her usual baggy hoodie and revealed a t-shirt that fit her properly. I loved that she was comfortable enough around me to fade back into the girl I saw in that picture when we were alone.

"Oh, you know, I was in the hospital and didn't call her. It's no big deal to people like us who have much bigger problems than that, but she just works at a diner, so this isn't her normal excitement!" I gave a reply that I knew was ridiculously smart-assy and laughed after I finished pretending to brush it off like it was no big deal. "I told Kathryn and Noah on my walk home today and they both almost tore me a new one over that and the fact that Jared is the same Jared that hit them that night." I turned to face Ellie who was leaning against the wall with her arms crossed, her full attention on me.

"I hate to say it and be that person, but you deserve it. How many times have I asked you, 'Dyl, have you called everybody back home to tell them what happened?' I know if it was me that you moved across the country from after years of being best friends, I would probably fly out here just to slap you for not telling me. The Jared thing, though, that I can understand your hesitation over."

"Noah didn't seem so upset with me for not telling him, maybe it's more of a chick thing." I shrugged and then realized what I said. I panicked for a minute, but then I remembered who I was talking to. If I was around Nat or Kathryn, I knew without a doubt in my mind that I would've gotten slapped or something would've been thrown at me.

"Do us both a favor and try to make being a chick sound worse. God, have all the women in your life taught you nothing about stereotyping, you sexist dick?" She fought back her smile as she scrunched her face up at me in a disgusted look that she was really good at making on the spot.

I have to say, one of the things that I thoroughly enjoyed the most about Ellie was her sense of humor and how it matched up with mine. I knew that even if I did just so happen to accidentally offend her, that she would hand it right back to me.

"You're pretty cool, you know that?" I looked up at her from where I was sitting on the floor.

"Yes, I do." She bent down and put her hand on my shoulder as she leaned over to look at the text that I had so far. "Wow, real nice and lengthy. Don't forget to mention to Martha that we are sort of playing house, but we haven't officially labeled or defined our relationship yet because our lives are so screwed up at the moment and we can't catch a break so we figured spending every night together at whoever's apartment and kissing from time to time is our best option." She took a deep breath after exhausting her lungs with that one sentence and then shrugged. "I think she'd like to hear all that."

"I want to fill her in, Ellie, not give her a heart attack and a reason to worry about my mental stability." I shook my head at her and turned my attention back to the phone.

"That's something that's going on in your life that she doesn't know about, isn't it?"

"Yeah, yeah, I'll mention it. I'm gonna make it sound a lot better though." I waved dismissively at her comment and tried to just focus on not making Martha worry with the rest of my text.

"Alright, Mr. I-have-all-the-answers, good luck with that. When it gets too hard to dance around just blatantly saying it, let me know how you end up wording it." She winked at me and walked into the kitchen.

It was quiet for a while before I heard Ellie's voice again. "Hey, Dylan? What's this envelope on the counter? Some oil splashed on it; I hope it wasn't anything too important."

"Oh, yeah, don't worry about it. It's no big deal."

"No big deal? Dyl, it's from Washington State University! Did you apply?"

"Yeah, I spoke to Natalie about it a little bit before she passed, I've been thinking about going and taking a crime scene investigation class, you know, just to see if I like it enough to even consider a career."

"I think that's a fantastic idea! You haven't even opened it yet. Oh well, I'll do it!"

"Hey, wait! It's illegal to read someone else's mail!" I ran into the kitchen, and chased Ellie around the apartment, trying to reach over or around her to grab the letter.

"Oh, yeah, okay. Go ahead, call the cops on me for opening your letter, I dare you." She ran into the bathroom and closed and locked the door just before I made it in there.

"Ellie, come on, this isn't fair."

A few more moments passed with my hands on the door frame, waiting for her to open up before the door swung open. "You got accepted!" She waved the paper in my face while she jumped up and down in front of me.

"Wait, what?" I let my arms drop to my sides.

"Read it!" Ellie handed me the letter and then drummed excitedly on my chest.

"*Congratulations, Dylan Fields, you've been accepted into the Fall Semester of 2021 at Washington State University. We look forward to speaking with you and working to form your schedule!* Did I really just read that right?! I mean, fall of next year is kind of far away still, but this is it! This is the start of working towards my potential future!"

"I'm so proud of you, angel. You're gonna be amazing. I can't wait to watch you prosper!"

Again, we found ourselves in each other's arms lovingly and this was the only place I wanted to be, good news or bad news.

I FINISHED the text for tonight but decided I would come back to it tomorrow at some point to make sure that I said everything that I wanted to say and didn't leave anything out. If it's all good tomorrow, I'll send it.

I got up from where I was sitting and walked into the kitchen where Ellie was.

When she noticed my presence, she immediately started talking. "What do you think of us staying here tonight instead of going back to my apartment?" She focused on cooking and didn't stop to look at me.

"We can do that if you want. It'll make me feel a little bit better to know that I'm not just paying for an apartment so it can collect dust." I teased her in an attempt to keep her mind off of her fear of Jared finding her.

"Good. I'll take the couch; I just need a blanket." She

regurgitated the exact line I fed her not too long ago and turned to look at me with a smirk. I don't know what it was, but in that moment, I felt such an urge to kiss her.

But we don't know what we're doing. We don't know what we are. I'm not going to shove the idea of us being together down her throat until I know that we'd both be ready for it.

Instead, I walked over to her and stood as close as I could without getting in the way. "Do you need help with anything?" Her perfume filled my nose.

"I don't think so, I'm almost done. You can preheat the oven to 375 degrees for me if you'd like. And maybe cut up some cucumbers for the salad? And make the rest of the salad?" She smiled at me like a little kid.

"Would you like me to grow the vegetables, too?"

"If it makes you happy!"

"Sounds to me like the only way you could be considered 'almost done' is if you stop working when you're done with that and let me finish the rest."

"Guilty!" She finished what she was doing and washed her hands before skittering into the living room, her socks making the hardwood floor too slippery for her to have any traction. "Toss that pan in the oven when it's done preheating and set a timer for 30 minutes, thank you!" She yelled from the couch.

I rolled my eyes and laughed. I internally made a bet with myself that she was probably already wrapped in a blanket with the TV on and when I peeked around the corner, that's exactly what I saw.

When I finished making the salad and throwing dinner in the oven, I joined her on the couch and groaned when I saw that she was watching the same movie that she's watched at least seven times since I've known her. "I'm not sure if you know this, but there are other movies."

"Yes, I do know that and none of them are as good as this one. Don't watch if you don't wanna see it again." She stuck her tongue out at me.

"Do you have this alarm in your head that goes off every time this movie starts? You always catch it within the first ten minutes. Or is it just that they play this movie *that* often?"

"I guess I'm just lucky. Now, sh, this is my favorite part!" She was sucked into the TV within seconds after she stopped talking.

I sat on my phone and played games and scrolled mindlessly through social media until the timer in the kitchen went off. Ellie paused the movie so we could go get our plates and we came back to the seats we just left.

I didn't really have much room for a dining room table and quite frankly, I wouldn't sit at one by myself anyway, so it would just take up unnecessary space that I could put to better use.

Ellie didn't press play on the TV when we sat back down with our food and I was thankful for that. I also knew that the second we finished eating, she would probably hit play, but as long as I got her attention during dinner, I didn't mind.

Everything she has cooked so far has been delightful and this was no exception.

"Do you have work tomorrow?" I asked her, my napkin covering my mouth.

"No, I get to burden you all day tomorrow!"

"Excellent. Do you want to go out and do something?"

"Sure, we can do that. I have to stop home in the morning before we do anything else, though. I didn't bring a change of clothes for tomorrow and all I have here is pajamas." She finished before shoving another heaping forkful in her mouth.

"Okay, that's fine." I wiped my mouth after finishing my

plate and offered to take hers to the kitchen whether she wanted seconds or was done eating.

As expected, she finished eating and was fully ready to jump back into her movie. We assumed our positions on the couch and basically just existed together for the rest of the night and I didn't have a single complaint... other than the fact that the movie was on again, of course.

CHAPTER THIRTY-EIGHT

DYLAN

W hen I looked over at Ellie about an hour later, she was already asleep, and I had no idea for how long.

Her phone rang while she was sleeping, and I grabbed it off of the coffee table before it could wake her.

Officer Gonzalez.

I answered the phone and walked into the bedroom as quietly as possible.

"Hi, it's Dylan. Ellie's asleep and I really don't want to wake her up just to tell her bad news. Can you legally tell me?"

"Legally? No, I can't tell you. But I see the way that you look at her and how you want to protect her and being that he's impacted your life, too, I can tell you this without taking a hit to my moral code. The domestic violence will just give her a restraining order against him, and he'll be on probation for a few years, but it won't send him to prison."

"At all? I thought the punishment would've been more significant." I sat on my bed and rested my forehead on the heel of my palm.

"If it will, it'll most likely take a while with the trial and all. He's being held here for now, but I don't feel confident telling you guys to pack up your lives and run because nobody deserves to spend a life where they're constantly looking over their shoulder. I just wanted to let you know that I'm not giving in. I plan to contact the police in Boston tomorrow and get any information they have on the accident with your sister. Once they know I have the guy they're looking for, they'll be extra cooperative. I'm going to keep digging until we get him, okay? Pass the message along for me, I'm sure it'll be better coming from you. I'll be in touch. Take care."

"Thank you for the update, I'll talk to you then." I hung up the phone and groaned before walking back out into the living room.

She was awake, pushing her hair back out of her face and stretching. "Hey, what's wrong?"

"That was Gonzalez." I held her phone up and shook it between my middle finger and my thumb.

"What did he say?" All signs that she just woke up had seemingly fallen off of her face, she was fully alert now, waiting for me to continue.

"Good news and bad news. Bad news, the punishment for domestic violence won't kick in right away, and I'm assuming the lack of evidence will probably hurt us depending on the attorneys on both sides. If he hires a really good one, he'll probably just get out with probation and a no-contact order. Good news, Gonzalez is not giving up until he's put away for a long time. He's going to get the information he needs from the Boston police regarding Natalie's accident, that should put the nail in Jared's coffin. We all want what's best for you so try not to worry too much, okay? You have people in your corner, I promise. In the meantime, get dressed, we're going out."

"Wait, what? What time is it? I told you I don't have

clothes with me, we'll have to stop back at my apartment. And also, you suck for dropping that bomb and then making me leave the house, you know that, right?" She crossed her arms at me matter-of-factly.

"I know, I give Satan a run for his money, don't worry, there's a throne in hell waiting for me right next to him. Come on, let's go. Throw your sweatpants on top of your shorts, put your hoodie back on and you'll be fine." I waved her up off the couch and tossed her hoodie in her direction.

"Can I at least know where we're going, or do you make my decisions now?"

"We're going back to that diner." I said, shrugging on my jacket.

"No, Dylan, please don't make me go back there." Panic overwhelmed her features and tugged at my heart strings.

I walked over to her and wrapped my arms around her as tightly as I could, trying my best to hold her together. "I know, El, I really don't want to bring you back there, but we need to get the surveillance from that night, it could really help us."

"I can't do it. Please just stay here, can't we ask Gonzalez to get his hands on it? They probably wouldn't even give it to us because we don't have the authority of a badge."

I pulled away from her and kissed her head. "I'll go give him a call. It's okay."

Ellie nodded weakly and sat back down on the couch. I really didn't want to worry her all over again, but I had no idea how to approach a situation like this.

I dialed Gonzalez's number and waited for him to pick up but eventually the only thing that answered me was his voicemail. I waited for his message to end before leaving one of my own.

"Hi, it's Dylan. After our conversation, I talked to Ellie and decided to try to bring her to the diner so we could get the surveillance from that night, but just the idea of going got her all worked up, so I was hoping I could talk to you about getting it. Maybe you could get your hands on it since you have the 'authority of a badge' as Ellie put it. Call me when you get this. Thanks, bye."

I turned around and Ellie was standing in the doorway with a blanket wrapped around her. "He didn't answer, huh?"

"No, but he'll get back to me tomorrow, it's okay. Why don't you get ready for bed? You need to get some rest."

She nodded. "You should, too. I have a confession to make... I don't think I can sleep alone tonight."

"That's fine, I wasn't going to let you take the couch for the night anyway. Believe it or not, I am a gentleman."

"Not." She snickered.

"Alright, out you go. I gotta get dressed."

"Nope! I refuse." She crawled across the bed to the side that she usually slept in at her house which was supposed to be my side here, but I let it go. If it would make her more comfortable, I would let her sleep wherever she wanted.

She yanked the sheet up above her head. "I'm not looking, go ahead!"

"You're such a child." I started changing into my pajamas, changing my pants first. When it came time to change my shirt, I had just finished pulling my shirt off over my head when I saw one of her eyes peek around the sheet. I pretended not to notice and stifled a smile as I threw my clean shirt on. I turned off the light and got in bed underneath the covers and waited a few moments.

As expected, Ellie scooched right over and held my arm like she has nights prior to this one.

Something about it wasn't good enough for her tonight. "Can I get closer, please? If it'll make you uncomfortable, don't worry about it."

I pulled my arm out from her grasp and wrapped it

around her instead, pulling her closer. "Come, it's all good." She came closer and I saw my opportunity. "By the way, I totally saw you peeking." I couldn't hold my smirk back as I felt her stiffen.

She shot upright and looked at me and slapped my chest. "I didn't peek! You're delusional!"

"And you're lying! Believe me, I'm flattered!" I sat up and wiggled my eyebrows at her.

"Oh, god!" She flopped down on her back and covered her face with her hands. "I think I'll take my chances and sleep at my own apartment tonight. I'll see you when I see you." She swung her legs off the edge of the bed and moved to get up, but I wrapped my hand around her waist and gently pulled her to face me.

Taken by surprise, she was easier to spin than usual and luckily, our faces wound up inches away from each other. There we were, sitting face to face, still, silent, and she seemed more herself than ever and I couldn't help myself.

"You're beautiful, Ellie, you know that?" I kissed her forehead.

"No, I'm not. I'm very bland and average, I've been working at being boring and blending in with the crowd."

"There's just something about you that's so special." I kissed her cheek.

"See, now, I know that's not true."

"Stop talking." I grabbed her face with both of my hands and kissed her. I let the meeting of our lips linger for a few seconds longer than a peck but the whole kiss was very middle school and that's all I wanted.

You could only imagine the surprise that washed over me when she grabbed a fistful of my shirt and pulled me back to her. She kissed me harder, with more urgency and passion than I've ever felt. When she pulled away, she gave the back of my hair a tug.

My heart was pounding, and I started thinking that this wasn't just the grief. It wasn't either of our traumas that made us think we were feeling this way; it was real.

She looked down at her lap and pushed all her hair out of her face. "I'm sorry," she whispered in the dark. I could barely even see her, but I knew she was beating herself up for what just happened.

I couldn't help but let out a small laugh, "Why are you sorry? That was better than I was expecting. It was fantastic." I grabbed her hand and held it.

"You know, I'm not usually like this, I don't know what came over me. I guess it's easier to be brave in the dark." It was quiet for a minute.

"Is it bad that I want you to do it again?" I watched as I brushed my thumb across the top of her hand.

"Only if it's bad that I want to do it again."

"It's not, I promise, but you're taking too long." I placed my finger under her chin and guided her face up to mine so I could kiss her again.

I felt her smile against my lips, and I couldn't understand what it was that this girl was doing to me. Does this change things? Is this going to be a regular thing or is this just tonight in the dark? I couldn't help but wish that my mind would be as silent as the room was. Here I am, kissing Ellie and completely drowning in her, yet I still can't stop myself from contemplating the what ifs.

We pulled away from each other silently and both laid in our designated positions in the middle of the bed. I felt my heart hammering in my chest, and I couldn't help but to think that she could probably hear it. I focused on my breathing and tried to slow my heart rate which made the problem so much worse.

She stayed quiet and I didn't try to get her to talk. I didn't bother talking either, I just laid there and wondered if her mind was racing like mine was.

This could be a major blessing for me provided that Ellie would be willing to talk about it and see where this could lead to. Or it could be a total disaster in the face of all the chaos and maybe she'll just dismiss it as a silly mistake that never should have happened.

The only thing I knew for sure is that kissing her tonight really clarified things for me and I knew that this wasn't just some desperate attempt at healing. If anything, being with Ellie that way filled a different hole that I didn't even know existed.

I've always wanted someone to love me in ways that I've never been loved before, but I never made it my goal to find someone to do that for me. I've read plenty of things saying that being loved by someone shouldn't complete you, but what if you're already whole and being loved by the right person makes you feel whole in an entirely different sense?

I know that I have to talk to Ellie about this sooner or later, but with everything that's going on, I'm really dreading having to put her on the spot. There's got to be a way around overwhelming her.

If she were to tell me that she regretted kissing me and wished she could take it back so we could just be friends, I knew I wouldn't be any less of a human being and I knew I wouldn't be any less me. Just having her in my life had proven to be enough for me, but just imagine if she wanted to actually give us a shot. I didn't know if I'd be able to contain myself.

I may have set myself up for failure. What if we're different people when we're healed?

I read a book once where this couple was together until they realized that they didn't need to hold onto each other anymore to feel safe and that they could survive on their own.

I just hope that the glimpse of Ellie that I catch when she's in her moments of healing will continue to blend with mine as well as they do now. I've found so many things to love in the healed version of her as well as the version that is still bleeding.

I stared up at the ceiling and thought about how much everyone back home would be teasing me right now. They've never seen this side of me, and I've made sure to keep it that way. I tried to come up with a few different ways that I could go about talking to Ellie about this and when I had a small list, I started to mull them over in my head and fell asleep somewhere during the process.

CHAPTER THIRTY-NINE

DYLAN

The next morning, I rolled onto my side and my eyes fell on Ellie's beautiful sleeping face. She's gorgeous and I can't help but wonder if she knows it. Maybe she did once upon a time, before Jared came in and made sure that there was nothing left for her to be confident in. Or maybe he brought the confidence out in her and then, when he knew she was stable and that she knew her worth, he decided to rip the carpet out from under her for his own sadistic pleasure.

For a while now, I've wanted to understand Ellie on a level that would leave no questions. I want to know who she was before anything significant happened in her life. I want to know who she was while she was in that abusive, toxic relationship. The person that I *do* know, the person that has fought tooth and nail to come back from the depths of hell that she got sucked into, has so much life behind her eyes. Life lived, life to live, life she's living. I just wanted to know everything about her.

I got out of bed and decided to just let her sleep as much as she could.

I threw on a sweatshirt before I walked into the kitchen to start cooking, feeling the air get colder when I entered the living room.

I was halfway through the batch of pancakes that I was making and had just finished cooking the bacon when Ellie padded into the kitchen. "Good morning," She stretched as she sat down at the breakfast bar.

"Good morning, how'd you sleep?" I started making her a plate and slid it in front of her.

"Thank you. As for how I slept, eh, okay. You?" She put her hair up into a floppier than usual bun and pulled her sleeves down around the middle of her palms.

"Good." I responded, my elbows locked as I leaned on the countertop.

"Can we talk about this?" We said in unison. We both smiled and looked at the ground.

"We should. The elephant is taking up way too much room in my apartment and that is valuable space that can be put to good use!"

"I'm really not even sure where to start if I'm being honest with you. Last night just felt different for some reason." She pushed her food around with her fork.

"Good different, I hope."

"The best possible kind of different! I'm just not sure what was different, but something was."

Our conversation was interrupted by my phone ringing from my sweatpants pocket.

"I can let that go to voicemail." I pulled my focus back to the conversation that we were in the middle of.

"No, it's okay, you should check it. It might be important." She assured me with a small smile.

"I'll be quick, I promise." I pulled my phone out of my pocket and saw that it was Gonzalez and excused myself into the bedroom. "Hey, Gonzalez. You got my voicemail. Do you think you'll be able to get the surveillance?" I spoke into the phone. The other line was relatively quiet.

"Dylan, is Ellie with you?" He sounded concerned.

"Yeah, she's in the other room, why, what's going on?"

"We just got a tip from one of her neighbors. They heard a lot of banging and shattering late last night and then nothing ever since it stopped. Where were you two around 2:00 a.m.?"

"We stayed at my apartment, she's terrified and didn't want to go home."

"Okay, good, I'm glad you kids are alright. Keep her away from her apartment, I'm heading down there within the hour to check it out. I'll give you a call back when I know more, okay?"

"Yeah, thank you for the update. I'll talk to you then."

He hung up and I have to admit, my level of curiosity has rarely been this high.

I walked out into the living room just in time to see Ellie scampering back to where I left her. "You were eavesdropping, weren't you?"

She looked at me with an innocent face for a minute but came clean quicker than usual. "Yes, but what else is new? You know I'm nosy." She looked at me with a sudden shamelessness.

"Believe me, I know you are. Anyway, that was Gonzalez. Someone called the cops concerned about the noises they heard coming from your apartment, but he asked me to keep you away from there. He's going there soon to check it out. Until then, we stay right here."

"Dylan, I can't just sit here and wait, can we please at least meet him at the apartment building and go up with him? I'm sure it's nothing, my neighbors are infamous for having sex at top volume and vacuuming at all hours of the night. There's a whole bunch of things that that person could've been hearing and who says it was coming from my apartment?"

"Ellie, please don't make me fight you on this, I just want you to be safe."

"Please? I promise we'll wait to go up until he gets there. I'll even let him go in for five minutes before I do."

I sighed. "Has anyone ever told you that you're a really shitty listener?"

She smiled at me from over her shoulder. "All the time."

"Alright, let's go."

"My hero! Just think about it this way, the sooner we go and find out for sure that everything is fine, the sooner we can come back to this awful conversation about feelings!"

"On second thought, let's take our time. We'll thoroughly check every inch of the apartment... you know, just to be safe." I nodded.

She threw her head back and laughed. "Yeah, that's what I thought you'd say."

The walk to her apartment felt shorter than usual and I think it's because I was dreading this. Something about it has my stomach in knots. For both of our sakes, I hope my gut is wrong this time.

Everything looked normal around the building and in the lobby. Nothing seemed off, as if nothing out of the ordinary happened and I started to get my hopes up that maybe she was right, and everything really is fine.

I was wrong. My gut was right the whole time.

Everything was not fine.

CHAPTER FORTY

E very time the front door to the building opened, I was terrified that it would be Jared, but it couldn't be. I sincerely think that I was more afraid of what I would have had to do to stop him rather than what would happen to Ellie. I knew I wouldn't let anything happen to her. Thankfully, we were only in the lobby for five to ten minutes before Gonzalez showed up and relief flooded my body. I took a deep breath as I walked over to him, letting the tension leave my body with my exhale.

"Well, well, well, look who it is. I see we didn't want to wait for my phone call after I checked out the situation."

"Only if by we, you mean Ellie. I'm here for moral support. I personally would rather not be here at all." I raised an eyebrow at her.

"I promised Dylan that we could wait for you and you can go in five minutes before us, but I want to be involved, I want to see what happened." She ignored my comment and kept her focus on Gonzalez.

"Okay, let's head upstairs. You kids can wait in the hallway while I check it out and make sure that everything's safe at the very least." Gonzalez turned on his heels while we walked to the elevator.

The ride up seemed to take forever and I imagined Jared standing there when the doors open, ready to kill all three of us. My stomach knotted further as my imagination got increasingly more active.

Relief washed over me again when the doors opened and the hallway was empty. I took Ellie's hand in mine while we stood outside her door, waiting for Gonzalez to call us in.

Shortly after, the door opened.

"Okay, the coast is clear. You guys can come in, just please try not to touch anything until I get pictures."

Gonzalez let us walk around on our own while he started taking pictures of every inch of the apartment.

When we opened the door to her apartment, it looked like a tornado rolled right through it. Her furniture was moved from all the usual places. Her drawers were ransacked. Her vase was knocked over and shattered into millions of pieces in the middle of the floor. Anything she had hanging on the walls was either now on the ground or hanging on by a thread. Her mirrors were shattered and every picture frame she had in the living room had clearly been chucked at the same wall.

She stood in her doorway, frozen, and I watched as she visibly swallowed.

I took her hand in mine and led her towards her bedroom. "Be careful where you step, El." I said as gently as I could manage through gritted teeth.

She let out a whimper as her eyes fell on even more damage in her kitchen. I was worried what the bedroom would look like, but I was surprised when I opened the door.

Her bedroom was even cleaner than how we left it. Her bed was made, which she would never do. There were rose petals all over the bedspread arranged in the shape of a heart and a note in the middle.

"Oh, god. I'm gonna be sick. I can't read it, what does it say?" She turned to face the other way.

I kept my grip on her hand fairly firm, praying nothing and no one would try to snatch her from me while I had my back to her. Or even worse, praying that she wouldn't just slip through my fingers.

I stepped towards the bed cautiously and reached for the note.

I might get locked up in a few days, but you'll never be rid of me. I love you too much to let go of you that easily. Don't believe me? Watch how well I know you.

I looked over at the back of Ellie's head and I heard her sigh. "How bad is it?"

"I'm not gonna lie to you, it's pretty bad, El." I set the note back down on the bed that didn't really feel much like hers anymore and wrapped my arms around her from behind, placing my chin on top of her head. "It's gonna be okay, we'll figure something out, okay? I'm not going anywhere." I whispered in the silence, desperate for answers.

She spun in my arms and tucked her arms under her chest, making herself as small as possible.

"You believe that everything happens for a reason, right?" She muttered into my chest.

"I do. It's the only explanation for life being so shitty sometimes. No way does the big man put us through stuff like this just for kicks. There's something better waiting for us at the end of all the suffering, there has to be."

"I want to read it." She pushed off of my chest gently, taking a step back from me.

"Are you sure? You don't have to; I can just give it to Gonzalez. He'll take care of it."

She nodded unconvincingly, "I need to know. I can handle it."

I grabbed the note again and handed it to her. Before she could open it, I took her other hand in mine. I gave her a nod to reassure her that I'm here and that she'll be okay.

I watched her face as she read it, waiting for the sudden change, but it never came. Instead, she laughed. Hard. "I can't believe this!" She bellowed in between cackles.

Gonzalez came over with a puzzled look on his face. "Everything alright over here?"

"I'm not really sure, what's happening. El, you lost me. I'm really not understanding the laughing." I couldn't help but let out an uncomfortable chuckle of my own.

She slowed her laughing down and caught her breath. "I'm sorry, I know this is a super inappropriate reaction to the situation, but-" She cut herself off with another couple of giggles. "I just can't believe that this is my life! I've always watched the girls who were in abusive relationships in disgust because they should know better and just leave him. I mean come on, it's always *so* obvious that he's abusive!"

I kept quiet, waiting for her to finish, and Gonzalez stepped away to give us a little bit of space.

"Not only did I become one of those girls, but he got so bad that I'm trying to get him thrown in jail for as long as possible and he's still harassing me! And the funniest part?! I don't think he'll ever stop! It's all just so pathetic!" She laughed again and her laughter slowed, but her gasping for breath persisted at the same pace. Tears started racing down her cheeks.

I stepped towards her and wrapped her small frame in my arms as tightly as I could, and she let me as her sobs shook her entire body.

"How did I let this happen, Dylan? Why didn't I just call the cops after the first time he hit me? Why didn't I just leave? I knew I deserved better; I just can't understand why I didn't fight to *get* better. I don't think I've ever been so mad at myself, but that was a whole new level of stupid. I basically signed up to keep getting hit. Everybody knows that it doesn't just happen once, there's always more and there will always be more."

"Ellie, listen to me, this is not something that you could have known was going to happen. You didn't walk into a relationship with someone who had 'Hi, I'm an abusive, obsessive stalker!' tattooed on his forehead. There's no way you could've known. People are really good at hiding who they are and pretending that they're perfect until all of a sudden, their true colors poke through and you realize how toxic they really are. People suck and will purposely try to trick you into falling for them just because they like the thrill of the chase and it just makes them feel some sort of sick satisfaction that they drew you in and did their worst." I tried to speak softer after hearing the anger in my voice.

"He made you second guess who you are as a person because he's a lost cause who will never be worth your affection. He is single-handedly taking away all the good parts of you and we have to fight this so we can get those parts back. It's okay for this to change you temporarily, but not forever. We're gonna get that girl in the picture back, okay? But you can't give up on me, you're too strong for that and he doesn't deserve the satisfaction of having changed you." I rubbed circles on her back.

"I don't want to live like this anymore, he's draining. Plus, what if I don't want to be that girl again? What if she's just gone forever? I know too much now. I was so safe and protected in that picture, how could I ever go back to that? Maybe it's just better that I grow into being someone who is happy rather than ignorant. Growth is important anyway and I think in some aspects, I've been stunted in that region of my life. Now, I'm free to grow to my heart's content. Well, I'll be free once he's gone." She raked a hand through her hair and gave it a frustrated tug.

"I know, El. The good news is that we've already started doing something about it. Gonzalez will do his job and then we'll figure out what our next step is going to be. For now, just know that I'm right here and as long as I'm here, I won't let anything happen to you. Do you want to go back downstairs while we wait for him to be finished?"

She nodded. "Yeah, I don't want to look at this stuff anymore."

"Alright, come on. Watch your step." I placed my hand on the small of her back and guided her out of the apartment that I can only assume had become her worst nightmare.

"I'm sure you really regret moving to Seattle now, huh? Then again, I doubt this was in your game plan. Meeting a crazy girl with a ton of problems in her life and a psychopathic, stalker ex-boyfriend? Was that on your checklist?" She smiled up sheepishly at me.

"I love Seattle. It brought you into my life and whether you wanna believe it or not, that's not at all a bad thing. The only thing that sucks about my life since I moved here is that I spent all my money on staying in that damn motel for those first couple months. Such a waste of money. Everything else has been just as I've expected it, if not better. Life is just full of surprises, huh?"

"Yeah." She sighed.

She sat in one of the most hidden corners of the lobby in a chair with extra slouchy cushions. She pulled her knees up to her chest and sunk down in her seat as low as she could.

I stopped where I was and just looked at her for a minute, taking her in from a distance for a change.

Her hair was a mess from her sleeping last night, her eyes red and puffy. She just looked miserable.

Unable to watch her sit alone any longer, I walked over and slumped down in a chair next to her. I didn't bother trying to get her to talk to me, understanding that she probably needs to sit in her own head for a while and process everything.

Knowing her, she wouldn't want to move out of this apartment to get a new one that doesn't have this tainted memory. She would want to stay and stand her ground just like she did with the entire city of Seattle. I understand what she's trying to do or what she's trying to prevent, but it would be so much easier if she just let herself be defeated, just this once.

Gonzalez left after he got everything that he needed and talked to both of us. He said he was going to ask around to see if anything suspicious may have been noticed, but we were officially without police protection again and it worried me a little bit. I knew we would be fine, and that Gonzalez is just a phone call away at any time, but it just feels different when he's around.

You'd have to be pretty stupid to commit a crime against someone with a cop around.

I don't think there's anything for us to do but wait. We just need to let the legal system do its thing and try to help out any way we can.

Before he left, he told us that he couldn't add the charges for destruction of property and breaking and entering to Jared's already accumulating list of charges because since he was still being held in jail, *he* technically didn't do it.

Ellie kept looking at the note, which I hadn't realized that she took, trying to figure out who it could be that was helping Jared harass her. "I just don't understand, this had to be him. This is his handwriting."

"Well, he's got nice handwriting." I looked over her shoulder at the note again. I remember not having any issues reading it, it almost looks like it was typed. I even ran my finger on the backside of the note to see if I could feel the ridges from where the pen was pressed down to write.

"Yeah, I was always the one with the 'sloppy' handwriting in our relationship. I used to have him write out the cards and stuff just so it looked prettier. It was the joke in our relationship that I had the little boy handwriting and he had the cute handwriting. Wait a minute, you have unnaturally pretty handwriting and you're a man." She teased and squinted at me.

I settled for sticking my tongue out at her, not being able to come up with a witty response.

CHAPTER FORTY-ONE

I really tried to not let any feelings of pity come through as I recalled that our entire relationship wasn't terrible, the terrible just overwhelmed any good that remained. I was afraid that if I did, I would fail to realize that the good and the bad is all one person.

There's the guy who hit me and threatened me when I 'stepped out of line'. The one who would yell at me and constantly accused me of being out to get him. The one who would give me the silent treatment for days on end and constantly accused me of cheating every time I had to work late. The one who wouldn't let me look him in the eyes when I talked to him when we got into an argument.

And on the other hand, there's the guy who would bring me flowers on a random day after work and pay so much attention to me on those days. Sometimes, I would come home to a nice, hot meal and he would tell me to relax and unwind and that he would take care of everything. He would remind me that he loves me and tell me to never forget. He told me he would give me the wedding of my dreams when he could save up enough money.

It was all the same person and I think that's the part that fucks me up the most.

He was terrible. The worst part is that he wasn't always terrible but with him it was always just to the extremes. There was no gray area, only black and white. He either loved me or hated me, respected me, or beat the crap out of me.

Actually, scratch that, the worst part is that I know I could still love all those good parts despite the bad ones. I knew who he really was and that the love and affection was a rarity, but I was always willing to wait for it. I figured it had to be coming eventually, so I'd just wait.

Thinking about it this way, it makes sense why I stayed for so long. I was hoping that the anger and the beatings that I took were just a rough patch in the relationship and if I could just be the perfect girlfriend for him, he wouldn't have to hit me.

If I could've just shaved off all the pieces of me that he hated or that he thought needed to be changed or that I should've been punished for, then he never would've had to hit me again.

"El? You okay?" Dylan's voice snapped me out of my trance.

I looked up at him and felt tears hit my cheeks, I didn't even realize I was crying. As much as I would love to say that I didn't know why I was crying, I know that it would be a lie.

"Yeah, I'm sorry," I wiped my face with my sleeve. "This is all just pretty hard; thinking that someone that I once swore I could love forever is now making my life a living hell and getting a kick out of it." I looked at my living room and it was definitely cleaner than it was when we first walked in earlier today, but it would never be the same as before. He, well, I guess it was his helper who ruined my home. I couldn't imagine myself ever feeling safe here again. The whole apartment feels tainted.

"I can't imagine what you're going through, but if there's anything that I can do, you tell me and I'll do it, okay?"

"I hate to be this needy, but I can't stay here, can we keep staying at your place for a while? At least just until this whole thing is figured out. Once Gonzalez has what he needs to lock him up, we can find me a new apartment and we can live in our own separate places again."

"Ellie, stop. We can stay at my place for as long as you need, there's no rush to get you out. Is there anything you want to pack up and bring over to my apartment to make it feel more comfortable?" I watched as he walked around the room, gesturing to things, and asking me if I wanted to bring them.

We wound up packing up a few things here and there, but most of my stuff just stayed here. We walked back to Dylan's with one box each and when we got in and set the boxes down, I turned to face him and wrapped my arms around his neck, our bodies pressed together as I stood on my toes to get my chin on his shoulder.

We moved slightly as his laugh bounced us. "What's this for?" He snaked his arms around my waist.

I pulled away but grabbed his hands so we could stay touching. "You."

"What did I do to deserve this?" He squeezed my hands quickly before loosening his grip.

"You're you."

He gaped at me. "I *am*?"

I shoved him. "Shut up, I don't know, you make me feel safe. I feel safe in your apartment, I feel safe in your bed, I feel safe in your arms, I feel safe when I'm just in your sight. I trust that you mean it when you promise you'll do anything to keep me safe." I looked up into his eyes and resisted the urge to look away.

"Good, because I mean every word of it, every time I say it. We're gonna take your life back, I promise." He stepped closer to me, pushed my hair back and cradled my face in his hands.

I stood up on my toes again and pressed my lips to his. His hands slid from my face down to my neck, paused briefly and continued down my back. When they reached my waist, he wrapped his arms around me and lifted me a few inches off of the ground.

I smiled into the kiss and tried my best to keep my lips closed to keep him from kissing my teeth. I felt him smile back and, in this moment, there was no one else in the world. No one could take this moment from us.

He set me down for what felt like half a second and then hoisted me up even further, so my legs wrapped around his hips. He carried me into his room and laid me down on the bed. Hovering over me, he whispered, "Can I tell you something?"

"Of course." I wrapped my hand around his arm.

"I'm falling in love with you." He paused briefly and sat up almost immediately after.

My heart started pounding the second his words fell on my ears. *His beautiful words.* I really thought that a point would come where I wouldn't get butterflies like a schoolgirl when someone would say something sweet to me, but I guess I was wrong.

I opened my mouth to say something back but closed it after nothing came out.

He's upset, Ellie. Say something!

"Hey, stop it, look at me, you didn't even give me a second to react." I sat up and scooched closer to him. I placed my hand on his cheek and tried to get him to look at me.

He gave in but wouldn't let his eyes meet mine.

CHAPTER FORTY-TWO

I couldn't believe what I said. There's no way that she feels the same way. There's no way that I didn't just screw this whole thing up for both of us. I swore to myself that I was going to wait to tell her until after this was all over, but I couldn't hold it in anymore.

"Dylan, look at me. I want you to be looking at me when I say what I'm about to say." She tried to pull my face to look at her.

I finally looked her in the eyes, and they were a little more glassy than usual.

"I haven't reacted yet and I'm not going to react until you explain why you said that." If she wasn't Ellie and the sweetest person I know, I probably would've reacted differently, but I understood where she was coming from.

I turned my body to face her and took a deep breath. "I'm falling in love with you. I've watched you go through some pretty dark stuff and I know that there's more that you haven't told me about, I can tell. I'm not in a rush to learn those things about you either because I know that they'll come out when the time is right and when you're comfortable enough to tell me. Not to sound like a total cliché, but you get my heart racing when you kiss me and sleeping next to you just makes sense. We've connected on another level from the day that we met, and I've never felt like another human has understood me the way that you do."

I tried to stop myself before I went too far.

"You know what, fuck it. I'm not falling in love with you, I'm just flat out in love with you, I love you, Ellie. I'm sorry to bombard you with this, especially with everything else going on, but I think we can be even stronger if the truth is out. I just had to tell you." I sighed after realizing that I just basically word-vomited all over her, but at least I never broke eye contact.

Small victories, I suppose.

"Are you done?" She asked me with an expression on her face that I couldn't read.

I nodded slowly, afraid of what was next.

"Good." She threw one of her legs over to the other side of my lap and pushed my shoulders, so I was laying on my back with her straddling my lap. She dropped down on her hands that rested on each side of my head. What came out of her mouth next was the only thing I needed to hear. "I love you, Dylan."

I grabbed the back of her neck and pulled her down to kiss her, rolling us over, so she was under me.

She let out a laugh that was probably louder than it needed to be, but that was something that I loved about Ellie. She was a little over the top when she was happy, and I loved seeing her that way.

"Are you sure?"

She looked at me while she gnawed on her lip and nodded. "Yes."

I've never been that vulnerable and exposed. I wanted to

273

give her every piece of me that always ached to be loved and that night, she took every piece.

We laid facing each other afterwards and I just stared at her, taking in every detail of her face. The hairs that were usually loose from her ponytail and framing her face were now slightly sticking to her skin. The rest of her hair was slightly bigger and frizzier than usual, covering part of her face.

I tucked her hair behind her ear and before I could pull my hand back, she grabbed it and gave it to her other hand to hold. Her now free hand found its way to my cheek and her thumb stroked my cheek gently. I allowed myself to melt into the way her touch made me feel.

"That was something new, huh?" She giggled.

"Yeah, I'd say." My eyes were shut, but I knew she was still looking at me, I felt her eyes practically burning holes through my skin. I opened my eyes and turned my head to look at her. "Are you okay?"

"Better than okay. I had no idea what I was missing."

"Well, I guess that makes two of us." I pulled her closer and kissed her forehead before closing my eyes again.

I felt myself slipping into the darkness as I fell asleep and I didn't fight it, I just pulled Ellie closer to me and held her in my arms before I was completely asleep. The last thing that I remember is her sleepily mumbling an "I love you" into my chest.

***

OVER THE NEXT WEEK, we kept in touch with Gonzalez so we could be updated on their progress with the case. Thankfully, we haven't needed any kind of help since the day we saw the shape of Ellie's apartment. We've been staying at my place since then and I have to admit, it's been nice staying in one place. It's something I under-appreciated while I was back in Boston.

I tried not to bring up Jared at all unless it was our daily phone call with Gonzalez, but I really wanted to ask her how she's been feeling about it all. She seemed better when she was distracted, so I've been letting us just live in our bliss and hoping that she'll come to me and let me know if she needs me.

On another note, we were really lucky that we found Gonzalez of all people to help with this case, he's been a phenomenal help throughout the whole process and incredibly patient with us both. Yesterday, he told us that he should be able to tell us what happens with Jared's sentence in two days.

You can only imagine how antsy we were.

As expected, Gonzalez called two days later around 2:00 p.m., just after the sentencing was decided, just like he said he would.

"Hey, Dylan. Put me on speaker." Gonzalez kept it quick and to the point, he knew that's what we needed.

"Alright, we're all ears." I propped my elbow up on my knee and held the phone in between the two of us so we could both listen and be heard when we decided to talk.

"Okay. Jared has been found guilty of having a weapon in his possession without a license, three counts of unlawful restraint and two counts of assault and vehicular manslaughter. He will be in prison for a very long time. You can relax now, Ellie, it's all going to be okay, he can't hurt you anymore." Gonzalez's voice flooded in through the phone and I don't think I've ever been so glad to hear it. I let out a laugh and squeezed Ellie's knee.

Her pain was over.

Now we could finally focus on us and our lives and where we're going to go from here. Thinking about a life and a future without the looming fear of Jared made my whole body feel lighter. Considering I've only been in this situation for a fraction of the time that Ellie has, I can't imagine how she feels.

I looked over at Ellie and there she was, sitting next to me with tears flowing steadily down her cheeks and a hand clasped over her mouth.

I grabbed her hand and pulled her in close to me.

"Gonzalez, can we give you a call back in a little bit? The news has to sink in." I spoke quickly.

"Yes, that's fine. Congratulations, Ellie, you finally have your freedom back." I heard the smile in Gonzalez's voice and couldn't help but wonder if he's always this emotionally invested.

We hung up the phone and Ellie looked at me with a happiness and relief that has never reached her eyes before today.

"Dylan, I can't believe this." She held my hand tight.

"I know, but you better believe it because this is just about as real as it gets. I don't want you to ever forget how you feel right here in this moment. Relief like this doesn't come around often."

She laughed lightly.

Her relief faded and I felt the excitement leave the room.

"I don't even have to ask, but I'm going to, just to make sure. You're worried about whoever did that to your apartment, aren't you?"

"Yes, of course, how could I not be? You saw the condition of the place. I'm just worried that he might have someone helping him that isn't currently facing a very long prison sentence. I guess that's just how it is though, one problem goes away and a whole bunch more pop up, right?"

"Ellie, I need you to know that I am here for you and even if bad things keep popping up, we will face them one at a time together. I think we need to get you out of that apartment as soon as possible so you have one less thing to worry about. If Jared actually does have someone helping him, they won't be of much use to him if you don't live where you used to and they don't know where you moved to, right?"

She was hesitant in her nod, but I continued anyway.

"So that's what we'll do! We'll get you a new apartment where nobody will know where you live, and we'll get you all new stuff so none of the old stuff will remind you of what happened! We can work around this; I promise we will find a way." I couldn't explain why I was excited all of a sudden, but I just wanted to do what I could to right his wrongs.

"Dylan, I love you, but I can't afford that again. And how do we know that his helper isn't always watching us? How do we know that they didn't bug my stuff with those really tiny nanny cameras or something like that? There's no way that he'll give up that easily, he always gets what he wants. He didn't have much growing up. One day, he told me that any money that his parents gave him, he would give to his brother, so he knew that he was eating. I started sneaking extra snacks from home or sharing my lunch with Jared. My parents caught on, but I didn't tell them why, I just apologized, said I would stop, and kept sharing my lunch."

"Why didn't you want to tell your parents?"

"I knew he was embarrassed by not being as fortunate as the other kids in our school and I figured he would want it to be our little secret that I was helping him out. Come middle school and high school, he started changing. He got a job the second he legally could, he would bring a few dollars to school for lunch once a week. I noticed how little he was eating, and I asked him about it, and he said he was saving his money. I didn't understand what he could possibly be saving up for that he would think he has to skip meals, but I tried to just leave it alone. He was buying brand name clothes so he would fit in."

"Yeah, I know how that feels. Nat and I always stood out at school, too. We were the kids with the dead dad. I tried to make us both sandwiches for lunch, but Nat said they were terrible and had way too much mayo." I smiled fondly at the memory.

"See, not everyone handles that kind of stuff like you did, though. Jared took it and ran with it. I have to say he spoiled me, too, he wanted me to have the best of everything. I think after a while, he just wanted me to match his image that he worked so hard to build. He got me, he got the image he always wanted, he got everything he wanted, and he decided not to stop there. He bullied his way through the rest of high school, stepping on everyone. It didn't matter who you were, in his eyes, you were beneath him. I thought I was special because he always had me on a pedestal. You live and you learn." She shrugged.

"Anyway, he's persistent and he won't stop until he gets what he wants and unfortunately, this time what he wants is me. I never thought I'd want to be unwanted so badly in my life." She huffed at the irony.

"I can't promise that he'll ever stop wanting you, but I know that we're meant for great things and I'm not sure how many great things can happen if we're stuck living in the fear that him or his little helper is just waiting for us to turn a corner before they attack. I will do everything in my power to take care of you, that promise will always stay true. Especially now that you've got me emotionally invested in you." I walked over and kissed her cheek.

"I wouldn't be so sure that we're in the clear with his helper." She's staring down at her phone, but there's no surprise on her face, she just looks exhausted.

I sat next to her and looked over at her phone. She tilted it towards me.

He may be in prison, but I'm still out and about. I'll do whatever I have to do.

The text came in from an unknown number.

"I'll text Gonzalez." I got up and there was no further discussion on the topic.

FIND ME ELSEWHERE

You can find me on Instagram, Twitter, and Youtube.

Instagram: @alyssalastella

Twitter: @alyssalastella

Youtube: Alyssa LaStella

Website: https://www.alyssalastella.com/

www.ingramcontent.com/pod-product-compliance
Lightning Source LLC
Chambersburg PA
CBHW071546110726
47908CB00007B/2010